Winter Mountain

(Book One of The Winters Series)

L.A. Liechty

The Winters Series:

Winter Mountain (Book one)

Hollywood Fire (Book two)

ISBN: 978-0-578-71845-3

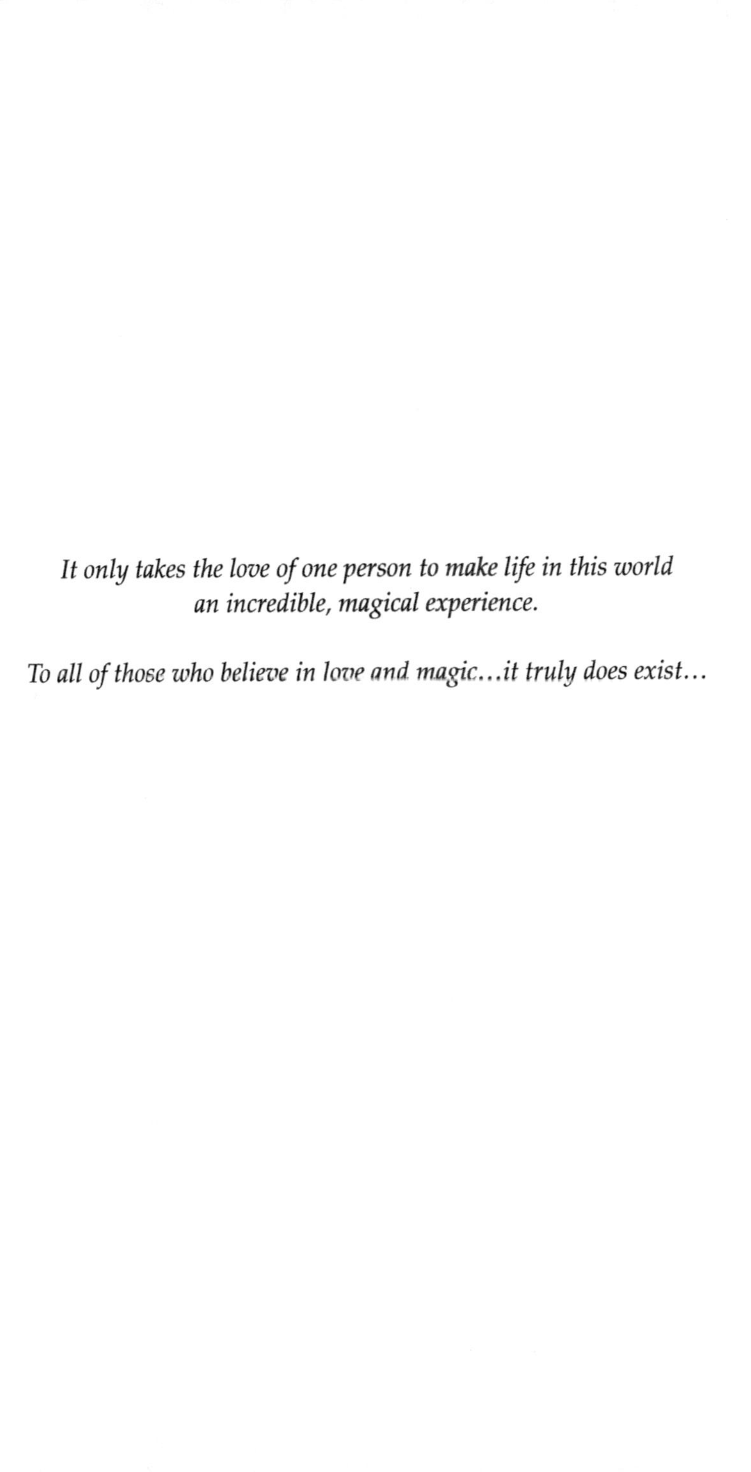

It only takes the love of one person to make life in this world an incredible, magical experience.

To all of those who believe in love and magic...it truly does exist...

Chapter One
Big Sky

The sun was just starting to pierce through the crisp sky above the Montana Mountains. Alease had a stunning view of it through the windshield of her new pickup truck. The black Ram had driven superbly well all the way from New York. New York…it already felt like another life. Good, that is exactly what she wanted; a new life. Leave the past behind. All she wanted now was peace and quiet. To blend into the background and not be noticed by anyone. A trick that would be difficult, she knew, even in this remote little town.

Alease Taynes, 28, was not exactly oblivious to her beauty, but even she didn't understand how fantastically drop dead gorgeous she really was. She would be the last person to realize that; but she knew men were attracted to her, as much as she tried to discourage it. She hated it. She longed for the ability to walk into a room unnoticed. Maybe the struggles in her life would never have occurred if she wasn't such a magnet. How strange to feel so lonely when at the same time being the center of attention. She didn't ask for it, but it always found her nonetheless. Whatever it was about her that sparked all the unwanted attention, it was enough, and it was time to leave.

Alease did not like feeling helpless. It had never been her

style to allow herself to be thrown around by the circumstances life shoved in her path; like a leaf at the mercy of the blowing wind. No. If she didn't like the course she was on, it was up to her to change it, hard as that may be at times. That was what she was doing now; helping herself. Others might see it as running, but to her, it was her best solution.

The sunlight streaked through the sky, exposing the snow covered tops of the mountains ahead of her. Wow, it really was as beautiful as she had imagined. When she rolled the window down a touch, the frosty chill of the late September air bit into her lungs. Winter was definitely on it's way, but she didn't mind. Wrapping herself up in layers was a bonus. Big sweaters would help her cover the cast on her right arm and hand. She didn't want anyone to see it and start asking the dreaded question of what happened.

It didn't hurt anymore. It did at first, but the physical pain paled in comparison to the emotional toll surrounding the entire ordeal. She tried to shake it off and focus on something other than the memories of it. In a few weeks, her new doctor in her new town would be taking it off and she could officially put the entire nightmare behind her. She hoped, anyway.

The sun was fully up now. It rose fast. She was glad for the light of morning. The dark of night had felt like an omnipresent enemy to her for the past few months. Sleeping did not come easy to her anymore. She tried to sleep last night at the motel off the interstate, but she couldn't. So, after making sure the small trailer she was pulling behind her was secure, she got back in her truck and hit the road. If she had to be in the darkness, she would much rather be in her truck, driving quickly, with her baseball bat beside her. That was her protection now that König was gone.

Every time she thought of him her eyes filled with tears of sadness, guilt and longing. König, her German Shepherd, was amazing. Alease had never known an animal with such a human soul. The bond between them was instantaneous and profound. Losing him had been an unjust dump of salt in the wound. The entire mess had caused a grave shift in her ability to believe in any good that life could offer her. It seemed that the minute she started to believe in the joy of something, she was quickly reminded it wasn't hers to keep. The loss of König hurt. He had been a better friend to her than anyone she had ever met.

She realized she probably felt that way because she didn't trust people very easily. She had learned not to. People never seemed to be who they pretended to be. Her trust in others was gone; maybe a weakness, maybe a strength…she no longer cared.

Her start in New York had such promise. She had been luckier than most in her field. Funny that a woman who hated attention fell into a career of performing on stage.

Alease had a gift; she could sing and she could write. She

had a unique combination of modern country with layers of emotion woven into the timbre of her voice. She had a way of making the strongest men in the audience feel through her ability to connect with each person listening. Her voice was something else.

Alease liked to think it was her voice and not her beauty that had caught the attention of Kenny Keep, the world renown country music star. He heard her sing and convinced her to write and record with him. The duet would have been a solid hit for them both, and paved the way for her own career as a singer/songwriter. It was a break most in the business would kill for, but, in Alease's case, it was the break that almost killed her.

The memory came into her head like an unwanted visitor. She tried to shake it off, but when it wanted to force itself into her consciousness, she could do little to stop it. The only thing as strong as the fear of what happened to her, was her guilt that it cost the life of her guard dog. It was her fault he died. The tears welled up in her eyes, almost causing her to miss the exit sign she had been looking for.

Big Sky. Here it is. She flipped her blinker on and took the exit, glad to almost be done with the long drive.

In an effort to lighten her spirits, she turned the radio on and found a local Channel that was already playing Christmas music. Alease did love Christmas. She turned the volume up. George Michael's "Last Christmas" was just finishing, and, as the next song began, Alease couldn't help but smile. Kenny Keep's voice whispered in, singing "Christmas Mountain." The song had been an overnight sensation and already considered a Christmas standard. Alease was glad for him. He was a good guy and deserved the huge success.

Kenny had tried to convince her to go forward with recording and singing, but after what happened, she was done. The attention it brought her felt like a curse and she didn't want it after that. It was enough for her to write a few songs here and there and let Kenny record and perform them as if they were his own. It made her a lot of money and she could go quietly about trying to fade into the background. Which was all she wanted now.

Alease didn't really know why she had chosen to move to Big Sky. She didn't know if she would like it. But it felt right. Something about the mountains. It called to her more than any other place did when she decided she wanted out. It was far away from New York and had lots of privacy. She arranged to rent a house for the winter, and, if she liked it, look for something to buy for the future. If she hated it, she would just pack up and try somewhere else. Freedom was her new best friend now.

The realtor sent her a detailed map along with the keys to the house, so she knew she was about 45 minutes from her new home. The clock on her dashboard said 9:00am. That was a little earlier than she wanted…the realtor had said she was meeting some repair men at the house to double check the heater. The older woman who owned the house, Mrs. Katrockuss, was a sweet lady, but she had forgotten to have the heater replaced before she rented it for the winter, and it had been known to conk out now and again. During a Big Sky December, that would not be a good thing.

Alease had no desire to be at the house when repair men were in there, and she had been told they would be done by 10:00am. So she just needed to dilly dally a bit in order to avoid them.

On her right hand side, she saw a big food store. Perfect. She needed fresh groceries anyway. This way, she could kill time and not have to go back out again once she got to the house.

She parked her truck and stepped out into the chilly morning air. A gust of wind pulled the baseball cap right off her head, and her long auburn hair came billowing out. *Great, so much for my hat*, she thought. It was well into the road by now, just missed the front tires of a Red Ford pickup truck that was turning into the lot. She thought very briefly about running after it, but that was far too embarrassing, so she let it go and went into the store.

Cal Winters had very few pleasures he indulged in, but the fresh baked croissants at the Elk Ridge Food Store bakery was definitely one of them…and the coffee. He did love a good cup of strong black coffee, but he never learned how to make it right, so he always got a cup when he was out.

The Navy SEAL had lived here since childhood and still loved the little town, but things had changed drastically since his last two deployments. Personally that is. The divorce had been hard on him. Well, truth be told, his ex wife's cheating on him had been hard on him. Kind of made the divorce a little easier; but the betrayal had devastated him. He knew it was moronic that he had trusted her. That he married her. All his SEAL buddies had warned him she wasn't right for him, but he was so eager to have stability in his life…a wife, a family. He really did want to be a dad someday, but now, all that seemed out the window. Cal was only 40, but for a Navy SEAL that felt ancient. He wasn't sure he would ever have the family he always thought he would. He wasn't even sure he wanted all of that anymore. Cal had always been a man of deep emotions, which made the betrayal of his ex all the more painful. It had been well over two years since the divorce was final, but Cal had still not regained any desire to date anyone. Especially these women who threw themselves at him. He hated the idea of being used. He hated the idea of being with anyone who couldn't see the real him behind the strong cheekbones, deep brown eyes and masculine physique. He wanted to be with a woman who could feel as deeply as he did. Someone who could love him for *who* he was and not *what* he was. He didn't think that existed. There just didn't seem to be anything left to hope for as far as relationships. Best to just focus on his horse, his dog and his property in the mountains. There wasn't need for anything more than that. He had a group of good friends; his SEAL buddies, their families, and of course, his sister Sophie and her son. He could settle with being a great uncle.

It's not that Cal *couldn't* get a woman, on the contrary. Women were not shy about putting their interest in him front and center. Cal knew he was an extremely handsome man, with a rugged masculinity that easily drew women in. That was not something he could, or frankly should, hide. What he tended to guard more carefully was his incredible depth of emotion. Cal was a kind of walking contradiction; he was the kindest man one could ever meet, cloaked inside of a badass killing machine - when called for. He knew if he ever met a woman he could fall in love with, he would be all in. That meant he had to be careful about allowing himself to be with anyone. He felt deeply and that tends to cause pain. He didn't like being that vulnerable. Truth be told, he was convinced more and more that there was no woman out there he could love. No one he met ever really sparked anything in him. Sophie kept telling him that he was purposefully convincing himself that no one was good enough just to avoid having to try all together. Maybe she was right. He didn't much care. His personal life was no longer his focus. Part of him had given up on that when he signed his divorce papers. He had been a Navy SEAL. What's more important than that?

His skills as a SEAL were impeccable. He was one of the sharpest shooters on his team and his observation skills were almost psychic. He could read people like a book. His intuition was unmatched by anyone, and his ability to balance both worlds of a SEAL and a Big Sky cowboy was second nature to him. He could air jump into Iraq one day to shoot high level terrorists in the head, and the next day be back home in Big Sky Montana to open the door for a lady with a smile on his face.

The blinker of his red Ford pickup was clicking in almost perfect time to "Christmas Mountain" playing softly on his radio. God, he loved this song. It made getting stuck at this notoriously long red light actually enjoyable. He could have pushed it when it turned yellow, but he saw the black Ram pickup turning into the parking lot and he chose the breaks instead. He always took note of cars he had never seen before. Habit from his training. This one had New York plates and a trailer attached. Someone passing through or checking in. Cal didn't know. As he sat at the red light he found his eyes following the truck to see who got out…and when she stepped out of the car, he felt a breath escape his body.

She was probably the most beautiful woman he had ever seen. Then, the white baseball cap lifted off her head, and he knew without question that she *was* the most beautiful woman he had ever seen in his life. Her long auburn hair flowed around her shoulders like an angel. Her face was stunning. Even from this distance he could see the perfect cheekbones and full lips. Her slightly faded blue jeans outlined her curves and long legs, leading to her black boots with high thick heals. She was wrapping herself in an oversized gray sweater fighting to keep the crisp air at bay. He was beside himself, lost in the sight of her.

The car behind him honked… he had been so distracted that he didn't see the light change. He turned into the lot, just missing the woman's baseball cap that had, for whatever reason, flown directly towards him.

When Cal entered the store, his first thought was no longer about the croissants he had come here for. He wanted to get a better look at this mystery woman. He spent the walk from his truck to the door convincing himself he must not have seen her correctly. She couldn't be that gorgeous. There was a part of him that needed to prove to himself that he was reacting to some kind of fake fantasy in his mind and that he needed to snap out of it and get his head back on straight.

He looked around when he walked through the door. There were a few other men in cowboy hats and jeans in the store picking up coffee and donuts as they always did before heading off to work their ranches and properties. Cal noticed instantly that all the men seemed to be looking in the same direction. He followed their gazes and, of course, it led him to the woman he had seen outside. She was on the far side of the store just turning down the first aisle with her cart, and then disappeared from his sight.

Cal walked over to the same aisle, but on the opposite end, and pretended to be looking for something on the shelf. He stayed near his end and gazed up from the random product he had pulled down.

He watched her from a distance. He admired the way she pretended not to notice all the men looking at her; at how politely she walked past them when they tipped their hats hoping to start conversations with her that she never allowed to begin. He could tell from the way she carried herself and kept her eyes on the shelves instead of the people that she was trying to stay hidden. How could a woman that beautiful think that was even possible?

Cal was surprised to find that, not only was she as gorgeous close up as he had thought, she was perhaps even more attractive. There was something about her that pulled at him. It wasn't just her obvious beauty…there was a magic around her that Cal had never seen before in another woman. A shyness even, which Cal found fascinating coming from a woman with such a magnetic presence.

He noticed her pace slow down as she got closer to his side of the aisle. Without even realizing it, Cal found that he had begun walking away from her to the next aisle. *What the Hell am I doing*, he thought? But his instincts were always one step ahead of him. Somehow, maybe he figured the man who walks away from her just might be the one she would say hello to? Jesus…he must be losing his touch. No wonder he hadn't been on a date in so long. His logic was ridiculous. Maybe he just got nervous and couldn't admit it to himself.

A few seconds later, he heard the clicking of her heels come around the corner into his aisle. He feigned interest in the dog toys he found himself in front of. He had to smile that he was smack dab in-front of a big Kong toy - the exact one his dog Max had destroyed the other day. Perfect. He picked it up and decided Max deserved a new one.

Her heels had stopped. He couldn't help himself so he looked up to see her just staring at a big bag of Blue Wild dog food. Funny, the same brand he gets for Max. She seemed lost in thought. He couldn't see her eyes from the angle he was in relation to her, so he was unsure what was going on in her mind.

He saw the cast on her arm peeking out from under the big gray sweater she had wrapped around her. Her other hand was resting on the bag, just gently touching it. She was absorbed in a contemplation that Cal could not quite read. He really wanted to talk to her. The thought of crossing over to her made him nervous. That surprised him. Cal being nervous around a woman…that just didn't happen; until today, but he couldn't resist it.

He walked over to her, careful not to get too close and startle her.

"Excuse me," Cal said in a deep but soft tone.

When she looked up and their eyes met, Cal felt a jolt of fire coarse through him. For an instant he felt like his heart stopped. She was unlike any woman he had ever met and yet something about her felt so very familiar. He realized he was lost in her gaze and had forgotten to continue his sentence. He gestured to the dog food bag.

"Did you need help with that?"

She seemed dazed at first, then a nervous smile formed on her face as she shook her head.

"Oh, no. Thank you." She paused for a second to catch her breath. Cal was hoping it was because she had felt the same reaction when she saw him, but this woman was harder to read than most.

"I thought maybe you could use a little help getting that in your cart. Hard to lift a bag that big with one hand," he pointed to her cast.

She instinctively pulled her sweater down a bit to cover it…which told Cal immediately that there was a story there. She let out a little laugh. Cal found himself warmed by it for some reason. This woman was pulling him in and he didn't even know why.

"How long have you had the cast on?" Cal asked.

"A few months. It's almost off."

He could tell she was trying to brush it off as if it didn't bother her, but he saw in her eyes that it did.

"What did you do?" Cal didn't mean it to be an intrusive question, he just wanted to keep talking to her, but he could see a flicker in her eye that he recognized. It told him she was about to skirt the issue.

She paused briefly before she answered with an honest, but rehearsed flare of humor.

"Well, I'm trying to figure out which sounds better. What do you think; Jumping out of a plane, falling down a mountain or slipping on my driveway?" Her charm and smile were infectious.

It was intriguing, the skillful way she was avoiding the answer. He was sure it must work on other people, but he saw through it. He had to admire though, that she was not choosing to lie to him, just choosing to avoid answering. That meant something to him. He went with it.

"Well, as someone who has jumped out of airplanes, and broken bones doing it, I would go with that one." He loved that she was laughing with him.

"Have you really?" she asked.

"Yes. I am a Navy SEAL, so that comes with the territory." He could feel himself smiling more than he wanted to. He still didn't understand why this woman was affecting him so much, but he was enjoying her company more than anyone in a long time, if ever…

"Thank you for your service."

Cal was struck at the deep sincerity with which she said

that. She really meant it. A lot of people say the words as if it's expected and not really connecting with the meaning. This woman…she meant it. He was kind of taken back by it.

"Thank you for your support," he responded.

"I have a lot of respect for what you guys do. It's remarkable actually."

There was a depth to her that Cal was just getting a glimpse of. He wanted more. He wanted to know everything about her, but he had a gut instinct that light conversation was the best way to keep her talking to him. *When in doubt, go with anything about dogs.*

Cal pointed back to the dog food bag. "So did you need some help getting that in your cart?"

"Oh,…no, I was just looking at it…"

He saw the beginning of tears forming in her beautiful brown eyes. It pulled at his heart. When she continued, he could hear in her voice the attempt she was making to mask the emotion she did not want him to see…but he did.

"This is a good brand…just nice to see that it's sold here too." She was trying hard to contain the emotions behind the walls that were building up in her eyes. Cal's instinct was to lighten the energy and try to put her at ease.

"Yeah it's great dog food. The exact same kind that I get for my dog." Cal smiled at her. He was sensing a warmth in her and a very real kindness. She could have just walked away, but she didn't. He didn't want her to. Her presence was very enjoyable to him. He liked how it felt. "What kind of dog do you have?" he asked her.

She paused slightly before she answered him. "German Shepherd."

Cal knew from the direction her eyes shifted as she said it that there was a level of deception in her answer. His quick calculation between the tears she was hiding and the answer she gave was that the dog was no longer with her. He wondered why she didn't want him to know that, but he let it go for the sake of keeping her talking to him.

"Hey, me too." *Ahh*…he saw a glimmer of camaraderie peek through her eyes.

"Really?" she smiled. Her smile was so amazing.

Cal could feel himself melt a little bit. What a strange effect she had on him. He found himself rather stunned at his overwhelming response to her.

"Shepards are the best," she said.

Cal reached out his hand gently to shake hers. "I'm Cal. Cal Winters." The beautiful woman in front of him was captivating him. Her shy smile and reserved caution were mixed with an honest kindness that Cal found so refreshing.

She kind of laughed as she apologized for having to use her left hand to shake his, gesturing to her cast and inability to use her right hand for the introduction. "It's nice to meet you Cal. How old is your shepherd?"

Her hand shake was firm, but feminine. Strong but

reserved. When he touched her hand, another bolt of fire raced through him. This woman was special, he could tell right away.

It did not escape Cal's attention that she did not give him her name, and her quick change in subject (by asking about the dog) was clever. Most men wouldn't have even noticed she had done that. Cal noticed everything. He wanted to know her name, but even more than that, he wanted to keep talking with her, so he redirected his thought process and answered her question.

"Max? He is 5 years old now. He was training to be a military dog, but he…well he flunked out. So I adopted him." He couldn't help but chuckle a little…he realized he was still a bit nervous talking to her.

She laughed. "He flunked out? That's hysterical. Why?"

It was the first moment of ease Cal had seen in her eyes. *Note to self,* Cal thought, *humor and dog stories, keeps her at ease.* Cal couldn't help but match her laugh and smile.

"Well, he doesn't like to bring things back. He will retrieve anything you ask him to, but once he gets it, he likes to keep it for himself. The military frowns on that, so they gave him an F." It was amazing the amount of joy that flowed through him seeing her laugh. Seeing her smile…at him. She made him feel like he was the only man in the world, though Cal knew full well the store was filled with local men who were currently pissed that he was able to strike up a conversation with this mystery beauty while the rest of them failed miserably.

"Yeah, that'll do it." She took a breath that Cal was afraid was leading to her moving on, so he jumped back in.

"So are you new in town or just passing through?" he tried to keep the question very light and casual.

"New in town. Just renting for the winter and then I'll see how I feel here."

Cal tried to conceal how thrilled he was to hear she would be here for a while. There were not too many food stores in town, so he was sure to find ways to keep running into her and hopefully enough of those would lead to him having the courage to ask her out. He couldn't believe that thought just went through his head. He had no desire to date anyone at all, up until he saw her in the parking lot. Then it was like his whole world changed.

"That's great. This is a really nice town. I've lived here my whole life, and I still love it. Local tip for you; this place makes the best fresh made croissants but you have to get them right at 9am when they come out of the oven or there won't be any left."

"Good to know. Thank you. I might have missed my window, but I will head over there and see if there are any left." She started to pull her cart away. Cal knew he shouldn't try to stop her, that he should let her go. Every fiber in his being didn't want to, but he found the strength inside to control himself.

"It was nice meeting you Cal." She smiled again. A real smile. Not a flirtatious smile. Not a fake smile. A real, warm smile. Cal felt like he had gone his whole life without a woman ever smiling at him like that. He didn't realize how much he missed it.

As she walked away from him up the aisle, Cal couldn't help it, "You forgot to tell me your name."

She turned over her shoulder. "I'll save that in case you get to the croissants before I do. I may need something to barter with."

Alease was hoping he couldn't see how he affected her. My God, that man was gorgeous. She had never met a man with more rugged masculinity coupled with the most amazing eyes and smile. Even in Hollywood films she had never seen a man more attractive. She felt herself shaking. God she hoped he hadn't seen that. Or heard the breath that escaped her control when she looked up and saw him. His smile…she had to be careful. Her first thought was how comforting it was. *Dangerous Aleas*e…

She spent the next few minutes in her head trying to convince herself that just because he was attractive didn't mean she was attracted to him. No, she was not interested in anymore bad things in her life. Foolish attraction to a man she just met was idiotic. She chastised herself for it. She was also upset with herself that her eyes filled with tears in front of him in the dog food aisle. Thank God he didn't notice. That kind of emotional exposure was a weakness she desperately believed needed to be kept hidden. Giving off an unbreakable air of strength and control was the best way to feel safe, and any outward loss of that appearance was a disastrous fumble she had been working on avoiding.

She hadn't wanted to let him know she no longer had König. Maybe if he thought she had a big dog with her, he would be less likely to try and get to know her. It was a safety thing. As well as an 'I don't want to get emotional in front of a stranger' thing.

Alease was aware that the other men in the store were looking at her hoping to get an opportunity to talk with her. She was always polite, but tried hard not to look up and invite any conversations. As she moved towards the cash register, she realized there was an intense heat flowing through her. Was that from Cal? Why should she be so affected by this guy? Her best course of action was to get out of the store as quickly as she could and get to her new home. What are the chances she would run into him again? She would be safe from all of this once she got to her house. The croissants were not worth the risk this morning. His smile was…disarming. She was getting angry with herself that she even had a moment of feeling comfortable with him. Jesus, had she not learned anything?

* * *

Cal very subtly kept his eye on her when she walked away. He couldn't help it. He felt an instant need to protect her. He didn't know why, he just felt a vulnerability in her that he wanted shielded. He knew he could not approach her again. Not now anyway. She was skittish around him. Didn't need to be trained in observations skills to know that. There was a fear in her. He saw it. He felt it. He didn't like it. He detested the idea that she would have any fear of him, but he also understood…a woman like that…she was bound to have had some bad encounters in her past. He wondered if that had anything to do with her broken arm. He felt an anger boil under his skin at the thought of anyone hurting her.

He saw her pick up her pace and leave the store. He knew there was a part of her that was running from something. She had no wedding ring on. No one with her in the truck. She was afraid and yet brave enough to move out here on her own; to a new town by herself. He admired her. *That is one hell of a woman,* he thought to himself.

One way or another, he was going to get to know her. He sent a prayer up to fate; *please help this woman to cross my path again. And again….and again.*

Chapter Two
Winter Mountain Ridge

The county road up to the private drive was long and beautiful. It opened up to reveal two homes. Hers was the one on the far right, and off to the left was the second home. The realtor said it belonged to a lovely couple who were spending the cold season in Texas. It didn't look boarded up for the winter, and the barn door adjacent to that house was open. Maybe that's just how they did things in Big Sky.

She instantly liked the look of that other home. It looked…warm and inviting. Like a modern log cabin, but on a slightly grander scale. It wasn't huge…two floors from the looks of it. Fenced off behind it was a beautiful piece of property that stretched down along the private drive. Alease admired the black horse grazing in the field. It was magnificent and looked very well kept. It looked almost like a show horse.

She turned her gaze to the little house she was renting. It was sweet. Smaller than the other one. Not a log cabin style. Just a simple little white house with a front porch, big moon shaped drive way and the most beautiful mountain scene right behind it. She was told there were private trails up into the mountains just off her house that led up to the top for the most glorious sights. She looked forward to walking them.

In-between the two houses was a large fire pit. She wasn't sure which house that belonged to, but since the neighbors weren't here anyway, she didn't think it mattered. There was a huge, well stacked pile of chopped fire wood along the fence of the other house. She looked on the side of hers to see a bunch of wood that had not been chopped or neatly stacked yet. *Great, that should be fun to do with one arm.*

It was peaceful here. When Alease pulled up to the house, she was disappointed to see the repair men were still there. Jenny, the realtor, came down the steps to greet her. Alease parked her truck and got out.

"Hello, you must be Alease Taynes. I'm Jenny. It's nice to finally meet you." She shook her hand, the left one again, but what else could Alease do.

"Hi Jenny, nice to meet you too. Still working on the heater?"

"Yes. It's taking longer than they thought, I apologize, but come on in and I'll show you around."

Alease looked over and saw the two men staring at her and talking about her to each other. They had that lust look in their eyes and she wanted no part of it. She politely shook her head.

"Oh, that's ok. I don't want to get in their way. Besides I've been driving for days and I could use a little fresh air. I'll just walk down the drive a bit and look around. I'd love to get a closer look at that beautiful horse anyway."

Jenny smiled and they exchanged a few more pleasantries, then Alease turned to walk down the drive and distance herself from the men in her new home.

The crisp late morning air felt good, cleansing somehow. She wrapped her oversized sweater around her tighter and casually walked down the private drive along the neighbors fence line. They kept their property in perfect shape. It was beautiful. She leaned up against the fence, the breeze blowing her hair off her face and behind her. She felt a sense of peace looking out at the horse, the mountains and the deluxe log cabin home standing so strong next door to hers.

The Horse across the field lifted his head and pondered at Alease. Then, to her surprise, he started to walk over to her, proudly swishing his long tail behind him. When the horse reached her, he gently nuzzled his nose into her chest seeking attention. Alease couldn't help but smile, it was really sweet for such a large, powerful animal. She was so taken with him that she didn't even hear the truck that pulled up just behind her.

Cal couldn't believe his eyes. *Holy shit. It's her. She is here.* His heart skipped several beats. Is *she* the one renting the house next to his? Of all the properties for rent in the area, this amazing woman chose the house right next to his. He must be the luckiest man on earth. If he ever had any doubts about fate before, he didn't anymore. He drove as slowly as he could to give himself enough time to figure out what he should say first. God forbid she thinks he is stalking her.

He slowed his truck down and rolled down the window. "Hi again," he said.

She turned around and seemed completely caught off guard to see him. Before she had time to get concerned, he spoke. "I see you've met my horse." He figured that was the fastest way to make sure she understood that he lived here.

"He's your's?" The black horse was still nuzzling up to her. "He is beautiful." She was stroking the horses nose with her free hand…and there was that smile again. Damn, it was like a weapon that just rendered him useless.

Cal turned off the engine, but stayed behind the closed driver's side door.

"So, you are the one renting the house next to mine this winter? Mrs. Katrockuss has been my neighbor for a while. Lovely woman. She lost her husband a few years ago. Between that and her getting older, I think she just can't manage the upkeep anymore. Especially in the winter time. She's been talking about selling it, but she just can't pull the trigger yet, so she is renting it out for now instead." He could tell that his subtle way of letting her know he really did live here was working. She seemed to be ok with him being there with her. "You know, my horse has never shown that kind of affection to anyone. He likes you. Animals are good judges of character. If he likes you, than you must be ok."

She chuckled. "It never occurred to me that a man would be concerned about a woman's character. Thought it was always the other way around."

"Hardly! Women can be horrible." His smile and humor enticed her to laugh again. He loved that he could do that.

"Well, I wish I could disagree with that, but you are right. Women can be horrible too."

His horse nuzzled at her again. Cal almost found himself jealous that his horse could get so close and he couldn't. Not yet anyway. He prayed there would be a time when he could.

"His name is Chase, and I've never seen him like this. I think he is in love with you."

He had a flash of nerves shoot through him when he said that. Almost like he was revealing his own feelings…but he couldn't be in love with this woman, he just met her. Of course he was talking about the horse…*right*?

She blew it off sweetly. "Oh, he is way out of my league!"

"*He* is out of *your* league? I think the New York craziness has messed with your brain."

"How did you know I'm from New York?" she asked.

"I saw the license plates on your truck." Her eyes told him she was a little nervous that he figured something out about her she didn't share.

"Observant," she said, as if reminding herself to be careful.

He looked to her house and saw the repair men on the front porch. *Ahh, that's why she is over here and not inside her new home.* He was putting the clues together…this woman is very on guard. He could guess why. Cal knew there were a lot of men on this planet that couldn't control themselves around a beautiful woman, and this woman was more beautiful than any he had seen before. He knew without knowing, and it bothered him to think that anyone had ever hurt her before, or scared her. She deserved to be protected and cherished. He really wanted to set her at ease. Cal knew he was the last person she needed to be afraid of, and he had to start finding ways to let her know that. It was important to him.

"Let me guess, the heater, right? I told Mrs. Katrockuss last year that she needed to replace that."

"Yeah, I guess she forgot to."

"Well, I know a few tricks to patch it up, so if it goes out on you, just let me know, and I'd be happy to help you." Cal was trying to sound as innocent and nonchalant as possible.

"That's very sweet. I hear these winters are cold, so I hope it won't be a problem," she said.

Clever response again. Cal noted the polite way she graciously acknowledged his words without any acceptance whatsoever of the help he was offering.

He really wanted to get out of the car and be closer to her, but he wasn't sure how to do it smoothly and without raising her defenses.

"So, now that you know I live here, have I earned the right to know your name?"

She laughed again and responded sarcastically. "Oh, I don't know that for sure. Just cause you told me? Men say the darnedest things." He chuckled at her response.

"Ok, I'll prove it to you." He opened his car door and stepped out slowly. He decided not to approach her so instead he just leaned back on his truck. "Max knows how to open the front door of my house. When I call his name, he will open it and come running over here. If he eats me, you will know I'm a stranger who doesn't live here. If he is happy to see me, you will know that I did not lie to you. Which, FYI, I would never do." He looked to the front door, whistled and then called out. "Max!"

True to his word, when she looked over, she saw the front door knob moving. A few seconds later, his German Shepherd dashed out the door running at top speed directly to Cal, tail wagging and nothing but love for the man standing across from her. Alease couldn't help but be touched by it. Max reminded her of König. Not as big, but the affection for Cal… König had that for her. Cal was so good with him. She saw how much love he gave the dog and it felt good to see. Cal looked up at her with a smile, and a slight air of arrogance.

"See? I did not lie to you. May I now have the honor of

knowing your name?"

She had no clever way out of it this time. So she gave in. "Alease. Alease Taynes."

"Alease. It's very nice to officially meet you." His smile shot through her again. She could not get a grasp on the feelings he sparked in her. She lowered her gaze to focus on the dog. Dogs were always safe. She knelt down as the shepherd came over to her, tail wagging and a bombardment of dog kisses.

"This is Max," Cal said.

"He is beautiful. He reminds me of König." She didn't really mean to say it out loud, but there it was.

"König, your German shepherd?"

She nodded in acknowledgment. She could hear the careful tone in Cal's voice as he spoke his next words.

"Would I be correct in assuming he is no longer with you?"

There was no reason to be aloof about it, he lived here and would see there was no dog in the house.

"Yeah. He died." She kept her focus on Max so he couldn't see the tears she was trying to keep from forming in her eyes.

"I'm so sorry. How long ago did you lose him?" his voice was kind. There was a tone in how he spoke that told her he understood the loss as only a dog lover could.

"A few months ago," she answered softly.

Normally the next question is always 'what happened' and Alease was grateful for the pause he gave the conversation so that she could change it's direction and not have to deal with the story she did not want him to know.

Alease took the moment and spoke before he could.

"I was told by the realtor that you and your wife were going to be in Texas for the winter. Did your plans change?"

She could see that the shift in conversation was not where he was going to go, but he took a breath and allowed her question to lead the way. Alease recognized the look of discomfort in his eyes before he responded, but to his credit, he answered her anyway.

"Ahh, well that's putting it mildly. Yes, our plans did change. My wife is actually my ex wife as of two years ago, and *she* was the one who moved to Texas, not me."

She couldn't help but be impressed with his openness about it. Her tactic when answering a question she didn't like was to play with words so she could answer without answering. He didn't do that.

"I'm sorry. That's hard." It was the only thing she could think to say.

He shrugged his shoulders. "Everything happens for a reason," he said.

"Do you really believe that?" It was a genuine question. He did not hesitate to answer.

"Yes. I do."

There was a strong sincerity about how he said that. It gave Alease a strange mixture of comfort and apprehension. She knew why. There was some deep part of her that really wanted to trust this man, and she felt a battle commencing inside with one part of her wanting to trust him, and the other part desperately demanding her not to. God, she hated herself for being so weak. How many traps must she fall into before she learns this kind of thing is just not meant for her?

There was a commotion at the house as the repair men and Jenny got into their cars and headed towards them. When they reached the spot where Cal and Alease were talking, they stopped and got out. The two men moved a little closer to Alease than necessary, and she stepped back instinctively. She saw Cal reading the look on her face even though she was trying not to seem uncomfortable, but she wasn't sure she was hiding it well. In a very gentlemanly way, Cal stepped up; almost as if he knew she was uneasy with the two men. It gave her a little comfort that he was there. She would, of course, have to chastise herself for that later, but in the moment, she was glad for him being there.

Cal addressed the men with a firm but polite voice. "So what's the story with that heater? Did you replace it for her?"

Alease could see the change in the two guys when Cal spoke. They moved away from her and turned their attention to Cal. They were clearly intimidated by him. After all, Cal was a six-foot-four Navy SEAL with arms that could break the men in half in the blink of an eye, and they knew it. It gave Alease a comfort she never quite felt before, and she found herself grateful for it. She was happy to let Cal take the lead for her. Again, a lapse she would have to lecture herself on later.

One of the repair men spoke up in a slightly timid voice, "Couldn't. The new unit is on backorder and won't come in til around Thanksgiving. We set up a temporary unit for now. Should hold til then."

As the conversation between Cal and the two men continued, Alease found it a bit funny that suddenly these two men seemed anxious to leave. Maybe it would be a really good thing for her to have an intimidating Navy SEAL living next door to her. Could keep all the bad guys away. The only problem left is, what if *he* is one of the bad guys too? Or worse…what if he isn't? She felt a slight panic in the realization that she did not know how to control these feelings that were threatening to start stirring inside of her. She really needed to just get inside and lock the door. She needed to not be near him. Avoidance was the only way to keep a lid on this.

When the conversation came to an end, Cal turned to her. "Can I give you a lift up to the house?"

It wasn't far, and her normal response would have been no, but she liked the idea of these two men seeing her with Cal. Maybe it would send an unconscious message to them to back off. She heard herself say yes to Cal, and then moments later found herself in his truck. So far, she was not doing a good job of the avoidance solution she had come up with.

He had even opened the door for her. Definitely not in New York anymore. She couldn't even remember the last time a man opened a door for her. Why did that feel so nice? Jesus, she really needed to get a grip.

His truck was clean and spacious. As Cal got into the drivers seat she noticed the croissants on the seat between them…and something else.

"My hat." Alease was really surprised to see it.

"Yeah, I saw the wind blow it off your head when you got out of your truck this morning. I found it when I came out of the store," he said casually.

"You *found* it? As I remember, it was blowing across the street."

Cal's laugh was so sweet and charming, she couldn't help but smile when he revealed it.

"Ok; full disclosure…I crossed the street looking for it for you. It's yours and I thought you should have it back."

Alease was slightly stunned. She didn't even know what to say. "That was so sweet of you." She could feel herself trying to diminish it in her head so she wouldn't be so touched by it, but she wasn't completely succeeding. "Thank you."

Cal was somehow very good at lightening the mood

whenever she started to feel things she didn't want to in front of him, and he did it again. He reached down and opened the box of croissants.

"Here, you have to try one of these."

Alease took a bite. "Wow, these are *really* good. You're right. Thank you."

He looked at her with such a meaningful smile. "Anytime, Alease Taynes."

He had hoped she would take him up on the offer to drive her up to the house. Even though it was less than a minute drive from where they were, any extra moment he could have with her felt good to him. It was obvious to him she was uncomfortable with the two men who had been in her home, so it was justifiable to him to step up and create a barrier of protection between her and them. He told himself he did it for her sake, even though he was acutely aware there was a territorial part of him that was happy to have those guys think she was his. A primitive pulse surged through him at the thought of being with her…in all of it's meanings. He was not denying to himself the incredible sexual attraction he felt to her…that was a given. It was the overwhelming emotional attraction to her that really had him at a loss. He couldn't explain why he cared for her so much so quickly, but he did.

It was the small trail of clues he was gathering that he found himself taking note of. The importance of the few things she said, and the many things she didn't say, that he was piecing together about who this woman is.

In the store this morning, she told him her cast had been on for a few months…interestingly, that corresponded perfectly with the answer she just gave him about when her dog died. She even said it in the same tone and cadence, which told him the two were connected. That left only a few possibilities…a car accident or an attack.

She was driving a brand new Ram truck. That could lead to the car accident theory…but an accident that would kill a dog and break a woman's arm and hand, would also leave other scars. There were no cut marks on her beautiful face. No cut marks on her free hand either. Not to mention, if she had just survived a car accident that killed her beloved dog, he doubted very much she would jump into another vehicle so quickly and volunteer to drive across the country by herself. And the obvious; a car accident would not explain her self protective behavior around men. He knew in his gut the truth must have something to do with an attack.

What he didn't know was the who, the where and the why…and of course, what exactly the attack entailed; but he knew German Shepards…if her shepherd died as a result of protecting her, than that meant the attack wasn't pretty.

He looked over at her as she took another bite of the croissant, happy that she was in his car, and a little embarrassed that he had to admit he went looking for her hat.

He was going to have it with him the next time he saw her in the store. It was his backup plan if he couldn't figure out how to approach her again. He had no idea she would be in his car and see it sitting next to him in the front seat.

She was looking out the window mentioning how beautiful the mountain off to the right was. He saw the scar on her neck. He was surprised he hadn't seen it before. He must have been so taken with her face that he missed it. He knew it had been made by a knife. He knew it. He had some just like it on his own body. Jagged edge knife. He wondered if it was from the same incident that caused her broken arm. He really wanted to find out, but he knew she wasn't ready to tell him any of that. She was purposefully keeping herself a mystery. It seemed to be a natural defense for her, and the clues he was gathering about her were making it pretty clear why. He questioned if she had ever been with a good man.

He had noticed her reaction to him opening the door for her: complete surprise, as if she had no idea men did that sort of thing. God, what kind of men had she been with before if something like that was unusual? This woman deserved more than he was starting too think she ever had gotten.

He drove up between the houses, but closer to her truck so he could get out with her and maybe try for a few more minutes of conversation.

He had every intention of crossing over to her side to open the door for her again, but she did it herself as soon as he opened his own door. He didn't think it even crossed her mind that he was going to do that. A slight twinge of disappointment flickered through him. She was not going to make it easy for him to show her he cared. This woman was not going to be easy to get through to. He had his work cut out for him, but he was more than willing.

He took a closer look at her trailer. It wasn't very big. No furniture, obviously. He wondered again about what she left in New York.

"Did you put your furniture in storage back in New York? That trailer only looks like it's big enough for several boxes, but not much more."

Alease was opening the back door of her truck as she answered him. "No. I got rid of it. Sold what I could and donated the rest. This truck with a trailer attached is about as big a vehicle as I feel comfortable driving."

"Didn't have anyone willing to drive a big truck for you?" He knew he was pushing the information barrier a little bit, but he couldn't help his curiosity.

She didn't give him too much help in that department. "No," was all she said.

Cal had a good view into the front and back seat of her truck and he saw several baseball bats. Interesting. One in the front seat and four in the back.

"You play?"

She looked at him completely confused about what he

was asking. "What?"

He pointed to the objects in the backseat. "Baseball. Do you play?"

There was that look again in her eyes…the one that comes over her when she is trying to figure out how to answer a question without answering it.

"Oh, no, not really. Well, ha, one arm right now anyway, so no."

He could tell she wanted to divert the conversation but she seemed at a loss of how to do it. He wasn't sure he wanted to make it so easy for her this time. "That's a lot of baseball bats for someone who doesn't play baseball."

She had no come back this time. That told Cal all he needed to know. He did a quick calculation in his head…one for the car (that was the one in the front seat,) one by the front door, one by the back door, one in the bedroom…the fifth one he wasn't sure…maybe she miscounted the number of doors in her new house. Oh, no, wait…he got it; one in the bathroom by the shower and bathtub.

The silence was making her uncomfortable, he could feel it, and he hated that more than not knowing what the real explanation was.

"Can I help you unload your trailer? Might be hard to do that by yourself with one arm in a cast."

He knew she would say no, but he hoped against hope she might surprise him.

"That's very sweet, but I don't think I'm going to do any unloading today. Think I'm just going to go in and rest. I've been up since, well, all night really."

She was so beautiful standing there in the sunlight trying to hold the weight of her entire world by herself. He had such an urge to wrap his arms around her and take the weight instead, but he knew he couldn't do that. Not yet anyway. He hated seeing her trying to take her grocery bags in with one hand…but he just knew she wasn't ready to accept any help from him. It took so much strength to allow her to push him away, but he promised himself he would find a way to change that. Slowly. He knew he had to go slow with her on every level.

"Ok. I'm right over there if you need anything," he gestured to his house. "Anytime, just let me know." He smiled at her and forced himself to turn back towards his house. One last thought hit him, "Did Mrs. Katrockuss leave you any chopped firewood? It gets cold at night and the front fireplace in your living room will really help to keep your house warm."

"I don't know. There is a bunch off the side of the house that I need to chop up. Do you know if she left an axe here anywhere?"

Cal couldn't help but laugh, "An axe? You're asking for an axe? How are you going to chop wood with one arm in a cast?"

"Slowly. With the other arm." She said it tongue and cheek, but Cal had a feeling this stubborn woman would actually try that.

"No. There is no axe. I'll bring some of mine over to you later. I'll leave it on your porch." He turned to walk towards his house before she could argue, which he knew she would. He would bet dollars to donuts this woman was not the kind of woman to accept things easily, especially help.

"You don't have to do that Cal. Just tell me where the nearest hardware store is and I'll go get an axe later."

She was stubborn. Cal turned back to her.

"Alease, I'm not going to let you try to chop wood with one arm. Just take some of my fire wood. I have plenty." She tried again to protest and he cut her off. "Alease, stop. I'm bringing over some of my fire wood and leaving it on your porch. Please use it and stay warm tonight. It gets cold, but I'm kind of hoping you like it here. It would be nice if you stuck around for a while." He smiled at her and turned before she could respond to him. He called over his shoulder as he walked to his front door. "If you need anything, just pop over and knock on the door. Anytime."

He said it as casually as he could, but he really wanted her to know that if she needed him he was there. He prayed that some part of her would need him, eventually. God, he would love to be needed by her.

Chapter Three
The House Next Door

Cal found himself constantly looking out his kitchen window towards the little white house, hoping to catch a glimpse of Alease, or to see her coming over to him for something…anything. She made several trips for the groceries in her car that she wouldn't let him help with. He saw her bring in a suitcase and the baseball bats from the back seat. He knew he was right about why she had those bats. He was determined to figure out a way to get her to talk to him about it, so that he could know and do something to help her. It was in his nature to do so, it's the SEAL in him, it's what they do. They help, they protect, they are needed… but with Alease…he knew it was more than that. The desire to protect her was coming from a much deeper, more personal part of him, and he was still at a loss to understand it.

All had been quiet over there for several hours. After her last trip in with the baseball bats, she didn't come out again, and he didn't see any movement through the windows. It was his guess that she was sleeping. He couldn't help but picture her lying in her bed, and he couldn't hold back the deep arousal from doing so. He was trying not to, but there was no way to stem the thoughts of being with her…being near her. He pictured himself on top of her and, of course, being inside of her. The big gulp of his beer did little to wash it away. Those images only made sense if she wasn't afraid of him…if she wanted him as much as he wanted her. Until she could look at him in a way that told him she felt the same, he wouldn't do anything of the sort. He would never. Still, the images and ideas of having her in his arms kept floating through his mind. He felt like he needed a cold shower.

When the sun started to go down, he saw her turn on all the lights. Occasionally he could see her silhouette through the cream colored blinds in her kitchen and living room, so he knew she was up and moving about. He didn't know why he was worried about her. Maybe he was just anxious to know she liked it here. To know she was comfortable, and not scared. Or maybe he has just lost his mind. He couldn't get her out of his head even for a second. This was so unlike him.

He left a big pile of fire wood for her right outside her front door. He did it right away, just to make sure she had it. It comforted him, somehow, doing what he could to make sure that she had everything she needed. Against his temptation, he had been as quiet about it as he could be, just in case she was sleeping. He was hoping she would have opened her door while he was putting it over there, but she stayed hidden inside. That was not surprising to him.

Cal leaned against the countertop of his kitchen island, and took another gulp of his beer. He didn't drink that often, usually only when he was hanging out with his buddies, but for some reason he felt like one tonight. He found himself walking around his house unsure of how to relax, which was strange for him. Usually a football game or some stupid TV show was all he wanted to do. Tonight, he felt…different. He pretended he didn't know what was bothering him, but every time he found himself looking over to the house next door, he was overcome with the bizarre realization that he missed her. Alease. Jesus, he just met her this morning and already he was pacing the floor trying to figure out what to do with himself. He just kept staring out the window hoping to see her front door open.

"I'm really pathetic," he said to no one, but Max cocked his head trying to understand him. "What are you looking at? You're just as pathetic. Hell, you kissed her the first moment you met her. Lucky bastard."

Cal took another chug of his beer in a futile attempt to wash away the feelings he knew had already begun.

Throughout the following week, Cal was unsettled to find the feelings stirring in him were not only refusing to fade, but they were growing every time he saw her. Even when he didn't see her, she was somehow all over his mind…and his body. He realized he was aware of everything about her; the lights she always turned on when it got dark out, her routine of early morning walks when the sun first beamed across the sky, even the damn to go coffee cups she had with her when she would come back from trips into town. Guess she found the place that makes the coffee she likes. Cal knew which one it was because of the bright red paper cups they used.

He had done his best to give Alease the space he thought she needed to get settled in, and also trying to continue a few interactions each day if he could.

She was tenacious, this one. He offered, manytimes, to give her a hand with the boxes that were still in her trailer but she kept refusing his help. Always politely of course, but she seemed to be trying to prove to herself that she didn't need him, which irked Cal greatly. He wanted to be needed by her. He wasn't used to a woman saying no to his help, and he certainly wasn't used to a woman who seemed perfectly capable of walking away from him, even when, at times, it looked to him like part of her didn't want to.

Each night he saw that she continued her pattern of turning on all the lights just as the sun was going down, and he never saw her turn them off again until the sun was well up in the sky the next day. It didn't seem to him that she was really sleeping at night either, because he could see her movements behind the thin shades in her windows through out the night. He wondered how she was really doing when the sun went down. It seemed to be a source of anxiety for her, from what he could see. He was waiting for the morning when she wouldn't lie to him when she answered his question of how she slept.

The sun had just come up, and sure as clockwork, Cal

saw Alease come out her front door. It was as if she paced through the night waiting for the light of day again, and as soon as it was there, she relished in it. He wondered what it was about the dark that scared her. He could guess every time he thought of her broken arm and the story she was not sharing with him.

Alease was dressed in her blue jeans and a thick sweatshirt with a pink scarf around her neck. Her hair was pulled back in a ponytail and she had on sneakers. Even dressed down she was the very definition of beautiful. She headed up the trail that leads to the multitude of winding paths on the mountain. Every fiber in his being cried out for him to run out the door and join her; to be her guide and show her the beauty of his land. He owned most of it on this side of the mountain, and he was yearning to be the one to share it with her. He would love to take her to the hidden gem of the mountain trail; the plateau that opened up to the most beautiful view of the canyon between his mountain and the next one. At the right time of day, the gaze from there had the viewer looking out above the clouds that layered below, brushing up against the mid section of the mountains. It was breathtaking. He would take her there…at some point. His heart pounded at the thought, but his instincts were telling him he should let her go alone again this morning. He hated it, but he knew he needed to. It pulled at the protective side of him. He wanted her to be comfortable and he knew, whatever the demons were that were haunting her, he didn't have his footing with her to help. Not yet anyway. He would though, at some point, he affirmed that to himself in his mind.

As he had since the first morning she moved in, he opened his front door to let Max out. "Go with her Max. Keep her safe." Cal wanted someone to go with her through the trails, for peace of mind. He gave him the command, and Max was off to join Alease, tail wagging and grinning from ear to ear.

He felt good that Max always went with her. He knew it would help her feel at ease. She didn't need to know it was his idea, just let her think Max was out anyway and chose to come with her.

Cal's phone rang. It was his sister.

"Hey Sophie, what's up?" he tried to sound as normal as possible.

"Your voice sounds different…what's going on?" she asked.

"Nothing. What are you talking about? Everything is the same as it always has been." He realized he probably tried too hard.

"Now I know somethings up. What happened?"

Cal knew that Sophie was very in tune with him and hiding anything from her would be difficult. He took a deep breath.

"Are you really going to make me confide in you right

now?" He was losing his strength to hide anything more about this woman who had somehow injected herself into his very soul.

"Yes. What is going on?"

Her curiosity was obvious, and not surprising to him. It had been a very long time since anything remotely different or out of the ordinary had happened in Cal's world, and he knew that any change, in Sophie's opinion, would be a good change.

"Ok, but you have to promise not to make this a big deal and not go all Sophie on me about it, ok?"

"Oh, I make no such promise. Come on, spill it." She pushed him, she knew she could.

"It's nothing. I just…I met someone that I find… interesting. That's all. No big deal."

She didn't even try to hide her over the top, giddy reaction. Cal instantly regretted telling her anything.

"Oh my God! Tell me everything! Who is she? How did you meet her, and how the hell did it come to pass that you didn't run in the other direction?"

"You know, your joy in making fun of me is really annoying, sis."

She was laughing, but also sounded genuinely excited to hear about this mystery woman.

"Oh come on. I have spent over two years watching you sulk around as women threw themselves at you left and right, while you pretended they didn't exist. Forgive me if I'm beside myself at the discovery that there is, in fact, a woman on this planet that has caught your attention…and dare I say your heart! Oh my God, who is she?" Sophie was not taking no for an answer.

"Fine. Sophie…Jesus, she is…well, first of all, she is gorgeous, but she is more than that…I'm beside myself. When I'm with her I… I can't explain it…I don't understand it…what the fuck is this? I have no idea what's happening to me. I haven't felt this way about a woman since…well, between you and me, since…ever," he couldn't believe he was admitting that.

"Even Becca…?" Sophie didn't hide her surprise at hearing him say this out loud. Cal knew Sophie always had her suspicions that his feelings for his ex wife were not as… deep as he said they were. She had spoken to him about it before, but he always denied it. "I have never heard this… sparkle in your voice before. You have never sounded like this about Becca, or any other woman for that matter." She waited for him to speak, but when he didn't, she continued. "Cal, you have always been a romantic. Even as a kid you used to talk about falling in love at first sight with an angel, and the happy ever after endings. I know, as time passed and all your friends got married and started families, that you began to doubt your belief in that kind of thing. I think you started to question your ideals and, perhaps, traded them in for the next best thing. Becca…well, she was a good image, but as far as substance, you know I was never convinced. I don't fault you for it, but don't let your experience with Becca ruin what you might find with this woman. Tell me about her."

Cal told her what he knew about Alease, leaving out his suspicions of the story behind her broken arm. Sophie listened without any interruption, which was an unusual feat for her. Cal was a little unsettled by it.

"Ok, you can speak now Sophie," he listened for her next words through the intense quiet that fell on her part.

Finally she spoke. Her voice was as real as could be.

"I'm speechless. Cal, I have never heard you like this. It's amazing. I have to meet this woman, she has done the impossible. She got right into your heart and you can't do anything about it."

Cal didn't want to hear any of it. "That's ridiculous." He let out a breath and stopped talking, as if he hit a brick wall. There was dead silence on the phone. Then Cal gave in, "Ok fine you're right. Sophie, what do I do? This is insane. I feel like I have lost all sense of reality."

"Listen, I know that this is probably very unsettling for you being a big Navy SEAL guy who is always in control of everything. Now you're not. Cal, it's ok. Just breathe and go with it." She paused and gave him a minute to hear her. "Listen, you are an amazing man, you have the best heart a man could have, and you have incredible intuition. Use it. If you're feeling something this strong, it means something is there…this is a feeling that you have never had before. Trust that there is a reason for it. Just go with it. Ask her out."

"Sophie I can't do that! Every time this woman steps outside anywhere, men flock to her. I've seen it. I've watched her avoid every man that tried to strike up a conversation with her. She is not interested in being hit on. If I ask her out, that makes me just like everyone else who runs after her." He took another gulp of his beer. "How do you let a woman, who doesn't want to be seen, know that you see her?"

Sophie was surprisingly calm. "Cal, you are not like every other guy. She is going to figure that out. Just keep doing what you do. Be yourself and give her the chances to let you in. I'm sure she will." She gave him a second to hear what she said. "I can't wait to meet her. When can Jake and I come up?"

Cal was listening to what Sophie had said, but his mind drifted off into thoughts of how best he could interact with Alease in a way that would offer her those chances Sophie was suggesting. It wouldn't be easy. Maybe it wasn't supposed to be.

"Cal? You still there?" He had forgotten to respond to her.

"Yes, sorry. I'm here. You and my nephew are always welcome you know that. Come up this weekend for a few days. But do not embarrass me in front of this woman. No comments and no letting her know anything I just told you, understand? Seriously Sophie, I have a feeling that she scares easy, so restrain yourself, ok?"

"Of course. We'll be there. Jake doesn't have school on Thursday anyway, so we can hit the road and be there in the late afternoon. He'll be so excited."

"Great. Tell him I love him. You too Sis."

"Cal?"

"Yes,"

"This is a good thing." He could tell she really felt that way.

"Then why is it so unsettling? I feel completely out on a limb." His voice had a little more emotion in it than he wanted it to.

"Because it might just be the most amazing thing you have ever experienced…and if it is, imagine how she must be feeling too?"

After he hung up with Sophie, he was restless, so he decided this was the perfect opportunity to continue chopping some more fire wood for her. She was going to need it, and it would be a great way for him to work off the excess energy he had since the moment he saw her. He threw on an old white t-shirt and jeans, his work boots and gloves, and headed to the shed for the axe.

The day passed faster than she would have liked, and

once again she found herself inside her home with all the lights on trying to keep away the dark of night outside. Alease sunk into her living room sofa, gazing into the fire she lit in the fireplace. It was a thankful contrast to the pitch black of night outside, which she still found frightening and unwelcome. Her escape to the little mountain home sounded good draped in sunlight, snow and isolation…but the dead dark of night out here left her feeling more scared than she had imagined. If it hadn't been for what happened in New York, she didn't think she would ever have heard each creek and crack the house made. She knew full well it would be a very long time until she slept again at night…if ever.

The fire was now at full blaze, after a bit of a struggle. She had to laugh at herself; making the fires had been harder than she thought it would be. She was really thankful that Cal had been leaving her fire wood; even though she kept telling him he didn't have to. This house was not as warm as she was used to, and she knew she would have been uncomfortable if he hadn't provided her the wood for her fireplace. He was right, it did add a much needed layer of heat to the living room. He also thought to leave her a box with kindling, paper and even matches. She reprimanded herself as she realized her enjoyment in believing he was that incredibly nice. It bothered her that she was so willing to credit that as the reason. She made a conscious decision to begin the effort of convincing herself it must be something else. Maybe he just thinks she is an idiot who can't light a fire, or that she is just a typical New Yorker…uhh, same thing.

She cozied back into the blanket she had around her, and sipped the cherry red wine she held in her left hand. Her thoughts and her body felt very disconnected. She was having periodic moments of calm, but then the wind would blow and she found herself startled with a burst of fear flooding through her. She had her baseball bat within reach and all the lights on. Just nerves…to be expected. She found ways to rationalize it and tell herself it was getting better. In a strange way though, she almost found those waves preferable to the other feelings that were in chase around her…and within her. Jesus, was that desire tapping at her? Longing even?

In the private corners of her mind, Alease admitted to herself that Cal had woken something in her that, perhaps, she never really let breathe before. Or maybe it never was there before Cal; but every time she was with him, she became more and more aware of this need that was stirring in her…it was more than just sexual. It was emotional too. It was both, and it pulled at her against her will.

Just *standing* across from Cal already made her past sexual encounters pale in comparison. She couldn't even comprehend what would happen to her if he touched her… kissed her…if he made love to her. She shuttered and threw back more wine to try and ease the rush of sensations that filled her. Just the thought of being with him was making her heart rate climb. She never felt this way before, and it scared her at the same time it thrilled her.

The idea of sex with anyone after that horrible night had not even been conceivable in her mind. She wanted nothing to do with any man having their hands on her. It has taken her all these months just for her to feel comfortable with her own hands on her. She made an effort, in the last month especially, to try and find a way to ease herself back into any kind of sexual joy or pleasure. She had gotten a vibrator and tried to entice herself back into the idea; alone, by herself with no one judging her. Only recently was she able to give herself an orgasm again. She couldn't always do it, but at least it was starting to come back to her. She was relieved when she did, because the one thing Alease knew that no one else did, is that the only orgasms she has ever had, were from her own hand when she was by herself. No man had ever been able to do it. It became normal to her. At least she was starting to get that back.

What was stranger to her now were these fleeting thoughts of sexual pleasure…and Cal. It had been so long since she thought of a man in that way…and with Cal it was even more…it was more than just sexual desire for him that was pulling at her…it was need. She couldn't explain it and she couldn't control it. She found herself imagining what it would feel like to lean against him…to be underneath him… to feel him touching her, kissing her…entering her. God, she could hardly breathe when the image flowed through her mind. Heat raced through her, her breathing quickened and her heart was pounding in her chest. She kept trying to pull herself back, and talk herself out of it. Letting herself believe his touch could feel that good was dangerous, misguided and foolish. Her mind was playing tricks on her. He would probably feel just like everyone else. Nothing more than what she could do for herself. But in the corner of her mind and deep down in her body, she couldn't help but wonder. Could a man's touch be that powerful? It was unsettling to her to be so electrified by Cal emotionally and sexually. It stunned her to realize that she was wondering what it would feel like if she brought herself to orgasm while thinking of Cal. A few more gulps of wine did little to settle her arousal. She pictured Cal's hands touching her…breath escaped her lungs she trembled. She stopped her thoughts and sat up. It was too much. Her entire body felt like it was on fire. She forgot about everything; her fear, her loneliness…everything was gone and replaced with this lustful need to be loved by this man; by Cal. She poured herself another glass of wine and tried to shake it off. She had never experienced this kind of need for someone and she didn't know how to handle it. It frightened her more than the creaking of the house and the darkness outside. Even just the idea of Cal loving her was so powerful, it took her breath away. It was tantalizing. It filled her with an equal desire to open herself to him completely and also to run for the hills, as far away from him as possible. She wasn't sure if she would ever have the strength to be with him; to even be near him. She wanted to hide now more than ever.

Cal woke with the sunrise in a sweat. His muscles pulsing and his sheets wet. He ran his hands through his thick brown hair, trying to get rid of the sexual images with Alease that haunted him all night long; or he was trying to hold onto them as if his life depended on it. Either way, he was helpless under this spell. His need for her was outrageous. Never had a woman had this tight a grip on him before. He was being tormented by the images of his lips on her body, kissing her stomach, licking her thighs and caressing her womanhood as he held her tightly in his arms. In his dream she held onto him with just as much need as he had driving into her. Cal tried to slow his breathing and snap out of it. He looked through his bedroom window towards her house. All the lights were still on. They had been on all night. He wondered if she slept. He wondered if she had any of the same kinds of thoughts that had been consuming him last night. The idea that she could be wanting him, even half as much as his want for her, made him hard as a rock again. Another cold shower would have to be the first step in order to start his day.

The cold shower helped his body, but his heart was still consumed with thoughts of her. He found himself practicing conversation tactics in his head to see which ones might lead to her opening up to him; about who she is and, of course, about what had happened to her. He knew she was scared to tell him anything she held close, and he really wanted to change that. He didn't want her scared, especially of him.

Cal wrapped a towel around his waist. The glistening water pearled on his chest and dripped off the muscles on his arms. In the mirror, he looked at the scars on his back from his deployments overseas. They are permanent proof of his bravery, his sacrifice and his strength. He wondered what Alease would think of them when…if…she saw them. His ex wife had always treated them as if they were something to be ashamed of. That hurt him. To survive the things he survived only to have her be offended by the marks they left on his body…that was hard to swallow. He kicked the thoughts of Becca out of his head and concentrated on Alease instead. She was different, he knew it in his bones. He had seen real admiration in her eyes when he had told her he was a Navy SEAL. That meant so much to him. He found himself wanting to talk with her about it; something he never did except with his SEAL team buddies. He felt a closeness to her that he still could not explain to himself, but he liked how it felt and he wanted to trust it. He wanted a lot. He wanted her wrapped tightly in his arms, as close as he could get her. He wanted her underneath him. A shiver ran through his body at the image. He admitted to himself he was a little nervous at the thought of being with Alease…of knowing exactly how to touch her. He would not be stopped by it, of course, but he admitted to himself he was nervous. He was pretty sure if *he* felt that way, than she must be terrified of it.

His phone rang, it was Joe. Joe Kimmey was the commander under him on his SEAL team, and had been Cal's best friend for years. They had deployed numerous times together and the two trusted each other with their lives; in and out of deployments.

"Hey Joe. What's up?" Cal was always glad to hear from Joe, and he was even more pleased to have his distraction this morning from the frustrating inability to get Alease out of his head.

"Breakfast. Come on. Get your lazy ass up and meet me." Joe's voice was always husky and deep with a even mix of tough stubbornness and kind heart.

Cal laughed and looked at his watch. "Sure, but you live four hours away. It would be lunch by the time I got there, not breakfast."

"I can't wait that long. It's a good thing I'm in your neighborhood. I drove down this morning. Twenty minutes out." He could hear Joe rolling down his car window, most likely to ditch his finished cigarette.

"No shit?"

"No, never when it comes to pancakes," Joe joked.

It was not at all unusual for the two to make the drive to

meet with each other for a meal or a quick visit, but usually a phone call the day before was part of the planning. It didn't matter, Cal was grateful for the drop in from his friend this morning, he could use it.

"Great. I'm getting dressed now."

"Meet you at Molly's?" Joe asked.

Cal thought for a moment. "No. Let's meet at Cafe Creme this time."

"OK. See you in Twenty."

Joe was already sitting in the booth when Cal got there. He was seated on the side facing the door (as SEALs always did…it was ingrained in them from their training.) Even if he hadn't stood when Cal walked over to him, Joe was impossible to miss, with his red hair and broad shoulders. Joe was just as tall as Cal and the two of them seemed to tower over everyone else in the crowded restaurant.

Cal slapped him on the shoulder and hugged him with a smile.

"Hey."

"Hey yourself," Joe said as he moved to the other side of the booth; allowing Cal to take the preferred position facing the door.

The waitress, an older woman who had a kind Grandmother type look to her, brought over two coffees as soon as Cal sat down. Cal looked up and smiled at her. "Thanks Betty."

"Always take care of my boys," she said with a grin. "Breakfast?"

Joe didn't even look at the menu she handed him, "Pancakes Ma'am. Lots of them! And Bacon," he smiled at her.

"Omelette, for me," Cal said.

"What do you want in it?" she asked.

"Surprise me," Cal didn't really care, he would eat anything.

"You got it." Betty walked away with the menus to get their breakfast order in.

Cal took a sip of his coffee. "So, how you doing? What's up?" he asked.

Joe tore open a packet of sugar and dumped it into his mug. "All good. Nothing new. You?" His eyes lifted from his coffee to Cal's, and Cal recognized the prying stare.

Cal released a breath and leaned back in surrender. "You and Dana spoke to Sophie, didn't you?"

Joe smiled. "Yep." He sipped his coffee continuing the stare down.

"My sister is a pain in the ass. What did she tell you?" Cal lowered his cup back down to the table.

Joe laughed. "Come on! You can't blame her. Not for this one. I've had my eyes on you for less than three minutes and I can see what she heard in your voice." Joe leaned back with a cocky grin. "God Damn, worth every minute of the four hour drive to get here." Cal tried to shake it off as he brought his coffee cup back to his lips. "Come on Cal, it's me. Let's have it." With that, Joe closed his mouth and kept his eyes on Cal. It was clear he was not going to let him off the hook in any way.

In all honesty, Cal had to admit he was glad to have the release. He needed to vent to his friend to help him unscramble his mind. "Jesus Joe, I think you need to hit me over the head with a shovel or something. I have lost it," Cal said as Joe laughed.

"Yeah, a good woman will do that to you." He sipped his coffee and waited to hear more.

"She is…amazing." Cal was half expecting Joe to poke fun at him, but he did no such thing. He just waited and listened. "Joe, she is…like magic. There is something about her that just…gets me. As beautiful as she is physically, I find myself seeing everything else about her even more than that. Every time I'm with her, or thinking about her…" Cal shook his head at a loss to explain it. "…Well, I've never felt less like a tough Navy SEAL in my life, I'll tell you that." Cal was uneasy, waiting for what he thought would be a slight chastisement, but to his surprise, it looked like Joe understood exactly what he meant.

"Cal, my friend, that's called love. Welcome to it." He lifted his coffee cup and toasted his friend who was looking at him stunned.

"How could this be love? Joe, I've only just met the woman."

Joe was snickering as he swallowed his coffee. "Cal, it only takes one second to fall in love. That first moment when your eyes meet the right woman…shit, that's what happened to me when I met Dana. Boom. That was it. Every tough guy wants to think that's a fairy tale, maybe that's a self defense tactic because there is no guarantee that will happen for everyone. You need to just realize that you are one of the lucky ones, and stop trying to convince yourself of anything else."

Cal found himself knowing Joe was right, but wanting to disagree with him for some reason. Joe must have seen that in his eyes.

"Listen, in all seriousness, between you and me…I know this is new for you. I spoke my truth to you about Becca, so you know I'm always gonna tell you how I see it. You are the toughest, most badass SEAL I know. I've never seen anything break you, even under circumstances that would have destroyed everyone else. You are not used to feelings that you can't control. Especially you."

Cal was struck by what he said. "What is that supposed to mean?"

Joe took a moment to think of how to phrase it, "You feel. Deeply. I admire that about you, I always have, but I've also seen how that has prevented you from being with a woman who actually means a lot to you. Not that you didn't care about Becca, or the other gazillion women you've slept with, but I've never seen you go deep. I think that's because you never had to. You have never crossed paths with a woman who got to you like this, and you are thrown off by it. But the situation is no different from any other challenge you have ever faced. You're a SEAL; grab the reins and dive in."

Cal listened. He heard him. He had no need to hide things from Joe. Joe was the one person he would share anything with, and he knew he was right.

Cal's eyes were drawn towards the front door. It amazed him, this invisible force that always pulled him where Alease was concerned. As soon as she walked into the restaurant, some part of him knew it, and he looked up. He knew Joe saw the look come over his face, because he turned eagerly to follow his gaze and then his unmistakable laugh came out as he turned back to his friend.

"So that's why you chose this place instead of Molly's. You knew she would come here didn't you?" Joe asked.

"I didn't know…just…hoped." Cal was caught and he knew it, but he didn't much care. He wanted to see her, and he was pretty sure that he wanted Joe to catch a glimpse of her too. "I've seen her with several of their to go coffee cups. Thought she might stop in for another one this morning."

Joe looked back at her again. As Alease ordered her coffee, Cal saw Joe study her and the people around her, gauging the fawning reactions from the men near her in line.

He smiled as he turned back to Cal. "Jesus, you weren't kidding about her being beautiful." He sipped his coffee again. "Ten bucks says the guy in the red shirt is going to "accidentally" bump into her and spill her coffee so he can buy her another one and get a conversation started."

Cal laughed. "I pegged that one already."

Sure enough, when Alease got her coffee, the man in the red shirt did exactly that, spilling her coffee on her coat, then going right into the conversation Cal and Joe knew he intended.

Cal watched as she tried to free herself from the man's attention. Part of him was always glad to see when she didn't want to deal with another man. Territorial, he knew it. She was usually good at getting away, but the crowd in the front didn't give her much room to back up, and Cal saw it. He stood without even thinking about it. Before he could call her name, her eyes looked up and saw him. She smiled.

"Come on over," Cal said with a wave, giving her the break from the annoying man that she needed.

She crossed over, shedding her coffee drenched coat as she did so. Joe's smile broadened and Cal shot him a warning. "Don't be an ass."

Joe laughed. "Never."

When Alease reached them, Cal could feel the heat flowing through his body as if he was suddenly standing inside a furnace.

"Hi," her voice was sweet and warm as always.

"Hi." Cal couldn't do anything about the smile that swept across his face. He gestured to Joe. "This is my best friend, Joe Kimmey. Joe, this is Alease."

Joe stood to shake her hand. He already saw the cast and took the initiative to reach out with his left hand instead of his right so that she could shake his as well.

"It's really nice to meet you Joe," she said.

"You as well, Alease. Sorry that guy spilled coffee all over your coat." Cal could see the very subtle assessments Joe was already doing of Alease, but he could also see the sincere approval in his friends eyes as well.

"Yeah, well, it's crowded. I guess he wasn't paying attention." Cal and Joe exchanged a look; they both knew she was feigning ignorance about the guys intentions. She knew exactly what the guy was doing, but was humbly pretending not to.

"Have a seat and join us," Cal said as he gestured towards the booth.

"Oh, I don't want to interrupt your breakfast," she answered shyly.

Joe spoke up. "Nonsense. Cal and I have breakfast all the time. You would be saving me from his boring conversation." Joe smiled as Alease laughed. "Besides, you might need to kill some time for that guy to leave before you walk over there again. Lord knows what the next thing will be he spills on you."

Alease's laugh filled Cal with such a breath of life, he was always stunned by it. Cal spoke with as much casual insistence as he could.

"You have to wait for your new coffee anyway. Come on, we would love to have you join us." Cal could see in her eyes that she wanted too. Not just because of the guy across the room, but he felt her enjoying their company.

"Alright. If you're sure I'm not intruding. I'll sit for a few minutes." Alease slid into the booth next to Cal and they all sat down as Betty brought over a fresh coffee to go for Alease.

"Here you go honey. Sorry about the idiot." She looked at Alease with a knowing smile, "Some men are so stupid. Might as well have pulled your pony tail," she laughed. "Now you are near the right guys." She gestured towards Cal. "Stick with this one, he's a real gentleman."

Alease laughed nervously and Cal saw her face flush red even though she was trying to hide it. He watched Joe reading every movement, every sound and every look on her face.

"Thank you for the coffee." Alease tried handing her some money to pay for the second cup, but Betty shook her head.

"No my dear. No charge for that one." Then she turned to get back to her other tables.

Joe laughed again. "You know, Betty is right. That guy did that in order to strike up a conversation with you."

Alease had that shy look cross her face again as she shook her head. "Seems like a stupid way to do that, doesn't it?"

"Well, some men get nervous," Joe said. "Some men need a minute to get their head on straight before they know how to handle a beautiful woman." Joe looked to Cal, double checking that he received the not so subtle message meant for him.

Alease laughed it off, being careful not to take what he said seriously, "Ahh, so spilling coffee on a woman is a typical first step in Big Sky Montana?" She sipped her drink as Joe responded.

"Well, for the idiots, yes. The second step would normally be him giving you his phone number, you know, pretending it's for the cleaning bill. In this case though, seeing as how you are sitting next to Cal, he will have Betty bring it over to you for him as he sneaks out the front door."

She laughed as if that was a joke, though Cal knew full well Joe was right. Alease turned to Cal and her smile shot right through him, as it always did. "So, how do you guys know each other?"

"Joe is on my SEAL team. We've known each other for years," Cal answered.

"We've been through Hell and back together," Joe said as

he lifted his coffee cup to his lips.

"I can imagine. I hate to think about some of the things you must have gone through. I do hope you have seen good things too." Her voice was very sincere, and Cal knew Joe felt it too. He could see it in his eyes. He never looked at Becca like that, that's for sure.

"Yes, we have. The good always outweighs the bad. I was just talking to Cal about the first moment I saw my wife. Most amazing second of my life. It's burned into my very soul. Erases all the bad, just like that. Still does every time I look at her." Joe smiled and looked at Cal as if reasserting everything he had told him before Alease joined them.

"That is so sweet." Alease seemed genuinely touched, but also, somehow, surprised to hear Joe say that.

Joe put down his coffee cup and gestured towards her cast. "So, what did you do?"

Cal was already very good at seeing the instant fortress that builds up in her eyes when she is asked something she does not want to answer, and there it was again. He saw the quick glance Joe gave him when Joe saw it too.

Alease took a moment and went into that rehearsed humor he heard the first time he asked her that question. She looked at Cal.

"Which answer did we decide sounds more exciting?" She laughed in an obvious attempt to keep things light. He knew she was looking to him for an escape, so he gave it to her.

He smiled. "I think you decided to take my advice and go with the jumping out of an airplane story."

"Right," she chuckled. Joe laughed with them, letting the humor stay, instead of pushing for a sincere answer. Cal knew he picked up on her avoidance tactics, just as he had when he first met her. "I hear that is standard practice for you guys, huh?" She sipped her coffee as Cal and Joe allowed her clever redirection of the conversation.

"Well, *I've* never broken bones jumping," Joe said with a cocky smile.

"That's cause you landed in a tree instead of on a boulder," Cal pointed out.

They all laughed. Alease turned her gaze to Cal and her smile, for the first time, seemed relaxed and filled with a deep sense of connection…to him. His heart pounded in his chest as his eyes locked into hers. Time froze and he was lost in her gaze. It amazed him how easily she could overtake his senses with those eyes of hers. She seemed locked in his eyes as well. Then, it looked as if she caught herself feeling for him…enjoying being near him, and he saw her defenses kick back up in her eyes as she shifted her gaze away and back to her cup.

Betty brought over their breakfast and set the plates down. She looked at Alease. "Can I get you anything honey?"

Alease shook her head, "No thank you. I have to be going

anyway."

"Don't go. Here, take half my omelette," Cal said

"No, I don't want to interrupt your breakfast."

Betty filled Joe's coffee cup and reached in her pocket. "Oh, I almost forgot. That idiot asked me to give you his phone number." She handed the piece of paper to Alease, who did not reach for it.

Joe and Cal both laughed. Joe spoke up. "Told you."

Alease looked to Betty. "You can throw that away."

Betty smirked. "Yeah. I had a feeling you would say that." Betty threw a knowing look to Cal, and then walked away to tend her other tables.

Alease turned to Cal, and that familiar but unexplainable bolt shot through him. "Thanks Cal."

He smiled. "For what?"

"For saving me…you know from the dumbass."

"Always." He could feel his heart pounding in his chest as he looked into her eyes. He saw her face flush again and she pulled her eyes away.

She looked to Joe. "It was really nice meeting you Joe."

Joe smiled warmly. "You too Alease."

As Cal watched Alease walk away, he felt Joe's eyes burning through him. After Alease left and the door closed, Joe's grin covered his face from ear to ear. "God damn, definitely worth the four hour drive!" His laughter flowed out of him.

"What is so funny?" Cal was trying not to let the smile on his face stay there, but he couldn't erase it.

"Seeing you try to battle the impossible! I never thought I would see the fight you could not win." Joe was enjoying this far too much. "Cal, just admit your feelings for her."

If it were any other person, Cal would deny it, but it was Joe. "Is it really that obvious?" he asked.

"Oh, good God!" Joe looked at him like he was an idiot. Then, in his confident, cocky style, he called Betty over. When she came to the table, Joe looked up at her. "Betty, tell me what you saw when that beautiful woman sat down and joined my friend at this table."

Betty answered very frankly and quickly as she filled Cal's coffee cup. "You mean the fact that it's forty degrees outside and I had to tell my manager to turn on the air-conditioning when she got close to him? Yeah, I saw that. Not to mention I could practically hear this one's heartbeat from across the room," she tilted her head towards Cal with that last statement before she walked away to pour someone else's coffee.

Joe turned to Cal with that told-you-so smile. "See?"

Cal felt completely lost under the weight of his feelings for her, and he knew Joe saw it.

Joe leaned in. "Cal, admit it. Stop trying to fight it, or even understand it. You have to admit it before you can figure out how to deal with it."

Joe was right. "Fine, I admit it." It was strange, but he did feel a sense of clarity when he said the words out loud.

"Helps, right?" Joe asked.

"Yes, but that doesn't mean she feels the same for me, or even anything close to it." Cal could feel his mind saying the words more than his heart.

Joe slanted his eyes at him in a challenge. "Oh come on. I'm calling bullshit. You are the most intuitive person I have ever met. No way in Hell you don't know she has feelings for you."

"She is…hard to read. You saw her, she constantly runs from me."

Joe put his coffee cup down and nodded his head. "Yes, but the way she runs from you, is very different from the way she runs from everyone else. You know it. I know you know it."

Cal released his breath, and the denial that went with it. "Yeah. I see it too." He shook his head as he uncomfortably revealed his bewilderment. "I'm just not sure how to do this with her. This is really strange for me."

"Cal, you are not used to having to work for it. You have spent your life with women throwing themselves at you, so you never had to think, you never had to fight, you never had to care about your next steps. Now you do." Joe sat back to eat his pancakes. "So admit what you want, and go get it."

"How? If I move too fast, I know I will spook her and she

will bolt."

"So proceed carefully…but proceed," Joe said simply.

Somehow, those words offered Cal a much needed sense of clarity. "You're right. Thank you. Guess I needed to hear that." Cal knew Joe was right about everything and was glad for the push.

Joe stuffed some more pancakes in his mouth and his energy changed to a much more serious tone. "Now, what's the real story with that arm?" he asked.

"Yeah, I picked up on that right away too when I first met her. She won't tell me. I haven't pushed it, but she finds very clever ways of trending off the subject when it's brought up." Cal ate a bite of his omelette.

"Yeah, I noticed that. Theory?" Joe asked.

Cal knew Joe had a gut feeling about it, the same as he did. He told him all he knew and confided that his guess was that she was on the receiving end of some kind of attack, but he wasn't sure what the details were. Joe listened carefully then spoke.

"Just say the word and I will have all my contacts on it. You know I've got friends in FBI, CIA, and more. I can find out everything you need to know," Joe said. Cal didn't need to be reminded of that, he had already thought about it.

"I know. Believe me, I almost called you right away. But I don't want to feel like I'm going behind her back. I really want to see if I can get her to tell me." Cal had been torn about it since he started to suspect what had happened, but he felt like he should hold off on Joe's help.

"I can have all the info for you in a few days. All I need is her last name," Joe offered again.

"I know. That's why I didn't give it to you. I know you have my back." Cal really was grateful for his friendship.

"OK. As soon as you need me to look into it, just tell me. In the meantime, ask her out," Joe said followed by another mouthful of pancakes.

"Joe, come on, you saw how every guy reacts to her and how she hates it. I can't ask her out and be like all these other idiots."

Joe laughed. "Yeah. I saw her blow off every man in this restaurant…except for one." Joe looked at him as he sipped his coffee again. "So you don't formally ask her out…but you just happen to be there when she turns around. One careful step at a time. I'm telling you Cal, she looks at you differently than she looked at everyone else here. And I know you know that."

Once again, his friend was right. Cal did know it. He felt it. Her fear of him was…different. He had to find ways of helping her fight it; to get her to give in to him and trust him, and, if he was so lucky, to see the day that, maybe, he would be loved by her in return.

Chapter Four
Facing Fears

The bite of the November chill was sharp against her skin. Alease spent far longer on her walk this morning than she intended to, but the peace of it today was exactly what she needed. Last night had been especially long for her because of bad dreams during the sporadic moments of dozing off on the sofa. She was frustrated with herself that the dark of night was always accompanied now with that heavy sense of dread and fear. She despised her inability to just forget about it and sleep; but she couldn't.

She loved that Max always walked with her in the mornings. He reminded her so much of König. Walking with him kept triggering the desire in her to get another dog, but every time she thought of it, she was filled with guilt about what happened to König. She couldn't bear to be the reason another dog might lose it's life, so she always talked herself out of the idea of getting another one. She had a guard dog once; if that wasn't enough, then she should be on her own to defend against whatever may come her way.

When she came down the mountainside to the house, she saw Cal chopping wood in the front. Her breath caught her off guard as it escaped from her lungs. He looked so amazing, she couldn't deny it. Her experience with men had been nothing like this. She was used to the kind of guys who needed time to dress up and groom themselves into presentable images. They had to work at it, but Cal…Jesus, just in his basic white teeshirt and jeans he was more desirable than all the men she had ever known combined, and then some. She couldn't remember ever seeing a man looking so…masculine, so strong and confident. His sweat drenched shirt was clinging to his incredible chest, his arms bulging and glistening with drops of perspiration. She couldn't believe how he took her breath away. She desperately tried to find ways to talk herself out of her incredible attraction to him, but she was failing miserably. Part of her wanted to run back up the mountain and hide until he went in, but he looked up and saw her. *Damn.* She couldn't turn back now, it would be to obvious. So, she continued her descent towards where he stood; the man who was capturing her heart and slowly leaving her defenseless. God, she needed to be careful.

"Good morning," Cal said as he lowered the axe and dried his chiseled face with a small towel. "How did you sleep?"

Alease was still trying to control her breathing and heart rate that had increased even more as she got closer to him. "Fine," she lied.

"I see Max went with you again this morning. How was your walk?" He put one leg up on the stump that was his base for chopping the wood, and leaned on it casually.

"Yes, I hope that is ok with you. He likes to tag along. It's fun to have him with me."

"Absolutely fine. I'm glad you had company. It's beautiful up there, isn't it?" His smile was infectious and she felt herself being warmed by it in the chilly morning air.

"Yes," was all she could think to say as she became even more aware of her physical reaction to being near him.

"There are a lot of hidden spots up there that will take your breath away. Whenever you would like a guide, I would be happy to take you to the best ones."

She hated how much she loved the thought of that. Of walking the trails with him. Of being near him, isolated with him on this beautiful mountain. As she was trying to convince herself she didn't want that, she heard herself admit the opposite out loud against her will. "I would love that." His smile grew and she knew she needed to get herself away from him before she lost her ability to hide the effect he was having on her. "I'm going to head in for a nap."

"Sleep well," he said to her in a deep voice that she took with her to her pillow.

Alease curled up in her bed, under the blankets with images of him. She couldn't help it. She tried to fight them off but she couldn't, so she gave in and drifted to sleep with thoughts of him all over her.

Cal saw it and he knew now for sure that she was

attracted to him. He could also see she was fighting it. Joe had been dead on. He was really glad Joe had come up and forced him to open his eyes and face his feelings. Ever since then, he had a clear determination of how he needed to proceed with Alease; a very careful, slow push closer to her, with space enough in-between for her to adjust to what she was feeling for him.

The sun had been glistening off her hair and she looked even more beautiful than she had the day before. It was probably a good thing that she ran for the safety of her little house because if she had stayed there much longer, the bulge under his jeans might have become too obvious. Every time he was near her, his body filled with desire for her.

When she closed her front door, he went back to chopping the wood. He hoped that would help relieve some of the built up passion flowing through him, but the images of her in her bed were preventing the easing of the fire burning up inside him.

The late afternoon sun over the mountain did little to warm the chilly air, but the sting of it was somehow refreshing. Alease needed to get out. Her body was restless and her mind overworked. As if adding salt to the wound of her losing battle to regain her self control and independence, Alease, once again, couldn't manage to detach the trailer from her truck with one hand. The last thing she needed was to ask

Cal for help, so she just decided to drive the truck again with the damn trailer attached to it. She needed to get out a bit and try to cool off the unsettling desires that kept waking her up from her morning nap. The relentless sexy dreams of Cal forced their way into her subconscious like a bull in a china shop; destroying every carefully placed barrier she had worked on to keep herself from ever having to deal with exactly what was happening to her now. She couldn't believe how hard it was to shake off the effect he had on her. A distraction and distance was what she needed, so she decided to do a little grocery shopping and driving around town.

Shopping had been fine. She managed to get a bunch of things she didn't really need, save for the red wine bottles in the bag. She had a feeling she would definitely need those. The grocery store only had the screw cap kind, which she was sure would not be as good as corked wine, but she had little choice.

When she pulled up in front of her house, she saw that Cal's truck was not there. *Thank God,* she thought. Now she could sneak into her house without another battle of standing in front of him trying not to let him get to her like he does. It was maddening to her that she couldn't control it.

She reached for one of the paper bags in the back seat and as she pulled it out, the bag tore and her groceries spilled out onto the dirt around her truck.

"Damn it," she said as the blueberries and strawberries

went in all directions. She unsuccessfully tried to avoid stepping on a bunch of them, as one of the wine bottles fell out of the bag and rolled towards her back tire. She was so distracted by her annoyance that she didn't realize Cal was pulling up in the drive next to her. She bent down to pick up the wine bottle that had miraculously not broken, but she lost her balance and found herself on the ground, "Fuck!" It was just after this impressive move on her part that she heard Cal's driver side door close and his strong boots hit the driveway as he got out. *Wonderful…graceful, Alease…*she was so embarrassed. The only thing she could think to do now was sit up, lean against her truck and act as if she didn't care.

"You ok?" Cal asked as he crossed over to her.

Alease smiled, twisted off the top of the bottle of wine and took a big swig. "Yep. Perfect. All is going according to plan." She took another gulp as Cal laughed kindly at her humor.

"Well, I'm told a good wine can be enjoyed anywhere… I'd say you're testing the limits. How is it?"

"Horrible. Dreadful. Screw cap, but it was all they had. Want some?" She didn't know why she offered him the bottle, but at this point, she had lost her ability to worry about how she was coming across. He was seeing her pretty much at her worst, so what more could happen.

Cal reached down accepting the bottle. "Yeah. Thanks,"

he took a gulp, "Yep, terrible." He took another guzzle and then handed her back the bottle. "I do know something that might make it better though."

Alease was curious. "Oh yeah? What's that?" she asked as she threw back another one.

Cal opened the back door to his truck and pulled out a big flat box. "Pizza." His teasing smile was intriguing.

"The grin on your face about that pizza has me curious," she said.

Cal walked over to her and opened the box. The glorious smell of the steaming hot pizza filled her senses and, against all her wishes, her stomach growled out loud.

"This is no ordinary pizza. This is a Cal Winters special…sausage, peppers, onions, mozzarella, basil…and wood fired to perfection." He shifted the pizza directly under her nose and within her reach. "Tell you what. I will share my pizza with you if you will share your wine with me."

She had no choice, her mouth and body overruled all her higher reasoning skills and she spoke before she could even think. "Done!"

Cal sat down on the ground next to her, placing the box in-between them. "Help yourself."

Alease didn't realize until this moment that she hadn't eaten a thing since yesterday. She was starving and this pizza was suddenly the most important thing in the world. She reached for a piece and savored the first bite.

"Oh my God is that good." She saw Cal smiling as he found his own piece and began eating too. "We must look like idiots sitting on the dirt surrounded by blueberries and mud, enjoying this pizza as if it was steak and lobster."

"I think it's perfect," Cal said as he kicked a blueberry away from his boot and stretched his legs out. He leaned against her truck and seemed completely at ease. She was amazed at how, once again, he was able to take a situation that had her uncomfortable and turn it into something…easy and calm. She laughed.

"What?" he asked her.

"Thank you for being kind enough to not make me feel like a dumb ass," she said.

He took another bite. "Why should you feel like a dumb ass?"

"Oh come on, you pulled up just in time to see me drop my groceries all over the driveway, then fall over as I tried to pick up this horrendous bottle of wine. Instead of pointing out how idiotic I am, you just sat down next to me and offered me pizza." She looked at him with sarcastic suspicion. "So what's your deal Cal Winters?" she asked.

He laughed at her question. "What do you mean?"

"How can you possibly be that nice?"

His laughter grew and he responded as he reached for the bottle of wine. "I know a few terrorists that would disagree with you on that." He took a swig of the wine and it looked like it was tasting better to him.

Alease gazed into his eyes more carefully than before and found herself interested in what was just under the surface of that comment. "Did you really face off against terrorists?" she asked.

He took a beat before answering. "Yes," he answered as he handed her the bottle.

Alease took another sip, and looked back at him. "I hope you killed them," she heard herself say. She meant it, but she wasn't sure where it came from that she actually said it out loud.

Cal's eyes scanned her, as if impressed that she held that opinion. "That wouldn't bother you?"

She brought the wine to her lips for a big chug before she replied. "I don't like bad guys." She hadn't meant for her answer to be shrouded in such raw emotion, but there it was. She blamed it on the wine and hoped Cal didn't notice it.

"Neither do I," he said calmly.

She didn't want to meet his eyes so she kept her gaze on the pizza instead, as if somehow that would shield her from the energy that was filling the air between them. Cal spoke again, and in his voice she could feel the purposeful care with which he continued.

"You've uhh…had some experience with that haven't you? With bad guys?" he asked.

Her heart picked up its pace and she was sure it skipped a

few beats in the process. She didn't want to fall into this conversation, so she reached into her bag of tricks to find a low key way to redirect it.

"Hasn't everyone?" She tried to keep it as light and breezy as she could, but when she caught Cal's eyes, she knew it hadn't worked on him. She felt that familiar fear of exposure creeping up inside her and found herself unsure of where to go from here.

"You don't like to reveal much of anything about yourself do you? Why is that?" he asked her.

"Habit. Just seems to always be the wiser choice."

She offered him the bottle again hoping to pull his attention to something else, but he kept his gaze on her. She could feel him looking past her eyes, deeper into her, and she didn't remember anyone ever looking at her in quite the same way. She had always wondered if a man could see past her face to who she really was, and now that she was faced with a man who seemed to be doing just that, she was incredibly unnerved by it.

"Is it that you don't trust me, or you just don't trust in general?" His question was direct and bold.

"I just try to stay hidden." It was all she could think to say. How could she explain it?

"Yeah, I've noticed that. I know you try, but you do reveal a lot more than you think you do. I see it anyway." He took the bottle and had another gulp of the wine.

She was fascinated by what he said. "What? Really? You think that?" She was either challenging him, or getting defensive about her failure as the guardian of her privacy.

"Alease, I hear everything you say and I hear everything you don't say." His confidence was unmatched by anyone she had ever met.

"You do that with everyone?" It was her turn for the wine and he offered it back without hesitation.

"Yes, but with you it's…different." He looked away as he said it, and Alease wasn't sure what she was reading in that.

"Why?" Part of her immediately regretted asking that question. This conversation was getting too real for her and her defenses were going off in her head.

"Because I care about you." That statement physically shot through her when he said it. She saw him look at her after the words came out, as if reading her face for a reaction that she was trying intensely to camouflage.

"You don't even know me." She was trying harder to convince herself than him, and she could tell from the look in his eyes that he knew it.

"Really? You want to test that theory?" The conviction in his voice told Alease he just might be about to say some things she did not want to hear, but she could think of no clever way to change the direction he was headed. "I know that you didn't break your arm slipping on your driveway, or jumping out of a plane. I have a pretty good idea what sharp object made that scar on your neck. I'm fairly certain that the loss of König is connected to one or both of those incidents." Alease felt her body flush with fear and she saw confirmation in Cal's gaze that he recognized it. "And I know you get scared whenever I ask you anything that could lead to you sharing something of who you are with me," he gave a slight pause before he continued. "I'm kind of hoping we can change that...that you will talk to me. I'd like to know you."

She felt at a complete loss. In one smooth moment, he disarmed her of all her normal avoidance tactics and called her out. He had been connecting the dots that she was sure she had been erasing. She wasn't clear on what he really knew, but obviously her ability to throw him off the trail had been unsuccessful. She didn't know how to cover herself with him.

"I'm ok Cal," she thought it sounded convincing.

"No you're not. As soon as the sun goes down you turn on all the lights. You don't sleep at night. You came up here to isolate yourself and you won't let anyone help you with anything. Do you really think you are supposed to be doing this all on your own?" He asked the question as if, somehow he doubted she really felt that way.

Her defenses kicked at her hard. "Life seems to be handing me plenty of lessons to suggest that, yes."

Cal thought for a moment before he spoke his next words. "You think maybe it's possible that life is handing you a few more lessons? That perhaps you might want to double check yourself to make sure you're learning the right things? I've been where you are, I've done that too. Thought my life was over when the truth is that it's not that life is *over*, it's that life is *starting over*. There's a big difference."

The sea of warmth in his eyes was almost too much to bear. She felt stripped of any and all intellect. He had rendered her speechless and she felt completely out of her comfort zone.

The sound of a car coming up the driveway was an extremely welcome relief to her. Alease had no idea who it was, but she was glad to have been saved from coming up with a response to Cal's last words. Alease focused up and out at the car, acutely aware that Cal's eyes were still reading her like a book.

The car pulled up and a young woman with very short hair got out. She had a girly smile and a folksy charm about her. Alease instantly liked her. She walked up to them looking down at the two sitting in the dirt with an almost finished bottle of red wine, and half eaten box of pizza between them.

"What am I looking at here?" she asked.

Cal laughed and smiled a very familiar smile to the woman. "Alease, this is my younger sister Sophie. Sophie, this is Alease Taynes, my new neighbor."

"It's lovely to meet you Sophie," Alease said in a perfectly pleasant tone, attempting to throw off any sign of discomfort from the previous conversation she had been having.

Sophie smiled back a warm, happy smile. "You too Alease." Sophie directed her attention to her brother, "Dear God, please tell me this is not your idea of a date. Pizza and cheap wine on the muddy ground leaning against a truck?"

Cal answered quickly. "No, no, this is not a date, Sophie. This is two adults just talking and eating pizza…on the ground because we were too hungry to make it inside to a table. Not a date. Right?" He looked to Alease as if to feel her out on the subject.

"Absolutely not a date. I'm sitting on smushed blueberries and squished strawberries…not attractive in the least."

Sophie laughed. "I'm sure you could be sitting on a pile of trash and you would still be the most attractive woman any man has ever seen."

Alease laughed uneasily. Cal spoke up. "Where's my nephew? Did you forget him at a truck stop or something?"

Sophie gestured towards the field behind Cal's house. "He wanted to say hi to Chase, so he got out half way down the drive. He's been sitting in the car for an hour so the exercise will do him good."

Alease could see a young boy running up to them as she said the words. He looked to be about thirteen years old. He was a little out of breath when he reached them.

"Hi uncle Cal!" He was clearly excited to see him.

Cal got up and gave him a big hug, then turned back to Alease who was still sitting on the ground, "Alease this is my nephew Jake. Jake this is Alease."

Jake smiled at her and said hello, then turned back to his mom. "Is this the woman Uncle Cal said is so gorgeous?" he asked.

Cal playfully tucked Jake's head in an arm lock and looked at Alease with some embarrassment. "You'll have to ignore him…tourettes…it's very sad," he joked.

"My son does not have Tourettes!" Sophie interjected in defense.

"Whats Tourettes?" Jake asked innocently.

"It's when you say things out loud that will make your uncle have to throw you in a pile of manure," Cal said jokingly.

"But you did say she was gorgeous. I heard you telling mom," Jake boldly replied.

Jake laughed and screamed as Cal lifted him up over his head. "That's it! The manure pile it is!" Cal had him far above his head and started to walk towards the horse field.

Alease was amazed at the ease with which he lifted the boy, as if Jake was lite as a feather to him. His strength was remarkable.

Sophie looked back at Alease with a grin. "He loves Cal so much."

"I can see that."

They chit chatted about the drive, and the weather. Alease could tell that Sophie was a good person and she felt very comfortable with her. Cal had Jake over by the fence line and was pretending that he was going to throw him over it. They could hear Jake laughing from where they were.

Sophie turned back to Alease. "So how do you like it here so far? Big change from New York, huh?"

"Welcome change. I like it very much. How long have you lived in this area?" she asked.

"Cal and I grew up here. Our family has had land here and in Bozeman for a few generations. When our parents died, Cal took ownership of this place and I took the one in Bozeman."

"What happened to your parents, if you don't mind me asking?" Alease was curious.

Sophie sat down next to Alease. "Our dad died in deployment over seas, and our mom passed away from cancer about a year after that."

"I'm so sorry Sophie."

Sophie's smile put her at ease. "It's ok. It was years ago and they are together again, so Cal and I have made our peace with it. What about you, do you have family?" she asked.

"No, not really. My mom died when I was little, and my father…kind of just disappeared after I graduated from high school. Guess he thought his responsibility was done at that point," she shifted her tone to try and lighten her words.

"I'm sorry. Sucks to not have family." Sophie's manner was genuinely sympathetic, and Alease found herself at ease with her. "I have been lucky to have Cal as a brother. He was there for me when I got pregnant with Jake. I was only 19. Young and stupid. I don't think I could have done it if Cal hadn't been so supportive."

"What happened to Jake's father?" Alease asked.

"Out of the picture from the word go. Told him I got pregnant and he ran off. Probably for the best, he wasn't the most responsible guy in the world."

"Well, you seem to be doing a fantastic job with him. You should be proud," Alease said with a smile.

Cal and Jake were headed back towards them, Jake still laughing and rough housing with Cal.

"You settling in ok here?" Sophie's question came as they watched the boys walk towards them.

"Yes. I mean, unpacking is going slowly," Alease chuckled and gestured to her cast. "Makes it tough to do things like carry boxes into the house. I'm getting good at dragging things though. One box at a time. I figure I should have them all inside by Christmas."

Sophie laughed. "Well, I know a thirteen year old that could use some physical exercise after the drive. Please let me put him to work for you!"

"I'm sure Jake would much rather hang with Cal. They

look inseparable," Alease said.

"Perfect. They can both help you," Sophie responded. When the boys reached them, Sophie looked at Jake.

"What? No manure?" she asked.

Jake laughed. "No. Uncle Cal would never do that to me."

"You just watch!" Cal jested back.

Jake looked at the trailer attached to Alease's truck. "That's a cool trailer. What cha' got in there?" he asked curiously.

"Oh, just boxes mostly. It's everything I brought with me from New York."

"How come you keep driving into town with the trailer on?" Cal asked with a slight smirk.

Alease could sense he knew the answer to his question but was trying to get her to admit it. "I have had a little trouble trying to unhook it with one hand," she answered attempting to downplay it.

Sophie looked confused. "Why didn't you just ask Cal to help you?" Her question was innocent enough.

Cal's grin was a bit cocky as he leaned in. "Yes. Why didn't you just ask me for help, Alease?"

"I guess that thought just didn't occur to me," she brushed it off.

Cal walked over to the back of her truck, and in less then a minute the trailer was unhooked. He looked back at her.

"See how easy that was?"

Alease swallowed her dislike of the intrusive lesson. "Thank you, Cal."

"Now, I'm sure I am correct that pretty much all of your boxes are still in here, right?" he asked.

"No, I've gotten one or two boxes out on my own," Alease answered with sarcastic pride.

Cal laughed. "OK Jake, you and I have some work to do. If you want me to order you a Cal Winters special, then you have to help me bring all of her boxes from the trailer up to her house."

"You don't have to do that you guys," Alease tried to protest but Sophie cut her off.

"Please. Let them do it. They will have it done in a half an hour I'm sure. Besides, if we don't do something to wear out my son, he will be up all night!"

"OK, Alease, Jake and I are going to help you, like it or not. Where would you like the boxes?"

"Fine." She gave in, telling herself the wine had something to do with it. "Ok, the front living room is fine."

Sophie's prediction was pretty accurate; the guys had it done in an hour. They probably could have done it faster but they were enjoying jousting with each other while they did it. Cal was a great uncle. It was blatantly clear that Cal would be an amazing father. Alease wondered why he wasn't. It seemed so natural to him. She wondered what had happened between

Cal and his ex wife. She took note for that to be her next topic of conversation with him. Not just because she was curious, but also because it would keep the conversation off of her.

Alease was in her kitchen thrilled to have her espresso machine out of the trailer at long last. It was too heavy for her to carry with her broken arm, but thanks to Cal and Jake bringning in her boxes, she finally had it up and running again. She was busy pulling shots for three coffees, and steaming the milk for one home made hot chocolate for Jake. Sophie was sitting at her counter chatting with Alease about espresso and how to make the perfect coffee.

"It must be the New York in you. This coffee is amazing! East coast coffee always this good?" Sophie was in bliss with the flavor in her cup.

"No. Not all east coasters know how to make it right. Just the ones who learned how to do it and which companies have the best coffee beans." She turned back to Sophie with Jake's hot chocolate. She called over to the boys who were bringing in the last few boxes from the trailer. "Here you go, Jake. A fresh homemade hot chocolate, with whipped cream all for you." Jake dashed over and took the mug.

He drank it and smiled. "Wow, this is the best hot chocolate I have ever had. Thanks Alease!"

"My pleasure. Thank you for all your work today." She looked up at Cal who crossed the floor over to them. She handed him the coffee she made for him and he accepted it happily with his large hands.

Cal turned back to Jake. "Jake, I saw one more thing in the back of the trailer, can you grab it and bring it in? Extra pizza slice for you if you do."

"Ok!" Jake dashed out the door happily.

Cal took a sip of the coffee Alease had made for him, and looked up from it with an honest surprise.

"Wow. This is amazing coffee. How did you get the flavor so good?" He took another sip.

"Barista skills and great coffee beans," she answered as she drank her own coffee.

"Were you a barista?" Sophie asked her.

Alease shook her head. "Heavens no. I just took some classes years ago because I like good coffee and wanted to learn how to make it better. I never worked in a coffee shop or anything."

This gave Cal an opening he seemed eager to jump on. "So, now that we are on the subject, what is it that you do? Or did in New York?" He sat down next to Sophie across from Alease with an honest curiosity as to what her answer would be.

While she was trying to figure out how to answer the question, Jake came back in, holding her big black guitar case in his hands. "Alease, is this a guitar?" he asked excitedly.

Alease really didn't want to elaborate on her music career before Big Sky, so she downplayed his excitement over the instrument. "Yeah. It's an old guitar. Acoustic, not the exciting electric guitars you probably like."

"Cool," Jake said as Cal turned to look at her.

"You play?" he asked.

"Well, not right now," she chuckled, "Kind of hard to play with one hand." Cal was still waiting for further explanation. This was clearly an aspect of her past that he had not guessed, and he had that look that he was not going to let her skate by with floating vague answers about it. "I dabble here and there." She diverted the attention back to Jake, "What kind of music do you like Jake?"

"Country! My uncle and I listen to it all the time," he said as he crossed over to join everyone at the counter.

"Yeah? Who is your favorite artist?" It didn't dawn on Alease that her question would lead them to the very topic she was trying to avoid.

"Kenny Keep. Same as uncle Cal, right?" Jake asked Cal.

Cal nodded his head. "Absolutely. We listen to his stuff all the time, don't we?" Cal responded. Alease stayed perfectly still trying to quiet the beating heart that was pounding in her chest. She did not mean to open this door and she needed to find a laid-back way to close it. She hid her face with her mug and drank her coffee. Cal looked up at her. "You know his music?" he asked her.

Alease nodded. "Yeah, I do," she said simply.

"Uncle Cal's favorite song in the whole world is

'Christmas Mountain.' He even listens to it in the summer time," Jake added before another sip of his hot chocolate.

Alease felt like she was having an out of body experience. She could feel an unwelcome buzz of nerves shoot through her body as she attempted to downplay any outward reaction as much as possible.

Cal smiled. "It is, without question, the best song ever. Great all year round. I love that one."

"Let's listen to it while we wait for the pizza," Jake said excitedly.

Cal turned to Alease. "We would love for you to join us," he said to her.

Alease was fighting down that battle inside her again. Part of her wanted very much to join them. She had no way of denying to herself that having Cal in her home was comforting. Being near him felt…too good. She could feel a yearning to wrap herself in him; to cover herself with his energy like a warm blanket on shivering skin. So, of course, she said no.

"I can't, but thank you. Have to be in town early tomorrow morning."

"What are you doing?" Sophie asked her as she finished her cup of coffee.

"Getting my cast off." Alease couldn't help the happiness that came through her voice.

Cal's eyes lit up. "Really? Thats great. Congratulations."

He cheered her with his mug. "Do you know where you're going? I can take you if you want."

Alease shook her head. "No, thank you. That's very sweet, but I will find it. You have your family here, I don't want to take you away from that."

Cal had that look he gets when his frustration at her stubborn refusal of his help irks him. "Fine. OK, but you must join us for dinner tomorrow night then. I insist. To celebrate your free arm." Alease was about to challenge him, but he cut her off. "No no's. There is no no. You're joining us. I will grill New York strips, in your honor. Please join us. I really want you to." The way he said it was so sweet and she could feel him drawing her in against the warning screams in her head.

"OK." It was frustrating how her voice seemed to speak without her permission.

After some more chit chat on various topics, and an additional invitation to join them tonight for pizza, which Alease politely declined, she walked them to the door.

She couldn't help herself, "Hey Cal?" He turned back to her with that warm smile of his while Jake and Sophie kept walking towards Cal's house. "I'm curious. What is it about "Christmas Mountain" that you love so much?"

Cal leaned against her door in thought for a moment about how to answer her question. "I'm not sure exactly, it just speaks to me. It's powerful. It makes me feel. It's like a memory that I haven't had yet. That song, it just…it feels like home to me. Why do you ask?"

"Just curious," she answered. As Cal walked away she couldn't help but find it fascinating. This song that affected Cal so much…and little did he know that she was the one who wrote it.

Chapter Five
The Next Step

Alease's reflection in her mirror was a mix of well covered fear with sprinkles of excitement for the evening she was getting ready for. Cal had been swirling in her mind constantly since last night, the part of her that couldn't wait to see him again was louder than the part that was trying to argue with her about it.

She had been in town almost all day dealing with the removal of her cast, which went well, but the office was so backed up that it took far longer than she had anticipated. It was a strange sensation having use of her arm and hand back. She hated how it looked to her…thin and still a little bruised. The worst was the line across her wrist where the restraint had cut into her skin; it looked like a neon sign to her. It was a painful reminder of what that man had done; of how quickly he had slipped the restraint over her hand and pulled it till she had no hope of getting away from him. Thank God he had only been able to get it over one hand. Though she was tied down by the arm with the restraint, she was able to use the hand she managed to keep free to reach the phone and call for help. Just barely. A few inches further and she would have been trapped there for God knows how long. But the force with which she had to pull to get her fingers to reach the phone had caused the restraint to cut incredibly deeply into her skin. She could only hope, in time, the scars would fade. For now, she would try to cover it with bracelets and long sleeves. Maybe if Cal had a drink right away, his observation skills would diminish and he wouldn't see it. She made note to open the bottle of wine she was bringing first thing.

She added the last few touches of her make up and ran a thick comb through her long hair. Her nerves were annoying her. *It's just steak and wine.* No matter how many times she repeated it to herself, she still couldn't quiet the butterflies in her stomach. Part of her felt like a lamb walking right into the lions den. *Maybe I should start right away with the wine too,* she thought.

Jake must have seen her coming because he opened the door before she even reached it. "Hi Alease!" Max burst out to greet her first with kisses and licks.

"Hey Jake."

When Alease walked into Cal's home she immediately felt comfortable. It was warm, open and beautiful. He had a big fire going in the living room fire place, and the kitchen was bustling with Cal throwing last minute seasoning on the steaks and Sophie tossing a salad in a large green bowl. Cal looked up as soon as she walked in, and that beautiful, disarming smile crossed his face and shot right into her heart.

"Hey Alease. Hows the arm?" he asked. Cal wiped his hands on a kitchen towel and crossed over to her.

"It's fine. Doc says it looks good."

"Let's see." He reached her and gently lifted her newly freed arm to look at it. Her bracelet fell back a little and he paused when he saw the mark on her wrist. Alease saw the flicker of concern in his eyes as soon as he looked at it. *Damn…didn't open the wine fast enough…distraction needed.*

Alease handed Cal the wine, "Here. I brought a good bottle of wine this time. Cork and everything, to make up for the horrendousness of the last one." Cal's eyes took a second, but then they deliberately changed their look, masking his thoughts. He took the bottle out of her hand with a smile. She wanted to convince herself that he didn't register what the marks really were, but she knew he was sharp. In light of the fact that she couldn't run from it, she chose to ignore it and was relieved to see that Cal, at least for now, was choosing to let it go.

"Thank you. I say we open it and get the steaks on the grill." His eyes stayed with her a moment longer then necessary, which told Alease that he didn't miss it, like she was hoping he would. All she could do now was lower her sleeve back down over her wrist and hope he would forget about it. There were colors of care in his gaze; a sympathy and a depth that pinched at her. It was strange to be looked at in a way that was so comforting and yet so terrifying at the same time because she could see him looking right *into* her, not *at* her like other men. She was pretty sure if Sophie and Jake hadn't been in the room with them, that he would not have let it go, and he would be asking her about the marks on her wrist right now. Thank God they were. Against her will, she had to admit to herself that she loved the way Cal looked at her, and she was not ready for that affectionate glimmer in his eyes to be replaced with pity, and the inevitable downfall into lack of interest; which would be certain if he knew she had been attacked. Victimhood was not attractive and she knew men didn't want that in the women they chose to be with. Not that she believed he wanted her, but she liked the possibility of it. It occurred to her as these thoughts pulsed through her mind that she really needed a drink. She followed Cal to the kitchen to begin washing the thoughts away.

Outside by the big fire pit, Cal flipped the steaks over, and the shooting flames spit up in the air, sizzling the meat on the grill plate that draped over one side of the pit. The flames matched the anger that flared up in him when he saw the marks on her wrist. He knew exactly what made those scars, and it infuriated him to no end. He was trying to keep it quiet, but it was taking him time to calm the internal vexation, so he stayed with the grill longer than he needed to.

He shifted his focus towards his kitchen window. Sophie and Alease were talking and drinking the red wine Alease had brought over. The sight of her in his home felt amazing, but was being overshadowed by the anger punching inside him at the restraint marks on her wrist. He boiled with rage at the invasive thoughts and images in his head of her being hurt and…Jesus…he couldn't let himself finish the thought. He wanted to kill whoever had done that to her. He saw the fear in her eyes when he met her gaze after looking at her wrist, so he tried his best to smile and let it go. Pretend he didn't notice it or understand it's ramifications, but he did. He was having trouble not wanting to barge in the kitchen and shake the truth out of her. He knew, if she could just let go and trust him that he could wrap his arms around her and shield her from the entire world. If she would let him. He took a big chug of the wine and directed his attention back to the sizzling steaks; but the thoughts refused to go away or even lighten up a little bit. What if this guy is still out there? He needs to be destroyed, and Cal relished the thought of being the one to do it. He couldn't wait any longer, he needed to know.

He pulled his cell phone out of his pocket and dialed Joe.

Joe answered. "Hey Cal. What's up? Have you kissed her yet?"

"Not yet. Still working on that. Listen,… I need your help."

"Anything. Shoot."

Cal really didn't want to feel like he was going behind Alease's back; he wanted *her* to tell him. But his concerns were growing, and after what he saw tonight, he was unwilling to wait for her trust in him before he helped her. She was so stubborn about hiding everything about herself from him. His concern now was too great and it pushed him to seek out the truth anyway he could. "I need to know who did this to her, and if this bastard is still out there."

"Did she finally confide in you about it?" Joe asked.

"No, but her cast came off today, and I saw something I didn't like. There were restraint marks on her wrist, Joe."

"Fuck," Joe knew what that meant too. "OK. All I need is her last name and I will find out what happened."

Cal hesitated. Joe would kill for Cal, would die for Cal, and the fact that she was important to Cal would make him all the more exceptional at finding what he wanted to know. No more waiting, he needed to find out.

"Alease Taynes."

"I'm on it. Give me some time and I will get you everything I can," Joe responded.

Cal hung up, looking back in the window at this woman he privately vowed to protect. He hoped and prayed that he could get her to talk to him before he found out through Joe. He hated feeling like he was doing this behind her back.

At the table, with full stomachs and empty plates, they all sat, laughing and talking as if they had done this together for years. Cal was amazed at how much he had enjoyed this evening. The combination of knowing Joe was on it, and the effect of Alease's presence on him had been extraordinary; his anger had diminished and was replaced with a peace he had never quite felt before. He was astounded at the way she filled his heart with everything he never realized he was missing. She managed, somehow, to almost make him forget his fury regarding the marks on her wrist; almost. The thoughts were still there, but he would strike his payback to the man that did that to her. You don't cross a SEAL and get away with it, and anyone who hurt *this* woman has crossed the wrong SEAL.

Cal let those thoughts go, and had been sitting back in complete surrender at the bliss he was feeling watching Alease discussing all things Christmas with Jake and Sophie. There was a sparkle in her eyes as she talked about the holidays which matched the love of holidays that Cal always had when he imagined spending them with a woman like her. Exactly like her. She felt like family to him. She felt like everything he had ever wanted and more. It was in this moment that Cal's inner voice said it loud and clear in his head…what he had known, but was not admitting to himself yet…Cal was in love with this woman. The realization shot through him like lightening. He had not expected this. It was almost funny to be so blindsided by the very thing he had wanted his whole life. Like buying a lottery ticket, hoping to win the millions, and then the utter shock when finding out you actually won. That's what Alease felt like. He thought back to the first moment he saw her in the parking lot…

amazing, he thought…that his whole world changed in that one instant. One moment can change everything.

"Oh, come on. Cal, back me up here, tell your nephew I'm right." Alease was talking directly to him and he suddenly realized he wasn't listening and had no idea what she was asking him.

"I'm sorry, what?" Cal asked.

Sophie laughed. "Haven't you been listening? Best Christmas movie of all time."

Cal snapped back into the moment. "Oh, has to be 'Miracle on 34th Street'".

Alease smiled. "Thank you. Told you Jake."

"Boring. 'Jingle All The Way' is the best one," Jake answered.

Alease's laugh was captivating and Cal could feel his heart beat through his chest. She was so beautiful to him it was almost unbearable to be that close and not be touching her. He couldn't believe how much he loved having her here, in his home, right across from him at his table. This is what he had always wanted his whole life and never had, and now it was all around him. He wanted it to last forever.

Alease was wondering what Cal had been distracted by. She had been enjoying the Christmas conversation so much she hadn't realized he might have drifted off in his mind. He had been smiling and watching her, so she figured he was listening, but clearly his mind had been somewhere else. She hoped against hope it wasn't because of the marks on her wrist. She fidgeted with her sweater again to make sure it was pulled down and covered the area.

"Well, I think it's time for Dessert Trivia," Cal said as he got up and headed to the kitchen.

"What is Dessert Trivia?" Alease asked curiously.

"It's so fun. Its when you have to answer the trivia questions correctly in order to get a piece of dessert. There are different categories; Uncle Cal gets to pick which one we do," Jake answered.

Cal came back to the table with a plate of beautifully decorated cookies.

"Tonights dessert; fancy cookies from the Elk Ridge bakery." He placed the plate in the middle of the table, and pointed to the biggest and most beautiful cookie in the middle of the plate. "This one is the final prize cookie. Who ever wins the last question wins this cookie and is the ultimate champion of tonights game." Cal headed over to the bookshelf that lined the back wall and reached for one of the boxes on the middle shelf. "Since we are on a Christmas kick, we will do Christmas Trivia tonight." He came back to the table unwrapping the box. "This is a brand new box with new, up to date Christmas Trivia."

"Oh boy! This is great." Jake was getting himself prepped

to be the champion.

As they played the game and answered the random questions on the cards, the depth of peace filling Cal's home was like an oasis of serenity and she cherished it.

"OK, we are down to the last question; the prize cookie and the title of ultimate champion is on the line. Who ever answers the next question first, and correctly, wins." Cal picked up the next card in the deck. "It's multiple choice. Are you ready?"

"Yes," Jake answered and they all sat quietly waiting for the final question.

Cal read the card. "Who wrote the Christmas hit "Christmas Mountain?" Jake and Cal both called out their answer in unison, at the same time Alease felt herself fill with a cold shock that buzzed through her body.

"Kenny Keep!" they both called out confidently.

"I said it first!" Jake announced as Cal playfully argued with him.

"You said it was multiple choice. You have to finish reading it before you can answer," Sophie insisted.

Alease was stunned into silence. She could not believe this question was in the card game. She had no way out of this one...unless the creator of the card game got it wrong.

Cal continued. "Is it A; Kenny Keep, B: George Michael, or C: Alease..." Cal stopped abruptly. Shock came over his face. He looked up from the card right into Alease's eyes, as if he saw a ghost. He flipped the card over to see the answer, then looked back up at Alease in utter amazement and disbelief.

"What is it?" Sophie asked as she tried to ascertain the look in her brother's eyes.

Cal almost couldn't find his voice, then somehow he managed to finish the sentence. "…or C: Alease Taynes."

A dead silence fell on the table as all eyes turned to Alease. She didn't quite know what to say. The silence in the room was heavy and she knew she needed to say something.

She politely cleared her throat. "Well, I'm guessing from the shocked look in all your eyes that it's pretty clear I'm the only one who knew the answer. That means this cookie is mine." She smiled and reached for the prize cookie, taking a bite of it as she did so. "I win." She casually got up from the table to get herself a little more wine.

The three were still speechless; shocked at the discovery. Finally, Jake broke the silence.

"*You* wrote 'Christmas Mountain'?" Jake asked.

"Yes," Alease said with a breath of unwanted surrender. She felt the weight of the room on her as she could do nothing but take another sip of her wine.

Cal was frozen on her, the look in his eyes was of utter bewilderment. He was at a complete loss for words.

Then he spoke. "*You* wrote that?" Even as he said it, Alease heard overtones of awe and astonishment.

"Yes. I did."

The silence hung in the air until Sophie broke it. "That's amazing Alease. That song is…amazing. I can't believe you didn't tell us that. Have you written other songs we know too?" she asked.

Alease nervously cleared her throat again. As much as she did not want the attention for it, nor to shine a big spot light on the part of her life that could lead Cal directly to what had happened to her, she also felt a nudge of guilt that she had been deceitful about it yesterday when Cal confided in her how much the song meant to him. She didn't want to do that again.

"Yes. I've written several songs for Kenny. I'm sure you know them all, actually." She looked at Cal. Behind his astonishment she could see the calculations going on in his mind about why she hadn't told him. Damn if this man wasn't always trying to piece together everything she attempted to hide from him.

Cal was silent for a few moments longer. Then he stood up. He crossed to the kitchen and filled his wine glass. Then he topped off Alease's glass as well. He picked up his big jacket that was on the stool next to him and softly handed it to Alease.

"I would *very much* like to talk with you outside by the fire." The warmth and depth in his eyes were colored with the myriad of questions Alease knew were swarming around inside his mind, and she was pretty sure she was out of clever tactics to dodge them. She gave in, took his jacket and put it on as they headed towards the door.

"What about us? We want to know too!" Jake said.

Cal turned over his shoulder to Jake and Sophie as he opened the door for Alease.

"You guys are on clean up duty. We will be back," Cal said.

With that he stepped out after Alease, and closed the door behind them.

Cal quietly followed Alease over to the bench in front of the fire pit, and sat down next to her. The flames were still strong and the warmth of the fire swept up around them as they sat down for the conversation Cal was not going to let go of this time. Part of him wanted to speak, but he found himself thinking that the silence might encourage her to go first, and he wanted to see where she would take it.

"I'm sorry I didn't tell you that yesterday. I should have. I just…I didn't…It's not a big deal really." She lowered her gaze pretending to be interested in her wine glass.

"Not a big deal? It's an incredibly big deal. That is my favorite song in the world…Why didn't you tell me that you wrote it? That's a big, amazing part of who you are. Why hide that?" He spoke in a nonjudgmental way. He wanted her to know he wasn't mad, just confused.

"I sang with Kenny for a little while. We toured together and I had several songs I had written that he liked very much." She paused before she continued, "But I decided I just didn't want that life anymore, so I stopped performing and wrote songs for Kenny instead."

"You are conveniently skipping over the details here. Alease, why did you stop?"

He could see she was struggling with how to come up with the right words. "Alease, just talk to me." Something in his tone forced her to look up at him. The look in her eyes was hard to read; a blend of apprehension and an honest loss for words.

"It's just connected to a lot of…ugliness that I didn't want you to know about. I like the way you smile at me and I didn't want that to change, so I just don't talk about it."

Her words, and the tone with which she spoke them, led Cal to connect the dots between her arm and the reasons behind the exit from her music career. Cal knew he was about to walk a fine line, but he felt the need to push her out of her comfort zone, so he wrapped as much protection around his next words as he could.

"Alease, what happened?" he asked.

She took a breath and, again, couldn't find the words. He knew he was going to have to help her through this conversation if it was ever going to happen.

"Alease…my intuition and my observation skills are

better than most. Whatever you think you're hiding from me, you're not. I've known since the moment I met you that someone, somewhere hurt you." Alease looked up with clear concern in her eyes, but Cal kept going in a calm and steady voice, "I already know that someone broke your arm and had a knife against your throat. Tonight, I saw the restraint marks on your wrist. Yeah, I know what those marks are. I don't know the details…but I know."

Tears welled up in her big brown eyes and it broke his heart to see it. He couldn't hold his distance from her any longer. He reached over with one arm and gently pulled her into him, wrapping his other arm around her as she folded into his embrace. To his delight, he felt her give in, and she rested her head on his chest. He held her silently in the firelight for several minutes before he continued.

"If you think for a second that diminishes how I see you, you are sorely mistaken," he said softly.

He squeezed her even tighter as he felt her trying to get a grip on the emotions she was still trying to keep from him. As much as he didn't want to, he released his hug and pulled away enough so that he could be face to face with her.

"Whatever happened to you, it's not your fault and it does not make you weak. Please tell me."

For a moment he thought she was going to tell him, then he could see her mind overriding her. There was a battle raging inside her and he had to give her the reinforcements she needed. Maybe direct questions about specifics would help ease her into the story.

"Did Kenny do this to you?" even as he asked it, Cal didn't think that could be true, but he thought the question might get her talking.

Alease looked up right away. "Heavens no. Kenny treated me better than most. He would never do anything of the sort. It wasn't him."

Good, he thought; *it's coming out now*. Cal kept going with the questions, it seemed to help her focus rather than get overwhelmed by the entirety of it. "Was it an ex boyfriend or husband?" Cal realized it hadn't even occurred to him that she could have been married until just now.

She almost laughed. "I would never date or marry anyone who could do something like this. My ex would have been far to worried about his own bruising to do anything of the sort."

Cal took note of her use of the word ex, and would circle back to that conversation later.

"Ok. Then who did it Alease?"

She had one more moment of struggle with the answer.

"It's really ugly, you sure you want to know this?" She was trying one last attempt at discouraging him, but Cal reached over and took her hand. He could tell instantly his touch calmed her, and he squeezed her hand lovingly.

"Alease, I'm a Navy SEAL who has been deployed in some of the most violent places on Earth. Of anyone, I can understand it and I can handle it. Please, just talk to me. Tell me what happened."

Alease took a long time to gather whatever internal strength she had in her. Cal sat quietly, patiently waiting for her next words.

"I was on stage with Kenny in New York City. We had just finished a duet, when he left the stage to me for a solo number. The lights went down and the spotlight had not reached me yet." She took a breath, then continued, "He came out of no where. Just jumped up from somewhere in the crowd. It happened so fast." She stopped again, probably hoping Cal would speak, but he chose not to. He wanted her to continue so he just waited. "I didn't even notice the knife. I just kept trying to pull away, but his grip on me was so tight, I couldn't really move." She closed her eyes trying to shake off the memory of it he knew she was experiencing. "Then König came running over and jumped him so hard he knocked him right off me. Somewhere in there is when the knife cut my neck. The blood freaked everyone out and created just the right amount of distraction that the guy got away."

Cal sat quietly waiting for her to continue. When she didn't, he spoke.

"I'm so sorry that happened." He saw the forced change behind her eyes; the one she calls on when she is attempting to block what is just under the surface. She was finally talking to him and he didn't want to let her rebuild the barrier that was starting to come down. He knew there was more to the story. "What's the part you are leaving out?"

She tried to hold onto the breath that fell from her lungs. "That wasn't enough?" She was trying to laugh a little, but she didn't manage to pull it off.

"Alease…," his tone was calm but insistent.

Her ability to deflect was at it's lowest point and he felt she was at the edge of surrendering to the steep fall off the cliff she had been fighting. He knew, even if she didn't, that he was right there to catch her when she did, but she had to make the choice to let go, so he waited patiently right next to her.

"Apparently his obsession with me was far greater than anyone realized. He found out where I lived. A few nights after that, I came home; later then I had wanted to but the traffic was so bad that night. My house was set back a little in the woods, no lights or neighbors near by, so I always left the porch light on. I noticed right away when I pulled up that the light was off. I thought it must have just burnt out. I should have been more careful." She paused, then continued. "König was with me. I let him out and he went off a bit in the front yard. I should have waited for him. I don't know why I didn't. I walked up to my front door…my thoughts completely on other things. I wasn't paying attention. I didn't expect it." Cal could see in the reflection of the fire light the memory in her eyes as they filled with tears and the fear he wanted so badly to erase. "Before my hand even reached the door handle, the front door flew open from the inside. He grabbed me, pulled me in and shut the door. I don't even know how he got the restraint over my hand so fast, but in one motion he had me inside my own home with König on the other side of the closed door."

Cal wrapped his hand around hers tighter and somehow was able to separate the rage inside from his voice. It took all his strength to sound calm and soothing in the midst of his inner SEAL wanting to destroy the man who did this to her.

"Keep going. Tell me what happened."

"I screamed. I could hear König scratching at the door, barking ferociously. He was trying to get in but he couldn't. I struggled. I managed to punch the guy in his face. I think that's when my hand fractured. The hit enraged him and he threw me down so hard that my arm smashed the coffee table. When I hit the ground pain seared through me. I tried so hard to move my arm, but I couldn't. I knew I needed to fight, but I couldn't move it." Her anger with herself came through as if she faulted herself that she couldn't fight with a broken arm. "He was quick, and ruthless. He strapped my arm to the foot of the sofa and pulled it so tight I thought that alone was going to kill me. I couldn't move. He had me trapped." She stopped again, most likely hoping that would be enough of the story for Cal. But he remained still, encouraging her with his silence to keep going and tell him everything. He could see she just couldn't say the words. Her tears overflowed past the barriers she was desperately trying to hold onto. He knew he had to say it for her, and he hated it, but he had the strength right now that she did not.

"Did he rape you, Alease?" his tone was as kind and as loving as he could make it. He knew the place for his outrage against this guy was not here. Not with her. He would have his revenge against this man if he was still breathing, that much was certain. No matter where on the planet he was, Cal would find him. This man was going to pay for what he did.

The involuntary breath that escaped her answered his question before she did.

"He started to, but my scream was so loud that I think it threw König into a panic. He jumped through the living room window." Her tears flowed even harder as the flood of the memory came crashing through her. "He went right for his throat. There was an intense struggle and then…silence. They both were still. Both bleeding. König had a huge gash along the underside of his belly from jumping through the glass. It killed him within minutes." She covered her eyes with her hands. "I shouldn't have screamed. Maybe he wouldn't have jumped through the glass if I just hadn't screamed."

Cal pulled her into his embrace as tightly as he could. He had so many things he needed to say to her, but he knew she needed a breath before she could hear anything. So he just held her and kissed the top of her head with as much care as he could.

"Alease, this is not your fault. Listen to me. König was going to jump through that window to save you no matter what you did. I know these dogs. He was already planning that as soon as he knew you were in trouble." There was more he wanted to say; needed to say, but the layers of guilt, shame, fear and pain that were swirling around her were too thick, and he needed to give it time to settle. So he held her in the firelight, softly caressing her hair and surrounding her with as much of himself as he could.

After several minutes, Alease pulled herself together, wiped her tears and sat up.

"I'm sorry for…getting all emotional," she said.

He stopped her before she could continue with that absurd thought process.

"Alease, do not apologize for that." He softly brushed away one of the tear drops she missed and caressed her face as he did so. He held her gaze softly. "Thank you for telling me." He couldn't quite read the look in her eyes, but he saw a tiny speck of relief under the remaining struggle of emotions still swirling.

There was one more piece of information Cal needed before he would attempt to lighten the energy and set her back at ease. "What happened to the guy?" he asked.

She looked surprised in a way. "König killed him. He didn't move the entire time I was waiting for the police. It felt like it took them forever to get there. I was lucky I had left the phone where it was. A few inches further and I wouldn't have been able to reach it."

Cal pulled her into him one more time. He hugged her with everything he had and whispered into her ear.

"You are safe now. It's ok." She held onto him and Cal felt his heart melt into her. This woman would never go through anything like that again as long as he was breathing. He swore it.

After several more minutes, the front door opened and Jake stuck his head out.

"Hey, we're going to watch 'Jingle All The Way!' Mom already made the popcorn. Come on!" Jake's excitement for his favorite Christmas movie was just the right shift in mood Alease needed, Cal could see it in her face when he looked at her.

He was glad for the smile she managed to bring to her lips. He softly brushed the hair away from her eyes and scanned her again making sure she was ok. When he was satisfied, he smiled and offered her his hand to help her stand up. She took it, and she didn't let go of it as he walked with her to the front door. He held her hand as if it was a lifeline to her and he guided her back into his home.

Cal and Alease took the big comfy sofa, Jake wanted to sit on the floor in front of them with a large blanket and his own bucket of popcorn. Sophie was happy lounging in the big love seat with her legs draped over the side. In the reflection of the fire warming them from the fireplace, and the big screen TV playing a light hearted Christmas movie, Cal had the woman of his dreams in his arms right next to him. It was magical. Throughout the movie, Cal found himself hugging her into him, and relishing in her acceptance of his embrace. When she rested her head on his chest again, he was sure she must feel the rapid beat of his heart as it pounded through his muscles. He wasn't embarrassed by it; he wanted her to feel it. To know how much she meant to him, how his heart filled with her. He brushed his fingers along her hand and felt her holding onto him with a release she had not offered since she met him. She was folding into him and he found himself completely overcome in the love of it; of her. He kissed the top of her head, and caught the smile on Sophie's face as she saw him do it.

Before the movie ended, Cal was aware that Alease had fallen asleep in his arms. Both of them were stretched out on the sofa with Alease snuggled safely in his embrace. Sophie quietly turned the TV off after the last line of credits cleared the screen. She motioned to Jake to be quiet so they wouldn't wake Alease.

Jake whispered. "Goodnight Uncle Cal."

"Goodnight Jake." Cal quietly gestured for Sophie to bring him the thick blanket that was on the other recliner. She brought it over and Cal draped it over himself and the woman he was holding. He had no intention of moving and losing this moment. He wanted her in his arms forever. Sophie kissed Cal on the cheek, "Goodnight," she said quietly as she and Jake headed up the stairs to their bedrooms.

The room was relatively dark except for the remaining light from the glowing fireplace. Alease moved slightly in her sleep, and Cal instinctively pulled her in and caressed her arm; letting her know he was there. She quieted and fell still again in his arms. He could tell from her breathing that an incredible thing had happened; it was the middle of the night, and Alease was sleeping soundly. He held her close, savoring the absolute pleasure that engulfed him. At long last, he allowed himself to close his eyes and follow her into sleep, but he refused to let go of her as he did so. He couldn't.

When Cal opened his eyes again, the first breath of light was just starting to peek through over the mountains. Out the window he could see the faint blues and pinks of the morning sky. Alease was still snuggled into him fast asleep. There was an extraordinary sense of calm and peace in the moment that Cal felt imprinted itself onto his very soul.

Alease stirred in his arms. Her breathing had changed so he knew she was awake, but she did not pull herself from his embrace. She stayed right where she was and he could feel her relishing in the comfort of his arms. It was an incredulous feeling of happiness that was unknown to him until this moment, and he was sure that Alease was feeling it too. He wondered how long it would be before she convinced herself she needed to run from it.

Several minutes went by and then Alease lifted her head and sat up, "Did I fall asleep here?" Cal sat up next to her and softly brushed the hair from her eyes.

"Yes, you did. So did I."

She had a shyness in her eyes this morning that seemed to reflect an uneasiness about all she shared with him the previous night. Cal was pretty sure she was already lambasting herself for it.

"I'm sorry. I didn't mean to do that." Her surprise that she was sleeping at all crept into her words.

"Don't apologize for that," he said as he smiled at her. "You seemed to sleep pretty well last night. How do you feel?" The question was layered, and he wasn't sure how in depth she would go in answering it.

"I feel…confused. I haven't slept that well in months." She looked at him with that reserved shyness again, almost as if she was embarrassed to admit it.

Cal smiled. "Yeah, me too." He looked in her eyes and for the first time since he met her, he finally saw a moment where she was not fighting him. A moment when the walls she had built behind her eyes were down, and he was able to see a depth of unfiltered emotion there.

Jake came bounding down the stairs and broke the moment.

"Good morning! Hey Alease, you're still here?" Jake skipped over to the kitchen.

"Yes, but I'm heading back over right now." Alease got up and the blanket fell from her arms back to the sofa.

"You don't have to." Cal really didn't want her to leave. She paused and he could see that shift in her eyes which told him her fear of exposure was pinching at her again. "OK, I'll walk you over."

"You don't have to Cal."

"I know I don't have too. I want to." He looked back at Jake, "I'll be right back."

"Pancakes when you come back?" Jake asked excitedly.

"Pancakes it is."

The morning air was getting colder and the ground was starting to get the frost of winter. Alease wrapped her arms around herself, pulling her big sweater tightly to stay warm; which he also knew was a convenient way for her to avoid the emotional vulnerability of physical contact with him. They walked most of the way in silence. He knew she was wrestling in her mind about how good last night had felt, and he was pretty sure that the more she thought about what he now knew about her, the more she was trying to convince herself that she should run from him. He was not going to let that happen.

"You ok?" he asked her in a soft tone that matched the peace of the morning atmosphere.

"Yeah. I'm fine. You?" she asked back.

"Better than I have been in a long time," he paused and then continued. "Alease, stop second guessing yourself about what you shared with me last night. I'm glad you told me. You needed to. It's ok."

They reached her door and she turned to him. He could sense her nervousness and her defenses struggling to regain themselves. Her voice had an almost childlike uncertainty to it even though she was trying to appear calm and in control. She clearly was not.

"Listen. I don't want you to feel…obligated. It's a lot, what I told you, and I know it effects…things." She was stumbling over herself trying to sound clear and rational, but her inner conflict was obvious to Cal. He smiled with an unapologetic, almost challenging smirk as she continued to try and give him every excuse she could to walk away. Instead, he moved closer to her. She instinctively backed up trying again to give him the room to run from her which he did not take. He moved closer to her again. She ran out of words and stopped talking.

"Alease, you can try all you want to, but I'm not going anywhere. I know you're scared of me, of what we have here, but I'm not. I am not walking away from this. I'm not walking away from you." He saw the fear and the longing in her eyes. She was losing her ability to run from him and he knew it. He moved in closer to her as she found herself backed up against the wall. He took his time, he leaned in slowly, carefully and purposefully. His gaze unbreakably fixed on her and his face now a breath away from hers. He gently brushed her cheek with the back of his hand…his touch was incredibly meaningful and soft and he knew she was overwhelmed with emotion and passion for him. He felt it and he saw the rate of her pulse quicken. She closed her eyes and tried to look down in a futile attempt to stem the rush that was pulsing through her.

Cal gave it one breath, but that was the last moment of running from him that he could allow. His hand gently moved down her face and then he slowly lifted her chin with his fingers. He brought her eyes back to his, holding the deep connection between them for a long moment. Then he leaned in. His lips met hers and he kissed her with such a bolt of emotion that he could almost physically feel it as it raced from his body through hers. He started the kiss soft and loving, then smoothly advanced to a kiss that seemed to be pulling her very soul from her body. It was surreal. It was magic. They both found themselves lost in it for what seemed like a lifetime or a split second. Time was no longer relevant or logical. Cal was mesmerized; blown away by the power of what was between them. At long last, he broke the kiss and pulled back slightly. When she opened her eyes and found his on hers, she looked as if she was completely lost. Her confidence and self assuredness replaced with a vulnerability that Cal took right to his heart. His breathing matched the speed of hers and the smoldering heat between them obvious.

"You are going to be the death of me," she said breathlessly.

"No. I'm going to be the beginning of you."

Chapter Six
The Inevitable

She couldn't get his words out of her head. Everything about him; his touch, his smile, his warmth, his protective energy…it engulfed her like an unstoppable flood drowning her from the inside out. She felt herself wanting him… needing him…all against her will. God forbid she allowed herself to get used to him being there for her, how could she ever go back to the normalcy of being alone? What if she trusted him; allowed herself to give in and need him, only to have life continue it's cruel tradition of wrenching those very things right out from under her? Were these moments of complete serenity really worth the bitter, cold slap of reality that was sure to come when that comfort would no longer be there? No, she had to stop this, for her own good. It's clearly lunacy to believe in this kind of magic. This exotic spark that flares between them, it must be in her mind. Believing in it any longer was getting too dangerous. She must end this fall down into the dark abyss…and just like clock work, there was a knock on her door.

It seemed to her that every time she made a conscious decision to rebuild her efforts to fight off her feelings for Cal, he appeared; reminding her that he was not going to let her drift from him that easily. Alease opened her front door to see

Cal, dashing as ever, with his perfectly shaped five o'clock shadow enhancing his strong cheekbones. He was standing in the late afternoon sun with Chase saddled and waiting behind him.

"Hi," was all she could say, as she simultaneously realized her entire pep talk with herself about ending these crazy feelings for him just flew out the window.

"Hi," his voice was filled with low tones of warmth and seductive enticement that seemed to cut past all of her resistance. "I'm thinking that you've been hiding in here long enough, and wondered if I might get you to come out and spend a little time with me. I'd love to take you for a ride up to that secret plateau on the mountain. The view at this time of the late afternoon is amazing."

"I'm not hiding." She knew she was lying but her mind wouldn't allow her to say anything else.

Cal smiled, letting her lie slide. "Great. Then grab your coat and come out with me." He leaned against the door almost challenging her to say no. She couldn't. That part of her soul that he breathed life into was pulling at her; begging her to submerse herself in his company.

"Fine. I'll get my coat." Cal waited by the door and when Alease came back out, he led her to his horse. He had put a double saddle on Chase so they could ride together, and Alease fluttered inside at the thought that she was about to be held in his embrace as they rode up the mountain.

Cal helped her onto Chase and then lifted himself on right behind her. Immediately Alease could feel the heat from his body even through his coat. His arms came around both sides of her to grab the reins and she felt him move his body as close to hers as possible, snuggling her safely inside the fortress of his physique. Cal gave a slight kick and Chase began the romantic trek up the mountain side as big snow flakes softly fell all around them.

Alease had never known such a tangible sense of emotional security before in her life, and no matter how badly she wanted to convince herself to overlook it, she couldn't. It truly was the most remarkable feeling she had ever known. She found herself closing her eyes and breathing in the sheer pleasure of it.

The ride up the trail was more enjoyable than anything Alease had ever experienced. Cal navigated the intense emotional and physical vivacity coursing between them by interspersed casual conversations on the different trees, plants and flowers that grow along the mountain. But she knew he felt it too, because whenever he stopped talking, he instinctively held her tighter, pulling her into him as if he couldn't bear having any space between them. She caught herself leaning into him and relaxing in his arms in ways she never remembered doing before with any other man. She knew, in her mind, it was dangerous to enjoy this so much, but she couldn't fight it. She was completely helpless against the power of the feelings he was drawing out of her.

They reached a point just before the trail they were on turned inward to the right. Cal pulled back on the reins and Chase stopped. Directly to their right the mountain side went very steeply up with trees and rocks scattered across it.

"This is it, just up over this incline. Hang on."

He grabbed her even tighter and she could feel all the muscles in his arms and legs embracing every inch of her body. He pulled the reins sharply to the right and gave Chase a kick. Before she even knew what was happening, Chase used his massive legs to pull them up the steep mountain side, negotiating with ease between the trees and the rocks, until with one final jump, Chase had them up on the top, onto a clear plateau. Trees lined three sides and directly in front of them was a beautiful view of the mountains on the other side of the canyon. There was a wooden bench and a fire pit perfectly situated on the far side.

Cal slid off of Chase and reached back to help Alease down. He took her hand and led her over to the bench as she lost her breath at the beauty of the mountains on the other side.

"Oh my God, this is amazing," Alease said in awe at the sight.

The sun was low in the sky right across from them, and the red and pink reflections danced on the clouds below them. The big snow flakes continued to flutter to the ground around them as Cal bent down to light the fire in the fire pit. The warm flames flickered in-between the wood and heated the air around them. Cal pulled a blanket from Chase's saddle and they sat down on the bench to enjoy the view, the fire and the moment.

"I love this spot. I always have. It's very peaceful. Helps me clear my head when things get…difficult to understand," his voice was so warm and comforting.

"What gets difficult for you?" Alease was curious.

He looked her in the eyes with that X-ray vision of his. "That's what I was going to ask you." When she didn't know how to respond, Cal took a breath and continued. "Can we do a Deep Dive here?" he asked her.

"What's a Deep Dive?"

"It's something my SEAL team and I do. Its when you have to speak the truth, no matter how hard it is, you have to be entirely honest." He looked her deeply in the eyes. "I know you are not fond of that, but I'm asking."

Alease saw no way out of this one, without rudely shutting him out which she did not want to do.

"Do I get a Deep Dive question too then?"

"Of course you do. You can go first. What's your question?" He was surprisingly open, and seemed almost eager to answer whatever she might ask. Alease had to think about what she most wanted to know.

"And you have to answer honestly, right? You can't lie?

SEAL team honor and all that?"

He chuckled at her. "Yes. SEAL team honor. When someone calls Deep Dive, you can not be deceitful in any way. You must tell the truth, the whole truth and nothing but the truth. I promise to always honor that. What's your question?"

Alease knew what she wanted to ask, but then she lost her nerve and wondered if she could come up with something else. Cal saw it in her eyes. "Don't change your question. What is it?"

She took a breath. "If you were physically attracted to a woman, but that was it, no deep feelings, no real care there, just physical attraction, would you tell her?"

"Yes." He didn't even flinch. No pause, no thinking about the answer, he just said it.

"Even if that might blow your chances of sleeping with her, you would be honest about that?" she tested him again.

"Yes." He looked into her through his gaze. "I told you, I don't lie. Listen, if you are asking have I ever just had sex with no real emotional connection; yes I have, but those flings were always mutual. Men are not the only ones who play games you know."

"I guess you're right about that." She paused and pushed for one more question. "Have you ever had more than that? I mean, I know you were married…was sex with her different? Did it mean something more to you?"

This time he took a moment to phrase his answer, but he didn't fumble his response.

"It definitely meant more…but, looking back now I realize it was missing something. That deep connection, just wasn't there. That's important to me."

Alease looked at him, almost bewildered at the tone of sincerity. "I never thought I would hear a man say that."

"You seem to have trouble believing that a man can actually love a woman. More than just physically. Why is that?"

"Is this your Deep Dive?" she asked trying to sound light hearted.

"Part of it yes." Cal was not going to allow her to skirt around it and she knew it.

"I don't have much experience with men offering more than sex. That's just all it ever seems to be about." She broke her gaze hoping to avoid his ability to see how deeply that admission bothered her.

"Much…or any?" his question poked into her confidence.

"Any. I've only chosen to be with a few men, and none of them were capable of much more than…getting what they wanted, and bragging about it to their friends later." She tried to brush it off, but she knew he would hear the hurt behind it.

Cal was quiet for a minute before he spoke his next words.

"So, am I correct that you always kept yourself

emotionally distant from the men you've slept with?"

She wasn't expecting him to see it that way, and it surprised her to hear that out loud, but she had to concede that he was correct.

"Yes, I guess that's true. I haven't really."

"Is that what scares you?" he asked her. She felt herself want to deflect the question but he was onto her. "Deep Dive; is that what scares you?"

She did not know how to answer him honestly. It felt far too exposed. "Please don't make me admit that."

He waited for her eyes to meet his again; his gaze on her was unbreakable, and he held it for a very long moment. She felt his fingers on her cheek, then her chin and that familiar gentle but firm pull as he brought her lips to his. He kissed her deeply, passionately, and did not relent until he chose to pull away. When he did she was speechless, her breathing couldn't be hidden, nor the flush in her cheeks.

"I know you feel that. I'd like to know if that is what you're afraid of. This…force between us that neither of us can control."

The word fell from her lips before she could breathe it back in.

"Yes. Jesus. I can't…I don't know how to do this," she stumbled over herself trying to regain her footing, which she could not. He brought his hand back up to her face and stroked her cheek with his strong, rough fingers.

"It's ok. Listen, I need you to know…" he paused trying to sort out the right words. "This is not just sexual for me. What I feel for you is…deep. Whatever this thing is between us…it's powerful and I know it scares you. Just…don't run from me. I'm not letting you run from me." He placed his lips on hers again, and didn't let go.

She should have been cold, but she wasn't. Her shivering had nothing to do with temperature and Cal seemed to know it. When he reluctantly let his lips part from hers, his eyes were on her again as he brushed her hair off her face. He took her hand in his.

"Come on, we should head back down while there is still sunlight left." He guided her to her feet and folded her into his arms as he turned them both towards his horse.

He held her tightly in his embrace as they rode down the mountain side. She could feel his arousal, his warmth and his hot breath on her neck. He kept her close the entire way down the mountain and she felt as though her entire soul was encapsulated inside his unbreakable fortress. He had been right; it was the overwhelming emotional reaction to him that was inciting such fear in her. His touch, his warmth, his body…his heart. She prayed with everything she had that his Deep Dive answer had been the truth, because if he was playing her, she was already done for. He seemed to be reading her mind because at that moment he pulled her even tighter to him and whispered in her ear, "Please don't run from me." Her heart froze and melted at the same time.

He stopped Chase just across from her front door, but did not immediately let go of her. He held her for a few more moments, then slowly released his grip and jumped off. He reached up to bring her down off the horse. He slid her down slowly. She glided down the front of his body, his strong arms pulling her into him as he lowered her to her feet. Standing face to face with him she found herself lost in the overwhelming sensation of being in his strong embrace. He kissed her with soft passion. His hands found their way to her face as his kiss deepened. Then he released her.

"You know where I am if you need…anything," his voice was so soothing. She felt lost. "Are you ok?" he asked, though he knew she wasn't.

"I'm just…overwhelmed." She didn't know how to say more than that.

Very slowly, he let go of her and took a small step back.

"Get some sleep. I'm coming over tomorrow to check on your heater." He smiled at her and grabbed Chase's reins. He waited until she was inside her house and reminded her again, "I'm right here if you need me."

Alease closed the door and leaned against it trying to release the rush of feelings flowing through her. Her body was on fire. It took everything in her not to open the door and run back into his arms. To let him take her to his bed and completely drown her in his masculinity. She felt so on edge that the wind could blow and it would lead her to an orgasm. She had to release it. She threw her coat on the sofa and headed for her bedroom.

As Cal walked towards his house, his mind was completely on Alease. He wanted to ravish her with everything he had, to fill her with all the love and passion that was flowing through him. He knew she was close to giving herself to him, but she was still too unsure of the intensity between them. Cal had to admit it was powerful even for a Navy SEAL. If it was powerful for him, he knew it must be overwhelming for her, so he forced himself to let her go so she would not have to make the decision herself tonight. He wondered if she would need to…please herself tonight, and if she did, how she did it. He couldn't help but picture her, wishing he could be the one to bring her release. His need for her was pulsing through every vein in his body. A cold shower would not work tonight, he needed to bring his own release…probably more than once.

At his front door, with the snow falling more now than before, he turned one last time, hoping against hope to see Alease running over to him. He knew she was too scared of it tonight, but he hoped anyway.

***

Cal's perceptions and intuition were so focused on Alease, that he didn't notice the extra set of large footprints by the back of his truck, or the foreign tire tracks in his driveway. A dangerous lapse for the Navy SEAL.

***

The next morning, the ground was covered with a thick blanket of snow. Alease found herself replaying the evening before and felt herself more and more defenseless against Cal's allure. He was naturally seductive without even trying. The way he could always read her mind…he had this way of knowing exactly how to phrase things she needed to hear. He was so good at lowering her defenses and getting her to talk to him. Which was a new experience for her. Most men didn't really care about what a woman said or how she feels; the objective was always obvious, but with Cal, he took his time with her. He was like the perfect mason; laying the groundwork and creating the strongest possible foundation so that what was built upon it would be secure. There were times when his ability to reach inside her soul frightened her to no end. Not because she thought he would hurt her, but because she felt herself needing him. Wanting to shelter herself in him. It threw her completely off balance to be filled with such an urgent desire for someone. Every time he kissed her, the passion that flared between the two of them was more intense than before. She had relieved herself last night, but it took three orgasms for her to finally relax. She couldn't sleep until the sun started to come up this morning, but when it did, she slept for several hours.

When she did get up, her house was freezing. She wrapped herself in sweaters and made the fire in the living room bigger, but it still didn't warm up. She took several hot showers, but froze again every time she got out. She found herself sitting right in front of the fireplace debating whether or not she should go ask Cal for help, but she couldn't do it. She didn't want to need him…then, of course, there was a knock at her front door.

When she opened it, she tried to hide how cold she was, but she failed. He saw it.

"Why didn't you just tell me your heater wasn't working?" he asked.

"I didn't want to bother you with it." He looked at her with that irked look in his eyes that he gets when she is unwilling to let him help her.

"Your stubbornness is exasperating." He stepped in and wrapped her in his arms, rubbing her body to warm her up, then holding her close. "One of these days you are going to learn that accepting my help is not a bad thing." Max came in right behind Cal. "It's Freezing in here. You should have told me right away."

"It's not that bad," but even as she said it, she knew her attempt to mitigate it was ridiculous.

Cal looked at her with a laugh. "Alease, you are wearing

two sweaters, a scarf and the fire has been blazing non stop in your fire place since last night. It's freezing." He moved closer to her challenging her to argue with him.

"OK, you're right. It's fucking cold. How do I fix this thing?"

He put his arms around her again, and pulled her into him, warming her with his body.

"You let me help you."

She gave in. "OK."

He leaned down and pressed his lips on hers, and in an instant, he had her heart pounding and her breathing quickened. He felt so incredibly good it was hard for her to keep from melting under the power of his kiss.

The only thing that broke her fall into the abyss was a shuffling noise coming from her bedroom. Cal heard it too and unwillingly pulled his lips off of hers.

"What is that?" Alease asked.

Cal saw that her bedroom door was slightly open. "I think Max got into your bedroom. Max!" Cal called.

Max intensified his wrestling around in there, and then came bounding out; proudly claiming something from her room for himself. Alease realized, in absolute horror, that Max had her vibrator between his teeth and was happily running past them with it through the partially opened front door. *Oh my God*, she thought, praying with everything she had in her that Cal did not see what it was Max had taken.

She would die. She would absolutely die.

"Max! Crap. I'm sorry. What did he steal?" Cal asked calmly.

Alease was hoping the red flush of absolute embarrassment was not showing on her face. She did everything she could to keep her voice as normal as possible.

"Curling iron," she lied.

"Really? I didn't see a cord."

"Cordless curling iron. Don't worry. It was old and I can get a new one." She tried to busy herself by straightening a stack of magazines on her sofa end table.

"I'll replace it for you. This is where Max's inability to bring things back becomes a problem," he said.

Thank God for that, Alease thought. She couldn't even imagine her mortification if Max walked back in with her vibrator and gave it to Cal. God bless that dog that he never brought things back! She hoped and prayed he was burying it right now somewhere outside; never to be seen from again. All she could think was thank God Cal didn't know what it was.

Cal knew exactly what it was. He was trying hard not to laugh. He knew Alease would be beyond embarrassed if he knew it was her vibrator. So he pretended he didn't know. It was actually hysterical to him. In all honesty, he was really glad to see it. To know she had it. It meant that all her attempts to convince herself that she didn't have sexual feelings or need for him were exactly what he thought they were; excuses because she was just scared to let herself feel those things. He knew it. He could feel it every time he kissed her. It was almost as if he could actually feel the physical sensations running through her body…and he could feel her fighting it. Letting go was not easy for her, he knew that. He couldn't help but wonder if she ever thought of him when she used it. He also wondered how she might handle the overwhelming sexual energy that sparked between them now that Max had conveniently removed her private way of dealing with it. Maybe now she might have to face her feelings *with* him instead of alone. *Good boy Max*, he thought. Cal could see her discomfort growing as she tried to settle the red flush all over her face. A change of subject is what she needed.

"Alease, I wanted to ask you something."

She looked up happy to have another topic to talk about. "What is it?"

"Well, we always celebrate Thanksgiving at Joe's house. Sophie and Jake always come, and my SEAL team with their families. I would really like it if you would come with me." He really wanted her to. The thought of it had been in his head for weeks now. She was important to him and he wanted her to be part of his world. He had a sense that her heart was fluttering a bit at the idea of celebrating the holidays with him, his friends and family, but he also believed, in his soul, that she would love it. He knew her feelings for him were growing even if she couldn't say it yet. He felt her inner core more than any other woman he had ever been with. He had been walking the line of pushing her to face it and giving her space to handle it.

"Are you sure you want me there?" She didn't really seem to be connecting with the words she was saying. He knew she was just stalling to give him time to reconsider. She always did that and he corrected her every time she did.

He pulled her into him with his arms looking directly into her eyes, "You know I do. I want you with me." He placed his lips over hers and took the kiss from her in a loving but assertive way. It was his way of communicating to her what he felt for her, without having to say the words. He knew she was not ready to hear it out loud and he was trying to beckon her in, not send her running. He had found that using his body to talk with her was a better way, at the moment, to get her to hear him. She could always fight with words in her head, but fighting the physical sensations that caught fire between them was a much harder battle for her to win, and since he had no intention of letting her pull her world away from his, he took every opportunity he could to destroy her insecurities and doubts. So far, kissing her had been his best tool, because every time his lips covered hers, he felt her melt under him… and he loved it.

He always brought her right to the brink and then he would softly release her lips. Her breathing repeatedly got away from her when he did that; he loved that too.

"I don't want to intrude on your friend's holiday," she was going to keep listing reasons why she shouldn't go, but Cal stopped her before she could get to the next one.

"Joe already asked me, several times, if you were coming. The group would love to meet you." He looked at her with those eyes of his. "I really want you to come. Joe has plenty of room. He has two bedrooms right across from each other on the far end of his second floor. Very private, you will have your own space and I'll be right next to you across the hall." He mentioned that so she wouldn't feel any pressure about the sleeping arrangements. Cal knew she was very aware that the next stage in their relationship was coming, and he knew it scared her.

"Ok. If you're sure. Then yes," her voice was timid, but he saw the warmth in her eyes that told him she wanted to come.

"Good. If you are up for it, we can leave for his place first thing tomorrow morning, that way we can get settled in there and help Joe and his wife prepare everything."

"That sounds great."

Cal kissed her again and he felt the need in her body rise. He reluctantly pulled his lips off of her.

"We should go in town and check on the status of your

new heater. Come on, I'll drive." He took her hand and folded it into his. As his fingers closed around her hand, he felt her whole body respond to him. He knew his touch was igniting a deep desire in her, and he saw her shiver. "You ok?" he asked her.

"Yes. Just…it's just cold in here." He was very aware that was not why she was shivering.

As they drove into town, Alease decided to broach the subject she had not asked Cal about yet, "Can I ask you something?"

Cal took his eyes off the road to look at her. "You can always ask me anything. What is it?"

"I'm curious what happened between you and your ex wife. Why did your marriage end?"

Cal did not seem thrown by the question at all. In fact, he almost seemed relieved to be able to explain it.

"Well, to start off with, she didn't like guns or war of any kind."

Alease kind of laughed. "You are a Navy SEAL. How was that supposed to work?"

Cal laughed with her. "Exactly. It didn't. She grew more and more…appalled at my place in our country's defense. She didn't understand it, but she created an arrogant disapproval of it in her mind. It caused a big rift between us. That was just one of the problems."

"What were the other problems?"

"I rushed into things with her for the wrong reasons. I needed stability, family and a greater sense of home than I could create for myself. I thought she could grow into the kind of woman I needed. She didn't. The last time I deployed, I came back to find her sleeping with someone else. So I ended it. My SEAL buddies threw me a congratulations party. They never liked her and they were glad I was free of the bad situation it was becoming."

"How long had you been married?" she asked

"A year. That was long enough." He didn't speak about it as if it caused him pain anymore.

"Were you in love with her?" Alease surprised herself that she asked that question and she didn't really know why she had.

Cal thought for a minute. "I convinced myself I was, but I know now that I wasn't. I was in love with the idea of it all, but not with her. A good lesson. I will not do that again." He looked at her as if trying to ascertain if she understood what he was saying. "How about you? A while back during our conversation at the fire pit, you mentioned the word ex. Were you married?"

"Yes. For about a year," she said it very nonchalantly, like she was recalling a grocery list. It wasn't intentional, it was just the way she thought of it.

"Really? I'm kind of surprised. You don't speak about it

like it meant that much to you," he said.

"It didn't," she admitted. "I mean, I cared about him, like a good friend, until I realized he wasn't." She looked out her passenger side window at the mountains they were passing.

"What happened?"

"He wasn't a very strong man. More of a model type. You know, the kind that looks good on a magazine cover, but if the wind blows he would be knocked over in an instant."

Cal laughed at her description. "How does a guy like that end up with a woman like you?"

"He was a safe choice. On the surface, it kept other men a little more at bay and it was…," she hesitated trying to figure out how to say what she meant without being too obvious about it, "…there was no danger in me losing myself in him."

"Is that what you wanted?"

"That's what I chose."

He let that go for now. "OK. So what happened?"

"He got another woman pregnant while he was married to me." Alease looked out the window again trying to distance herself from the memory.

"*He* cheated on *you*? What the Hell was wrong with that guy?" Cal seemed genuinely confused. He turned the truck into the parking lot of the Heating and Cooling store as she continued.

"It was not entirely his fault. I didn't make it easy. My life…the constant barrage of other men testing their limits right in front of him. I don't think it was easy for him to be with someone like me. I just don't think he knew how to love me," she felt a little exposed when she said that and she wished she could take it back.

Cal parked the car and looked at her. She could feel him waiting until she brought her eyes back to him, which she finally did.

"He sounds like an idiot; and it was *entirely* his fault. A real man would know exactly how to love you." He reached over and seductively pulled her to his lips. He kissed her as if they were the only two people on the planet. As if telling the world outside to stop and wait for them, which it felt like it did. Her breathing quickened and she found her hands clinging to his beautiful face as if she was afraid of letting go. In the depth and power of his kiss it was as if she could hear him telling her it's ok to let go and give in. She hated how much her need for him was growing. She pulled herself away and tried to shield the desire in her eyes. He paused, tossing a question around in his mind before he decided to ask her.

"Alease, have you ever been with a man with passion? With a man who needed you with everything he had?"

Alease was a little shaken by the directness of the question, but lying was not in her nature.

"No. I haven't. My experiences are limited to very few, and the ones who I chose to be with…they were all very safe choices, as far as passion is concerned."

He caressed her hand. "Don't you want that?" She knew he saw the flash of fear that swept through her eyes. "Why does that scare you?" he asked her.

"I guess I just always chose safety over passion."

"You know you can have both, right?" He was looking at her with that look he has that rocks her world and always throws her into chaos inside. "You know, all the scares you is not evil."

She lost her breath when he said that and he kissed her again. She took him in and felt herself allowing him to erase some of her fear as she did so. It was a rush she had never felt before. To allow, just for a second, to be that vulnerable and choose to let go even a little bit. When he broke the kiss and looked at her he smiled.

"I will teach you that." Her heart skipped a few beats and then pounded so loudly in her chest she was sure he must hear it.

In the store, Cal took the lead again and spoke with the men about her new heater. Somehow Cal managed to get them to agree to put the new one in tonight. Alease didn't like the idea of the men being in her home after dark, but Cal would be there so she knew she would be ok.

Alease felt Cal's arm pull her into him as they were waiting for the final paperwork. She looked up at him and saw his focus was across the store. "You ok?" she asked him.

He brought his attention back to her. "Yes. I'm fine." She

followed the path of where his eyes were, but all she saw was the front door of the store closing.

They got the paperwork and headed out to the cold parking lot. A beat up old pick up truck was pulling out and she saw Cal looking at it. "You ok, Cal?" she asked again.

He put her at ease with his smile. "Yes. Sorry. I just always take note of cars from out of town, that's all. Habit from my training. I say we get home and sit in front of a fire. I've had enough of this cold for today." He kissed her and opened the passenger side door for her.

Cal closed her door and found himself looking at the truck that had pulled away and faded down the highway. The man driving it had been in the store briefly huddling behind the airconditioning section. Cal caught him several times looking at Alease. Maybe he was just having a territorial reaction to another man eyeing his woman the way he was. Cal had to give some level of allowances, after all, Alease was incredibly gorgeous, but the vibe bit at him even more as he saw the truck the man was driving. He crossed to the driver side door as he tried to swallow his questions about what the man was doing looking at airconditioners in the middle of November…in Big Sky Montana…and driving a truck with New York license plates…

Just before he opened his door, his phone rang. It was Joe. Cal answered it as he opened his drivers side door.

"Hey Joe. What's up?"

"You have a minute?" he asked.

Joe's voice had a tone of seriousness that Cal picked up on right away, and he knew it was not only important, but private. He started the truck and motioned to Alease that he needed a moment to take the call, then he stepped back out in the cold and closed his door. He wandered casually a slight distance from the car.

"Yeah, what's going on?" Cal inquired.

"Something strange. I'm running into some red tape regarding Alease's attacker. I'm not sure what's going on, but my spider senses are up that something is not right here."

"What could that possibly be? The guy is dead, so why should there be any issues with finding out who he was?" Cal was confused.

"I know. I don't get it either," Joe answered. "Maybe it's just a glitch...but it shouldn't be this difficult."

Cal looked back towards his truck at Alease, careful to hide the concern that was washing over him.

"OK. Listen, she is coming with me tomorrow. We are going to leave early, so we should be at your place by late morning. Mind if I get in on the next call with your contact?"

"Not at all. My lower office here is as private as can be. We will call him when you get here." Joe paused. "Listen, we're going to figure it out. Maybe it's just a glitch in the system. I'm pushing my contact on it hard and he promised to get back to me tomorrow, but even he is confused why he can't get to the files. Something here…it's not right."

"Yeah…I agree."

Joe shifted the tone in his voice. "I'm really glad she is coming, though. You finally had the guts to ask her, huh? Took you long enough! Christ, it took you forever just to find the balls to kiss her," Joe laughed.

Cal couldn't help but chuckle too. "Yeah. I'm just… proceeding carefully."

"I know. I'm just fucking with you. Dana is really looking forward to meeting her. Everyone is." Joe couldn't resist his next question. "Everything…progressing between you two? I'm trying not to pry, but damn if I'm not curious as Hell."

"I know you are. I uhh…have not slept with her yet. Still working up to that," Cal said.

"You are officially the strongest Navy SEAL ever…I know what she looks like."

"She is…so much more than that," Cal said.

"I know." Joe took a moment before continuing. "I know she means a lot to you. I saw it."

He had no reason to hide it from Joe. "Yes, she does."

Cal could feel Joe smiling on the other end of the phone. "Good. You deserve to be with someone who means the world to you. Listen, don't worry about the info on this dip shit or what he did. Just focus on her. If there is anything to find here about this guy, I will get it. In the meantime, get your asses up here so the rest of the gang can finally meet her."

"Will do."

"Great. Drive safe. See you tomorrow," Joe said.

Cal decided not to let Alease know about his conversation with Joe. He didn't want her to know he was looking into it, especially if there might be any concerns there. It was hard enough fighting off all her defenses without adding the discomfort of this into the mix as well, so he made every effort to conceal the matter when he got back in the truck.

"Everything ok?" Alease asked him.

He smiled at her. "Yeah. That was Joe. Just talking about what time we are getting there tomorrow. Earlier the better he said...ok with you if we leave early morning?"

"Yes, that's fine."

He felt her gaze on him and he didn't want to give her the chance to ask any questions that would lead to him having to tell her anything more about the conversation with Joe, so he jumped in.

"How about we pick up some take out on the way back so neither of us have to cook tonight? Chinese sound good?"

"Sure." She smiled at him and he felt like he was successful at hiding the unease that was thundering through his mind about the circumstances surrounding her attacker.

The sun was just setting as they pulled back into the drive

way. Alease was glad to be back and done with being out in the cold. It dawned on her if Cal hadn't done this for her, she may very well have frozen tonight in that little house of hers.

Cal parked the truck as he always did, half way between the two houses. "They should be here within the hour to replace that heater" he said as he turned the truck off.

"Thanks for doing that Cal," she said.

"Of course." He looked at her. "I know you are not thrilled about them coming at night, but I will be there. In fact, if you want, we can wait at my place so you don't have to be there at all."

She didn't want to admit she was uneasy with it, and allow herself to seem weak. "No it's ok." It was a good effort, but she knew it didn't fly. She released her breath, and in a rare moment of openness, she let her guard down, "It really shouldn't bother me that much, should it?" she kind of laughed at herself.

Cal stroked her face. "It's ok if it does." His touch was always the right mixture of strength and gentleness. She could not figure out how he did it, but he always managed to make her feel safe when he touched her.

"Well, I do need to pack tonight so we can leave for Joe's in the morning."

"OK. So lets go to your place, we can eat while you pack."

They walked up to Alease's front door, and the light on

her porch flickered. It flickered again and then went out with a zap. Alease froze. A flood of images and fear rushed through her like a dam breaking that was holding back an ocean she didn't know was there. She lost all sense of where and when, and felt herself transported back to that horrible night. She didn't even think she was breathing. All she knew was that her body felt paralyzed and trapped. She was hearing König barking and scratching at the door, and she heard the voice of the man who was on top of her claiming her body as his own. She was reliving the moment; under the weight of the memory, desperately trying to pull herself back.

She heard Cal's voice… "It's ok. It's just a memory trigger. You are ok. Hey, I'm right here."

She snapped out of it just as quickly as she had fallen under. Cal was right in front of her holding her hand.

"Jesus," was all she could say. She felt tears falling down her cheeks and her breathing had shot through the roof.

Cal wrapped his arms around her, holding her close to him.

"I've got you. You are ok," he repeated it in her ear until her breathing came back to normal. He kept his hands on her face as he released her from his embrace. His caring eyes found hers and he held her gaze. "It was just a memory trigger. It happens to everyone who goes through that kind of trauma. It's perfectly normal. You are ok."

She felt her hands shaking as much as she didn't want

them to. Cal held her hands with his and pulled her into him again. "Come on, lets go to my place. We can pack your stuff tomorrow before we leave."

Cal guided her back to his home. As soon as he got her in his living room, he got the fire going in the fire place, turned the TV onto a channel showing Christmas movies, and brought her a hot brandy to help her relax. He sat down with her on the sofa under that big warm blanket that covered the two of them that first night she fell asleep in his arms.

He knew exactly what had happened to her from first hand experience. From his deployments over seas, he knew what it was like when a sound, or a visual, kicks up the overbearing memories of an unpleasant event. It was more common than most realize. He made note to change the bulb for her when he went over to let the repair men in.

For now, she was warm and safe in his embrace and her heart rate felt to him like it was back to normal. He loved that he was able to shelter her from the memory and bring her back to a feeling of safety. She needed that, and he felt like it was pulling her into trusting him more and more.

The sound of a van in the driveway pulled Alease's attention to the window.

Cal was already on his feet, "They are here." He bent down to kiss her, and he held her lips for several moments before slowly letting go. His voice was soft and deep, "Just stay here with Max. I'll take care of it." He stroked her face and sent her heart racing again. As soon as he closed the front door, Alease downed the rest of her brandy in one gulp to try and ease herself. It didn't work. She laid back on the sofa, under the big, beautiful blanket that had kept her warm in Cal's embrace that night she fell asleep in his arms. She longed for that again. Quieting the yearning was getting harder and harder for her. She closed her eyes and without even realizing how tired she was, she fell asleep.

It's closer this time; the Tsunami. Alease was standing on the beach, the same spot as the many dreams before. The only thing that seems to change is that wave, that gigantic wave, it's closer each time she finds herself here; and it's bigger each time. The size of it seemed to double every time she had the dream.

She didn't have to look around; she knew she was the only one standing on the beach about to face the inevitable, save for that voice that always speaks right before she wakes up. It always sounded like it came from someone standing right behind her...she wasn't sure. The voice was always the same; deep and masculine, kind but relentless. It was not there to stop the wave, or her fear of it. It was only there, to ask the same question of her each time she found herself here; "Are you ready yet?"

This voice that encapsulated a wisdom beyond hers...an understanding that she did not have. It offered no protection from the wave, only guidance through it. The voice always spoke right into her ear...there seemed to be a silent suggestion that she should trust it, and allow the wave to overtake her. Her consistent answer was always no. The tsunami was huge...like the equivalent to a baby bird being engulfed by the entirety of Niagra Falls...she wouldn't survive it. She felt herself take a deep breath as the tsunami arched right over her. She knew she was out of time...and when the voice asked her the same question this time, she did not hear herself say no...

Alease woke up, and found herself laying comfortably on Cal's sofa with the blanket tucked in around her, and Cal on the love seat next to her. She sat up, and her long hair dropped to one side over her shoulder. The moonlight through the window revealed big snow flakes falling softly in the dark of night outside.

Cal looked over to her and smiled, as he turned off his cell phone and placed it on the table. He leaned forward and brushed her hair away from her eyes, "I didn't want to wake you. It's nice to see you sleeping so peacefully." His touch was so masculine and yet so gentle.

"Yeah, that doesn't happen a lot."

"I'm glad Max makes you feel so safe." He lowered his

hand, his arms resting on his knees, but his eyes still very much on her.

Alease couldn't stop the words from coming out. "Cal, it's not Max that makes me feel safe."

She surprised herself that she admitted it, but the look in his eyes removed her apprehension. It meant a lot to him, she could see it in his face and hear it in the breath he let out when she said it. He kept his smoldering gaze locked onto hers as he leaned into her and brought his lips to hers in a kiss that seemed to mean the world to him. The intensity overtook her heart and she lost herself in it. She found herself pulling him onto her as if her need had a mind of its own. He followed her direction willingly, and moved his body on top of hers. It was breathtaking the way he did it; even with his obvious, and very intense desire for her, he was still careful not to crush her as he placed himself on her; protecting her as he advanced on her…it was thrilling…it sent a rush of feelings through her that overpowered her. The emotional sensations were incredibly intense…the equal contradiction of comfort and uncontrollable passion; of safety, but at the same time standing on the edge of a fall to the death. The extremes were overwhelming. She found herself holding onto him like her life depended on it. He lowered more of his weight onto her, as if making sure every part of his body was touching her. It was territorial, it was powerful and, to her surprise, she felt gladly submissive under it. There was a safety underneath him that she felt to her bones. The wave inside of her was raging only to be overpowered by the external wave that she knew was coming down on her. The absolute surrender to this man that she could no longer keep herself from.

He was taking control of her body and she knew it. She couldn't stop it. He controlled the speed of her heart rate, her breathing and even her movements. Her body followed his lead regardless of her instructions. She felt him slowing the last wave of passion. He slowed her down with his kiss as his hand reached up and held her face as if she was a priceless treasure to be protected at all costs. She felt him linger on her lips and then pull his away slightly. She opened her eyes to meet his. The burning desire in him was carefully clothed in disciplined control that she wished she had, but knew she didn't.

His voice was rough, soft and deep. The sexiness in his tone was almost unbearable and she shivered as he spoke to her, "Alease…as much as I desperately want to be with you… if you are not ready for this, it's ok." He stroked her hair and her cheeks with his loving fingers. "I know the power of this scares you." He paused as if trying to read her mind, which he was pretty good at doing. "It doesn't have to be all or nothing. You can stay here on my sofa if you want, where you will be safe and warm with me in the next room. Or…you can come with me to my bed…where you will also be safe…and warm…" Alease could feel her heart racing, but what really made her internal firestorm flare was that she could feel his heart racing just as fast. She knew with her next words she was about to open a flood gate of power, passion and physical sensations that she had never experienced before. She was terrified…but more terrified of not feeling it.

The words came out as she surrendered herself.

"Take me to your bed, Cal."

Cal swept her up in his arms as he kissed her, holding his control over the feverish blaze threatening to explode from his very core. He carried her to his bedroom, his domain. He gently closed the bedroom door and swept her over to his bed. Her breathing matched the rate of his, and he could feel her heart pounding in her chest. He reminded himself that he must keep a tight reign on his desire for her…if he completely let loose his lust for this woman, he was afraid he would crush her. It was like a powerful grizzly bear making love to a butterfly. She felt so fragile to him and yet he could feel the flood of passion just behind the remaining walls of her self protection that he was dismantling. He knew it was a matter of trust; that's all, and he would make sure every step of the way he reaffirmed to her that he was the man she could trust. He slid her body down, ever so gently, and they stood at the edge of the bed in each others embrace and lost in the need pulsing between them. He slowly allowed his hands to explore her body, instead of rushing in and tearing off her clothes. He wanted to saver every moment of being with her. He needed to take it one step at a time, not only for her sake, but to keep himself from exploding with his need for her. His hands found their way down her lean arms and then back up through the small of her back. He felt her hands tracing the same movements on his body and his skin was tingling at the touch of her. Her mouth was intensely on his, and he could feel her yearning for more. Cal gently placed his hands under her shirt and teased her bare skin. She shivered at his touch and moaned softly as he caressed her smooth, hourglass figure. She felt amazing. He slowly lifted her shirt above her head and let it fall from his hands. He moved his lips to her neck…to her shoulder…his hands released the clasp of her bra and it fell to the ground, leaving her beautiful, bare chest exposed for his exploration. His hand softly cupped one of her breasts and he savored the feel of her, as his lips found the other breast and kissed it over and over again. When her nipple was inside his mouth her head fell backwards in ecstasy and her hands reached around to grab onto his broad shoulders. She clung to him as she breathed heavily in his ear. Cal reached her lips again and kissed her with more force and passion than he had so far, and she responded in kind. He picked her up and placed her in his bed, hovering over her like a lion claiming it's pray.

* * *

She pulled his shirt over his head and threw it to the side. He looked magnificent. His body was incredible. Alease could see his eyes smoldering with lust as he looked at her underneath him, and yet, even with the raging passion that she could feel was flowing through him, he very gently lowered himself onto her, covering her completely with his body. His warmth and strength felt phenomenal on her. They were skin to skin and yet she still felt as if she couldn't get close enough. She pulled him to her as tightly as she could and he followed willingly. He kissed her neck again as his hands danced up her sides. His touch had her on edge. His hands came back down and swept across her jeans. His fingers flirted with the space between the top of her jeans and her skin just underneath. He flipped the button open then went back to her sides, giving her a moment to accept that her pants were now undone and about to be taken off. It was thrilling her that he was about to touch her. She felt as if she would explode. His hands came back and slowly undid her zipper. Her excitement forced her to place her hands on his face and bring his lips back to hers again. He kissed her with a primitive dominance that she found titillating. He broke the kiss and lifted his body off of her enough to sit back and pull her jeans off of her. He did it slowly, carefully, but with complete purpose, his eyes on hers the whole time. The outline of his body was like a dream…he was so masculine, so powerful above her. He managed to get his jeans and underwear off in one swift movement, and then was lowering himself back onto her in the same breath. His complete nakedness sent a rush of desire through her very core and she reached back to pull him closer to her as he carefully lowered himself onto her, resting his manhood on top of her silk panties. She let out a gasp when she felt his center rest on her. Jesus, he was huge. She had never been with a man who was this big and she wondered if he would even fit inside her. As if reading her thoughts, she could feel him slow the pace, his kisses deepened and loaded with emotion. His fingers began tracing up her legs further and further, then ever so lightly glazed on top of her panties over her womanhood and teased her clit. She shivered again. Even over her panties his touch was outrageous. Then he teased the edge of her panties with his fingers sliding just under them on her skin. She moaned again in his mouth and, with his kiss, he seemed to take her very soul into his. He gently removed her panties and slowly traced his hands back up her legs as his body met hers again. He kissed her stomach, he licked her bellybutton, and then his lips fell lower…and lower…until they were breathlessly dancing on her clit. Sound escaped her mouth as she fell under his control. His lips and tongue were so soft on her, and he moved on her so perfectly…smooth throbs of pleasure began sweeping through her. She was being over taken by sensations she had never known before. What he was doing to her felt so incredible, she felt herself begging him for more.

He knew exactly how to work her body, how to get her in such need for him that she could do nothing but plead for his entrence into her. Her breathing was on edge. He slowed the pace of his tongue and her breath stopped…dangling on the edge until he freed her with another stroke of his tongue. He gave her what she needed and licked her in a long and slow sweep. She moaned at the unbelievable arousal just as he slowed his tongue again…as if begging her to ask him for more. Her back arched, she was in such need for another, her body sizzling, waiting, pleading for him…he made her wait for what felt like an eternity, then he released her with a full, slow sweep of his tongue that sent searing pleasure through her entire body like lightening. She was on fire, in need like she never had been before. Words fell from her mouth, "Oh God" she exclaimed breathlessly. Cal's fingers were now running up her legs, across her belly and down to where her world was in his hands. He taunted her desire as he danced his fingers across her clit, down slightly just to the entrance then back up again. He had her completely on edge, teasing her with his hands. His fingers came back down again, tracing the entrance into her body…then, slowly, his fingers entered her. He explored inside her with one, then two, then three fingers. He drove them deeper into her. She let out another sound of pleasure she couldn't control. His lips covered hers as he played back and forth with his fingers inside her, slowly driving her to the edge she was just about to fall over.

* * *

She was so wet. She felt so good. Then suddenly, he felt her hot hands on his shaft. He let out a deep moan that caused him to break his kiss from her and breathe in the pleasure of her hands on him. She was stroking him with her soft, but wonderfully tight grip. Her fingers clasped around every inch of him, masterfully massaging him into a monstrous desire he could no longer control. He could feel her pulling the raging core of pleasure right out of him. He was wild with need for her. He slid his fingers inside her again; she was ready for him and he needed her, as he had never needed another woman before. He pulled his fingers from inside her and steadied himself over her body. As much as the primitive side of him wanted to just drive right into her and fuck her brains out, he knew he was bigger than most men, and he had to go slowly the first time. Her breathing was on the precipice and her legs opened for him. He reached for her hand and clasped his around hers. He pressed his lips on hers and lowered his core onto her. He felt her breath escape in his mouth as he caressed her clit with his rock hard shaft. He rubbed his manhood on her flaming spot of pleasure and she moaned under him. His tip found her entrance…he teased her again just as he had done with his fingers. Up and down he brushed her like a canvas. Then, at the entrance again, he stopped…he held the moment as he kissed her, feeling her body begging him, pleading with him to take her over the edge. Then, he released them both, and he entered her. Her canal clinging to him, holding him in as he pushed further into her. She let out a gasp as her arms grabbed his body and held on for dear life. The pleasure that shot through him was like none he had ever had before. He could feel her all over him, pulling him in, gripping him like a glove. He moved in further, pulled back almost all the way out, then pushed back in again. Over and over, quicker and quicker. His entire body was on fire, boiling, crying for more. The wet heat between them lubricating their way to overwhelming euphoria. He couldn't hold back the explosion, he was a slave to the power her body had over him. He reached the top, he came, shooting his manhood deep inside of her. He screamed his pleasure as his load shot from deep inside him to the depths of her core. He collapsed on her, careful to use his last bit of strength to keep from crushing her. He pulsed inside of her, he quivered and chills ran the gambit of his body. He found her lips and kissed her with everything he had in him.

He lowered himself beside her, quickly shifting her so that he could enter her again and have her in his arms. He cradled her as he continued to pulse inside of her. He felt her trembling in his embrace, her body still gripping his. He held her as tightly as he could and kissed her neck and face. He found himself bewildered at how incredible it felt with her. Like no experience he ever had before. His love for her suddenly endless and more powerful than he could have imagined. He wanted so badly to tell her, but he knew she was not ready to hear the words, so he told her with his body. With his embrace. With his lips.

He felt her body relax in his hold. Her breathing calmed and he could feel her melt completely into him. As he laid there relishing in the heaven inside his arms, he felt her fall into a deep sleep. He covered her with his arms, his legs and the big comforter, protecting her in his bed. His eyes closed and he followed her into sleep.

The next morning Cal woke up with Alease still in his arms, the length of her long naked body pressed into his and her small hand inside of his. Her hair billowed all around his chest. He traced his fingers on her shoulder and down her arm. He felt her breast resting above his heart and he kissed the top of her head as he pulled her even closer. Last night had been amazing, and the sheer thought of it made him rock hard again. She stirred and softly turned over keeping herself locked in his embrace. He rolled over towards her and pressed his body against hers. She woke and the flames between them seemed to spark instantaneously. He was on top of her as she responded to his need with her own.

Cal was trying to hold onto the flood gates with everything he had. He knew this was not the right moment to take her again. When he made love to her, he wanted all the time in the world with her, before, during and after. They didn't have that right now, and he would not be rushed. Not with this woman. He did his best to slow himself and dial down the passion threatening to explode between the two of them. He slowed her down with his body, his lips and his breathing. She responded in kind and they broke the kiss reluctantly.

"I'm suddenly regretting that I said we were coming to Joes," he said as he brushed her hair from her eyes.

She smiled at him and her eyes glistened with colors of trepidation behind her desire. Though he could still see it, he could also tell that her fear was lessoning, and that made him more confident his patience with her had been completely the right choice.

"How late are we?" Alease asked the question in a very sleepy, sexy voice that almost made Cal lose his control.

"Three hours late…so far." He kissed her again and found himself unable to stop.

"So what's a another hour? We'll bring extra wine." Her smile, her naked body and the heat between her legs was all too much for the Navy SEAL. He couldn't hold the flood gates. He needed her and would not be denied. Her hands found their way to his manhood and stroked him in long steady glides that drove him to the brink of insanity. He had to pull himself away from her touch or he wouldn't last. He knew how to get her under his control. He slid his tongue down her belly and danced near her inner thighs; then slowly to her pleasure center and her world seemed to stop under his touch. He stroked her with his tongue slowly, deliberately and her legs opened for him as if he found the combination for the lock and controlled it himself. He inserted his fingers to tease her more.

He wanted to get her even more on the edge of ecstasy so that her body would take him in, all of him. He drove his fingers inside her, then pulled them out to dance on her clit again. He lowered his lips on her clit and stroked her with his tongue. He played with her body like this until he felt she was on the verge of desperation. Her fingers were clawing into his back, her arms pulling him into her with such passion he could no longer wait.

She was even more wet than the night before. He was bursting for her. He brought his lips back up to hers and felt her hands on him again, guiding him into her with a need that matched his own. He drove into her and she screamed in pleasure. He went in far, her body gripping him the whole way, begging him to drive further. He went all the way in, then slowly all the way out, repeating the drives until he exploded in ecstasy. His load shooting inside her as she held onto him with every bit of strength she had left.

He collapsed on top of her, sweat falling off of both of their glistening bodies.

"Now we are really late," Alease said with a breathy gasp. He could hear in her voice that she was still trying to quell the lust that had shot up in her. He loved the sound of it.

He kissed her deeply and then moved off to the side. "I know. Before we go, I want to check to make sure your heater is working, but it looked like it was working fine last night."

"Thank you. I'll pack while you do that. It won't take me long."

After a shower and another flare up of passion that cost them an additional hour, they had their clothes on and headed over to her house. As soon as they walked into her home they could feel the warmth.

"What a difference," Alease said. "I didn't realize how cold it had been in here since I moved in."

Cal went to look at the new heater while Alease packed a few things. When she went into her bedroom, Cal quickly inspected the heating unit, but his real goal had been to put his eyes on her house and just double check that everything seemed ok. His concerns over what Joe had said were eating at him as he slept, and he woke with an apprehension about it that he couldn't shake. He didn't want to leave anything to chance, not where her safety was concerned, so eyes on her house before they left was important to him.

Her house seemed fine; nothing out of place, no damage to the locks, windows or doors. He was careful to check everything without her noticing what he was doing. He didn't want her worrying.

When Alease was packed, they headed to his truck with two fresh coffees, and Max jumped in the back seat. As they pulled out of the driveway, Cal felt an amazing sense of peace and calm in the warmth of the truck under the falling snowflakes. He took her hand in his. The sensations from being inside her still rushing through his body. The incredible love for her that he felt…it was extraordinary. He kissed her hand as he put the truck in drive, happy to be entering the holidays in the company of the woman of his dreams.

***

From up in the mountains behind the trees, a camera shutter snapped several times capturing close up images of the man driving the red ford pickup truck… and her. His cold heart raced and he licked his lips. The woman he wasn't done with. He had been given a second chance, and this time he was going to finish what he started. He wasn't used to following orders, but the man behind the money that bought his freedom and paid for his ability to track her down, was not to be double crossed. He knew that much. Fine. The money man could do whatever he wanted once he was done and handed her over. He didn't much care as long as he got what he wanted first. He snapped a few more pictures, and then checked to see if the tracker he had placed under the back end of the red pick up truck was working. Bingo. Now he had them. All he had to do was find a way to separate her from the man and take her to the rendezvous point.

Chapter Seven

Joe's

Even an hour into the drive, Alease could still feel her body tingling from being with Cal. She found herself readjusting in her seat in futile attempts to quiet the buzz rattling through her. He had not let go of her hand since they got in the car; his thumb gently rubbing back and forth on her skin. He lifted her hand to his lips several times, kissing her gently and lowering her hand softly back down on his thigh. It made it impossible for her to dowse the fire inside her that was still burning as hot as it was last night…and this morning.

Alease felt a slight shift of energy in the last twenty minutes though, and it had her defenses beckoning to be reinstated. Cal's thoughts seemed heavy and guarded. He had gotten quiet and his eyes gave the impression of someone in serious thought. A sense of unease started to emerge in her gut. She wondered if maybe he was regretting last night. She felt her grip in his hand loosen and her mind started to instruct her to pull away, which her body must have heeded because Cal noticed it.

He tightened his grip on her hand and took his eyes off the road to scan her face.

"Are you ok?" he asked.

She felt a little off guard since that was the question she probably should be asking him.

"Yeah," was all she could manage to say.

He squeezed her hand and pressed her. "I know you better than that by now. What is it?"

Maybe just getting it out there was the best way to cut through it and know where he was with everything.

"You just seemed…far away in deep contemplation. I wasn't sure if maybe you were…having second thoughts about…what happened last night."

The shocked look on his face indicated that, either his acting skills were top notch, or, she was completely wrong in her assessment.

"Oh God, no. Not at all. Are you kidding?" He kissed her hand again and did not release his grip. "Last night was… amazing. I mean it. Jesus. No, that's not where my mind was."

She wanted to believe him but her defenses kicked in, and flipping that switch off was really hard for her to do.

"Cal, listen, if being with me was not what you thought it would be…you don't have to -"

He cut her off without apology.

"Alease, stop. That is not at all what I was thinking. Last night…being with you…it was incredible. Honestly, the only second thoughts I'm having right now are about going to Joe's instead of pulling off to a hotel and spending the next

few days alone with you in bed. Last night was remarkable…
and this morning. Listen, I'm happy to do a Deep Dive about
it right now if you want to," he challenged her with his smile.

She knew she was not ready for a Deep Dive into what
transpired between them, so she switched off of that.

"Then what were you thinking about?"

He took a moment to gather his response.

"I was thinking about the guy who attacked you. I wanted
to ask you some things about him, but I didn't want to upset
you, so I wasn't sure how to bring it up."

His response caught her off balance, she was not
expecting that was on his mind.

"Really? Why were you thinking about him?"

"Just curious who this guy was. Did you ever get his
name?"

His question seemed casual enough. "No. I never asked."

"So after he was pronounced dead, and the police report
was finished, they never told you who he was?"

She hadn't really thought about that. "I never read the
final police report. The last communication I had with the
cops was at the hospital when they brought me in. I don't
really remember much from that except that I just wanted to
leave and be done with it."

"Did they ever give you a final cause of death on the
guy?"

He seemed really preoccupied with it. "Cal, why are you

asking this?"

His eyes softened and he squeezed her hand. "No reason. I just want to know the details. It's the SEAL in me…we always need specifics. It's part of our training."

That made sense to her. "In all honesty, I don't know anything past what happened in my house. When the cops showed up, my mind kind of shut off. It was all too much for me. I didn't ask any questions and I didn't really listen to anything they were saying. As soon as I was able, I left. I never returned any follow up phone calls from the police. I didn't see the point."

"Can you describe what you remember when the cops got there?"

She thought about it. "They cut me loose and took me out to the ambulance. It was quick."

"Do you remember what the cops were doing as you were in the ambulance?"

She hadn't really thought about that before, but she searched her memory.

"The cops were in the house standing over the guy. Several of them. They had their guns out. The paramedics ushered me right out into the ambulance," she paused for a second. "I remember seeing another ambulance and cop cars heading up the driveway with their lights flashing. They must have also answered the call without knowing someone else did already." Cal's eyes were steady and she couldn't read them. "Why?"

He softened his gaze again and gave her a reassuring smile, "Nothing. I just wanted to hear what you could remember." He kissed her hand again.

He didn't want her to know about his concerns. Why worry her if he didn't have to. Just then, Cal's car phone rang. They could both see it was Joe from the caller ID.

"Uh oh. We're in trouble for being late," Alease warned.

Cal laughed. He knew Joe was concerned about where they were and why they hadn't shown up yet. Cal was never late, and today, they were over four hours late. He answered the phone, quick to make sure Joe knew Alease could hear him.

"Hey Joe, you're on speaker and we are both very sorry we are running late. Everything is fine. It's uhh, my fault. I had trouble wanting to get out of bed this morning." It wasn't a lie…he knew Joe would understand what he was saying.

They could hear a raspy chuckle from Joe on the other end. "OK. You had me worried…why is your cell phone off?"

"Shit." Cal had completely forgotten to turn it back on. He had turned it off when Alease fell asleep on his sofa. He didn't want it to ring and wake her up. "I forgot. I turned it off last night…totally forgot to turn it back on."

"Alease, you have him flustered. He never does stuff like that," Joe chuckled again.

"I certainly didn't mean to," Alease laughed.

"I should have let you know, Joe. I was just…well, flustered," Cal admitted.

"No worries, just calling to bust your balls for not being here to help us set up the tables. How are you, Alease?"

"I'm fine, Joe. You?" Alease asked.

"All good. Everyone here is very much looking forward to meeting you. How's your drive going?" Joe inquired.

"Good. Sorry we got a late start," she uttered shyly.

"No problem. Just wanted to check and make sure all was…good," Joe answered.

"Yeah. Everything is fine. Just a late start," Cal reassured him again.

"Well, Cal, you're on trash duty when you get here. How far out are you?" Joe asked him.

Cal looked at the clock, "Probably about an hour."

"OK. Everyone is here. The team is waiting. See you guys soon."

The team is waiting… that was code…it meant there was information. Joe had something to tell him. Cal pushed the gas a little more to increase his speed.

One thing was made clear to him from his conversation with Alease…she had no confirmation that the guy had died. She just assumed it. She might not have known. A body can appear to be dead, but be very much alive. Unless she had confirmation from authorities, she wouldn't have known the truth. Considering what she had gone through, it was logical that she needed to believe he was dead and so, she just accepted that as if it were fact without really knowing. Cal was more anxious than ever to get to Joe's and start pushing his connections for the truth of what was going on with this guy. If he was still out there, Cal needed to finish him.

He didn't like that her defenses started kicking into gear again when he allowed his thoughts to wander. She got the wrong idea about that and he knew, if he didn't nip that in the bud immediately, she was bound to go down a deep hole of self doubt and pull herself away from him again, which he desperately did not want to happen.

"So, are you doing ok about last night?" He saw her shrink into herself a little bit, but he kept going. "How do you feel about it?" She had that look in her eyes, the one that reveals her desire to deflect any real answers.

"I'm not used to a man asking a question like that," she said.

"Well, I care about how you feel and I'd like to know. How was last night for you?" She seemed completely blindsided by the question. He found it curious. "Has no one ever asked you that before?"

"No. I have never had to talk about it before." Her cheeks were flushed and she was clearly out of her comfort zone.

"Boy, you have definitely been with the wrong men."

"Clearly," her response seemed multifaceted.

"OK, so if I was just one of your girl friends and she asked you how it was, what would you say?"

She couldn't hide the smile that forced itself on her face. "I would say…it was unbelievable." She looked as though she wanted to say more, but her voice just stopped working.

"So, you're admitting that it felt good. That you enjoyed it." He knew he was pushing her further than she wanted to go, but he needed her to.

"Yes," her cheeks flooded again with red.

He already knew she liked it, he could tell by the way her body responded to him; but there was one aspect he was not convinced about, and he needed to know so he could fix it.

"I need to do one Deep Dive here," he said.

"Oh boy. Do I need alcohol for this question?"

"Probably, but we don't have any at the moment. Deep Dive?" he asked.

"OK. What?" her voice was nervous and he could tell she was unsettled.

"Did you have an orgasm?" he asked it as casually as he could, but there really was no other way then to just ask it.

A bolt of embarrassment shot across her face.

"Oh my God. You go right for the jugular, don't you?"

"Don't take it like that. It's just, it's important to me. In some ways, I feel like I can read your body pretty well. I know it felt good. I'm pretty sure there were several moments that were…building up, but I couldn't quite tell if you ever climaxed. Did you?" He saw that she was extremely uncomfortable with the question, but he didn't want this unknown to be in-between them, so he pushed her to face him with the truth of it. "Please just talk to me and tell me."

She took a breath. "It's not your fault, Cal. It felt amazing, please believe me. It was better than anything I have experienced before in my life. I promise you that. It's just… the orgasm thing…I don't know, it just doesn't work with me…my body is broken or something. Please don't think twice about it."

He couldn't help but laugh at her ridiculous statement.

"Alease, your body is not broken. Far from it. Your body is the best body I have ever felt in my life. Let me ask you this, were you close?" He could tell she didn't really want to answer but to her credit she did.

"Yes. Several times, very close. So don't feel bad about it, please."

"Alease, stop worrying about how I am feeling about it. I'm not turned off by it, if that is what you are concerned about. On the contrary, I'm very…interested in correcting it." He kissed her hand again, but could tell she was bothered by the subject.

"Just don't think about it. I don't want you to focus on that, cause if it doesn't happen, I don't want you to get frustrated." She clearly was afraid of his reaction more than how it effected her.

"Why wouldn't it happen?" he asked her. She looked out the window unsure how to answer him. Then a thought dawned on him. "Alease, you have had an orgasm before, right?" It didn't occur to him until that moment that maybe she hadn't.

"Of course…you know…by myself. Sure." She was getting very fidgety.

"Are you telling me no man has ever made you come before?"

"This is so embarrassing, are we really having this conversation?" She shifted herself in her seat again.

He tried to relax her with calm in his voice. "No, it's not. There's nothing to be embarrassed about. It's ok. Just talk to me." She hesitated and then reluctantly answered him.

"No. No man has ever been able to do that. See, my body is broken, I told you."

He couldn't help but smile. "It's not your body that prevented you…it's your fear. It's your mind." He took a beat to find a way to elaborate. "I'm sure, for you, allowing yourself to come with a man is a vulnerability that scares you, so you shut down and block it." She was quiet and unsure how to answer him, but he knew he was right. "Let me ask you this, when I was touching you and it was building up, did you stop it by reaching for me and…distracting me from what I was doing to you?"

She took a breath. "I might have done that, yes." He

didn't speak, he wanted her to continue. "Yeah, you might be right, but I think I did that cause I didn't think it was going to happen and I didn't want you to get frustrated."

"I'm going to have to call bullshit on that one. I think you did it because it was overpowering you, it scared you, and your first reaction was to try and control it so it wouldn't control you. Am I right?" He knew he was right. The more he thought about last night, he remembered her reaching for him every time she was building up. He could kick himself now for not noticing it then, but her touch was so incredible, he lost his focus every time she put her hands on him, and when she stroked him into her…he was overpowered by his own build up. He would not let that happen next time.

"I don't know. Maybe," she said.

He could tell from the look on her face she was not even aware she had done it.

"I think your defenses are so second nature to you, that you may not have even realized you were sabotaging your own pleasure out of fear of losing control." He kissed her hand again. "Well, we are going to work on that." He knew what to do, and his arousal burned through him in anticipation.

The sun had just gone down as they pulled into Joe's long private driveway. Even in the dark under the moonlight Alease could see how beautiful it was. The snow was piled up on both sides of the drive, with big pine trees gracing each side all the way up to the house. It was an exquisite, luxury log cabin style home. Alease had never seen one so big, it looked like three floors, four if it had a basement. The entire outside of it already had Christmas lights hanging from it, sparkling in the reflection of the snow and ice hanging from the roof.

There was a smaller log cabin style guest house off to the left of it which was also adorned with Christmas lights.

"Wow, his home is beautiful," she said.

Cal smiled. "Yeah, it really is. He stole the idea from me. This is what I would like to do with my home and property. As soon as Mrs. Katrockuss is ready to let go of her home there."

"Wait. I'm confused. If you own the property, how is it her home?" Alease didn't quite understand the story there, but she saw a sadness in Cal's eyes she had not seen before.

Cal slowed his truck as he took the turns up the drive. "The land is mine, but I sold the land inside the footprint of that house to her and her husband…sold is not really accurate…there had to be a financial transaction for it to be legally theirs, so I sold it to them for one dollar. The only stipulation was that when they no longer wanted to own it, that they would sell it back to me."

There was a level of emotion behind what he was saying that she still didn't understand.

"Cal, who are they? Why were you so generous with them?"

The sadness in the breath he took before he gave his answer was powerful, and Alease felt it pierce through her heart.

"They are the parents of a SEAL team member of mine who did not make it back from one of our deployments. John Katrockuss." Cal fell quiet at the mention of his name, and a painful emotion filled the air around him.

She placed her free hand on top of his and held it. "I'm so sorry Cal."

"John was their only family, and when he died, they were crushed. My whole team stepped up. We had that house built for them, moved them in, and I gave them that piece of land so they would feel that it was really theirs. When Mr. Katrockuss died, it was hard for her to manage the winters there by herself, but that house was the last thing she had of her husband. She didn't want to let it go." Cal parked the truck at the top of the driveway and turned the ignition off. "She asked me if she could rent it out this winter so she could still hold onto it, and then decide in the summer if she was ready to let it go and move on."

Alease was so moved by the story she had tears in her eyes. She reached up and brushed her hand along his cheek.

"You are amazing Cal." He turned his moistened eyes to her, and she pulled his face to hers, offering him a deep kiss blanketed in emotion. He took it in and pressed himself into her for more. Alease could feel him yearning for her comfort and she gave it a thousand fold.

The front door of the house opened and a myriad of voices flooded out in chaotic greetings.

"Oh for Pete's sake, let the poor woman in from the cold before you smother her like that!"

"Come on Cal, kiss her later. We want to meet her!"

They broke their kiss and looked over to see a clutter of men, women and children all clamoring to get a look at this mystery woman they had not met yet. Cal smiled.

"Alease, this is…everybody."

Cal was able to guide her inside the house, navigating her through the crowd of eager beavers all wanting the long awaited glimpse at this woman who had captivated their friend. Joe and Dana were kind enough to try and ease everyone back so they could get in and shut the front door to keep the cold outside.

"We started to worry about you two. With all the snow and icy roads." Dana turned back after shutting the door and stood in front of Alease and Cal.

Cal lowered his arm from Alease's side. "Alease, this is Joe's wife, Dana."

Alease shook her hand as Dana smiled warmly. "Hi Dana, it's lovely to meet you," Alease said.

"You as well, Alease. We've heard so much about you." Cal could hear in Dana's voice that she took an instant liking to Alease, which didn't surprise him in the least.

Joe spoke out from behind Cal. He turned to see Joe crossing over with two steaming mugs in his hands.

He handed one to Cal, then hugged him like a brother. He turned to Alease.

"Hi Alease. I'm so glad you came." He gave her a kind hug, then he offered her the mug in his hand. "Here. Hot cider. I assume spiked is ok for you?

Alease laughed and took the mug. "Yes! Hit me!"

Cal continued the introductions. "These two lovely young ladies are Joe and Dana's daughters, Kathy & Jenny." The girls smiled at Alease and said hello. Cal turned to his SEAL buddies who were all grinning from ear to ear. "and these bozos are Dan, Eddie and Tom, my SEAL Team." Alease shook all their hands as they all greeted her warmly. Cal directed his attention to the three women standing with them. "These are their wives, Elizabeth, Sarah and Erika."

"Its so nice to finally meet all of you," Alease said with that smile Cal loved so much. Alease looked to the kids who were huddled in the back. "And who are you two?"

Cal introduced them. "This seven year old terror is Johnathan; he is Eddie and Sarah's son, and this beautiful 12 year old is Stephanie, daughter of Tom and Erika."

Jake and Sophie came bounding in from the back door

warming their hands in the welcomed heat of the house.

"Hi Alease!" Jake called.

"You guys made it! Finally," Sophie said as she took her hat off.

"Hi Jake. Hey Sophie." Alease's voice was bright and warm.

Cal hugged his sister. "Did you guys just get here?"

Sophie hugged Alease as she answered him. "No. We were just doing a last minute room switch."

Joe turned to Cal. "Yes. Dana and I thought maybe you and Alease should have the guest house and Sophie and Jake could have the two rooms on the second floor. Little more privacy for you two." Cal smiled his thanks to Joe. Clearly Joe had picked up on the fact that he and Alease had spent the night together and he was doing what he could to ensure their relationship was not…interrupted by the visit.

"Thanks Joe." Cal really appreciated that his friend arranged that for him.

"Can we eat now? I'm starving!" Stephanie called out.

Dana laughed. "Yes. Come on everyone." She led the way to the dining room table.

Alease was immersed with the joy in the house. It was an amazing feeling of family she had never experienced before. The overwhelming love and comfort here was more than she anticipated.

Sitting at the dining room table, empty plates and full stomachs, she felt completely at ease with the group she found herself part of. She looked around as she sipped her hot spiced wine and took in the scene. The house looked like it came right out of a movie. They had a huge Christmas tree up by the picture window in the living room. It was glistening with multi colored lights and the kids were all placing decorations on it, laughing and teasing each other as they did so. There was a large, cushy three sided red sofa that complimented the poinsettias that were beautifully decorated throughout the house. The fireplace on the far wall was the biggest Alease had ever seen, and the heat from the blazing fire warmed the large room beautifully.

The conversation at the table drifted from topic to topic, as Joe handed out more drinks and Dana brought over a plate of cookies and petite fours.

Cal had his chair moved as close to Alease as he could get it, his hand holding hers and the other clasping his brandy glass. He looked amazing. His rough, chiseled cheeks off set by that beautiful smile of his. Alease still couldn't believe the incredible mix of strong masculinity and warm kindness that emanated from him. She could tell by the way he looked at his friends that they meant the world to him, and he them. It was a new experience for her to see such brotherly love between men, and it was incredibly comforting to be around. To know these guys would do anything for each other…it was an extraordinary thing.

Alease took note of the affection each of these men had for their wives. What a contrast from the relationships she was used to seeing. Even as the guys talked with each other, they still had their arms around the shoulders of their wives, or holding their hands. Just as Cal always had part of his attention on her, even in the midst of a conversation with Dan about his faulty tractor, or Eddie about teaching his son Johnathan to shoot in the back yard. It surprised her how at home she felt here, with this group…with Cal.

There was that unwanted fear again that flashed through her. Warnings under the surface of her inner voices reminding her how much it would hurt if she were to lose this. It was too late to not get used to it; she knew she already had. She had been breathing this feeling in since…well, since the day she met Cal. It was already attached to her. How the Hell could she shake this off now?

Cal squeezed her hand. She looked up and saw him gazing into her eyes. He brushed her hair back from her eyes and smiled at her.

"You doing ok?" he asked her softly.

"Yes," she realized that Joe and Dana had their attention on them. "I was just trying to remember when I have ever had a meal as incredible as this one. I don't think I have. Joe, Dana, your home is so lovely…thank you for inviting me here."

Dana's face filled with joy. "Of course! I'm really glad you came. I know this SEAL team crowd can be a bit overbearing, but I'm very glad you found the courage to come face us!" she laughed.

Cal pulled her close to him and kissed her head. Alease saw a smile on Joe's face as he watched Cal doing it. There was a tenderness in Joe's eyes, as if he was really glad to see his friend so happy; but there was a little something else in there too she couldn't quite read. Joe caught Alease's attempts at reading his look and his energy changed.

"Well," Joe said cheerfully, "if you liked this dinner so much, just wait until the big Thanksgiving meal tomorrow." He stretched his feet out and placed his hand on his wife's arm. "This one makes the best roasted turkey ever."

"It's the duck fat coating on the turkey. That's the trick," Dana said humbly.

Dan chimed in with a bright laugh. "Bets on if Sophie burns the marshmallows again on the Sweet Potatoes?" They all cracked up, even Sophie.

"Dan you were supposed to remind me! Instead you distracted me with a stupid video on your phone!" Sophie was laughing as she responded.

"I think Sophie should be demoted from Sweet Potato duty and put on something less…flammable," Dan suggested.

"Yeah, ice," Eddie chimed in.

Joe laughed and looked to Dana. "I'll leave the delegating

to you. The boys and I will get on trash duty while you do that." He stood up and Alease saw him look to Cal.

She felt Cal pull her to him and whisper in her ear. "I'll be right back, ok?"

She turned her eyes to his and smiled. "Yeah. All good." He pressed his lips to hers and kissed her warmly. She wasn't sure if he would do that in front of his friends, but he did not hesitate. When he broke the kiss, he ran his hand across her cheek before letting her go. Just a simple gesture, and yet it made her heart flutter.

The men grabbed their coats, a few bags of trash and went out the front door. Alease was well aware it did not take five Navy SEALs to take out a few bags of garbage…she knew they wanted some guy time, which she completely understood.

She turned her attention back to Dana and the women and they talked about the meal for tomorrow as they cleared the table and cleaned up.

The night air was ice cold, but the SEALs didn't flinch. On the far side of the drive, Joe flicked his match and lit a cigarette. He took a puff and released the smoke into the night air. He looked to Cal, "I told them what we're looking into, I hope that's ok."

"Yeah. We're family," Cal answered.

"I'm sorry that happened to her. She is an amazing

woman," Eddie said to Cal.

"Yeah she is. Really glad you found her," Dan agreed.

"Thank you," Cal answered. He looked back to Joe. "So, what's going on? Any more information?"

Joe took another drag. Cal could see the unease Joe was feeling with what he was about to say.

"Cal, I don't think this guy is dead."

Cal knew it in his gut, but hearing it out loud caused another bolt of anger to fly through him.

"Yeah, I'm starting to get that feeling too. I prodded her a little bit about it today…sounds to me like they ushered her out so fast when they got there that she didn't know." His hands ran through his hair in frustration. "Fuck." Cal gathered his thoughts and pushed his emotional reaction aside. "OK, what do we know?" he asked Joe.

Joe took a moment. "I don't have any of the answers I should. Even Darrin at the CIA is under some heat for asking about this guy."

Cal was just as surprised as the rest of them at hearing that. "What? Why?"

"I don't know. Neither does he, but it's made him even more determined to figure it out, so he has some calls into his connections higher up. I'm hoping to have some answers by Friday. I doubt he can get anyone to reach back tomorrow being Thanksgiving and all. He said we should call him tomorrow morning anyway just in case he can get his hands on something he was looking into."

Eddie spoke up. "Did you learn anything else?" he turned to Dan. "What about your friend in the PC's office?"

Dan shook his head. "He couldn't even find the file."

"That doesn't make sense. Why?" Cal asked.

"It was moved," Dan responded.

"Where? And why would they do that?" Eddie questioned. Dan shook his head, he clearly didn't know.

Joe's face hardened. "This guy is masked in a whole bunch of fucking red tape…why?" Joe's eyes pinched together as he looked at Cal and he exhaled the smoke from his cigaret slowly. "I know that look in your eyes, Cal. Listen, don't let this get to you. We are going to find out everything, it's just going to take a little time. Maybe it's nothing. Maybe this guy really is dead and they just let the file drop. Even if he is, somehow, still alive, you have a whole team here ready to take this son of a bitch down for what he did to her. You know we've got your back…and hers too."

"I know that, but straight up; if this guy is alive, I'm the one who takes him down." The quiet nods from them was all the reassurance he needed that he would not be deprived of ending this bastard if he was still breathing.

It was pretty extraordinary seeing the five 6 foot plus Navy SEALs walking together into the house towards them. Alease could see how intimidating they were just in jeans and casual shirts; she could only imagine how they must seem with all their gear on and heading towards anyone they were intending to obliterate. It was an amazing image. The fear they must drive into their enemies…Alease could only imagine it.

Cal was very good at disguising the thoughts in his eyes, once again, she could not quite read him. She wondered what the general consensus was regarding her; she knew his buddies had one, and that, perhaps, that's what the huddle had been about.

When Cal reached her, he drew her into him, holding her near him as Dana handed out warm brandy drinks to the guys who wanted them. Cal took his, keeping his other arm around her protectively. It warmed her even though she wasn't cold.

She leaned back and softly whispered to him, "Everything ok?"

Cal flashed that reassuring smile, kissed her lips and answered calmly, "Yeah. Just SEAL stuff," he said as he hugged her closer. She felt herself fold into him, even though there was that little voice in her head stirring up some apprehension, but Cal was so good at easing that out of her that she already felt it fading as he held her, rubbed her arms and kissed her cheek several times as they all continued the conversation about Thanksgiving tomorrow.

After all the duties were assigned for who was to do what tomorrow, Joe piped up.

"So the only question is, will Cal be able to pull himself out of bed in the morning?" The guys laughed.

"No one would blame you if you couldn't," Dan said with a smirk.

Alease felt her cheeks flush, as the group enjoyed the tease at the new couple.

"Well, the least we can do is help him out by turning in now so he has some extra time," Dana said kindly.

"Everything is set for you guys in the guest house, towels, soap…anything else you need just holler," Joe said as he put his glass down on the counter.

As the 'goodnights' passed through the group, Alease got the sense that the SEALs liked her. She caught the approving looks between them and Cal and she certainly felt a good bond with the women. Perhaps she passed the test. She was fairly certain, if they did not like her, that she would have known it by now.

The brief walk through the back patio to the guest house was colder than Alease thought it would be, but Cal kept his arm around her and held her close until they got in the little house and closed the door. Cal locked it, and followed Alease into the romantically lit living room.

The fireplace was two sided; one side was in the living room, and the other side opened into the bedroom. Joe had already lit the fire for them, and a few soft night lights were on throughout the house so they could see their way. It was incredibly cozy and warm. There was a simple kitchen off to the left, and the door to the bedroom suite off to the right.

Alease took off her coat and Cal placed it over the loveseat, not wanting to take the time to hang it up in the closet. He moved close to her and gazed at her face with deep affection in his eyes. The reflection of the flames bounced off the strong outline of his cheekbones and the smoldering look was making her knees weak. The heat flowing from inside her was suddenly more powerful than the heat from the fireplace. She could see in his gaze that he had the same heat flowing up through him, and she knew, within seconds, she was about to be swept up in it, once again under his control.

His lips lowered onto hers and the sudden swell of emotion and passion consumed them both. Before she knew it, he had her in his arms and was carrying her off to the bedroom, where she knew she would be lost in ravishing pleasure underneath him.

He slid his hands under her sweater, caressing her bare skin with his rough fingers. Shivers shot through her. He traced his hands over her belly and around her hips to the small of her back. She arched in the pleasure of his touch and with one swift move, he had her sweater off. His hands came back around her front, slinking their way across her breasts. He found the front bra clasp with ease, and with a flick of his finger, it was undone and falling off. The whole of his hand captured her breast completely in its grip. He let out a moan of pleasure at the feel of her and Alease was overcome with desperate need thundering up from her lower core. His lips found her nipple and kissed it, sucked it, teased it till she lost her senses. Within minutes he had them both free of all their clothing, and he seemed to be ravishing in the sight of her nakedness in front of him.

Then he very gently picked her up and placed her down in the middle of the bed, onto the fluffy feather comforter. It enveloped her and felt as if she had been set down on heavenly clouds. He held his body over her, and slowly lowered himself so he could kiss her again. He held his body a breath away from hers, kissing her deeply, intensely, forcing every inch of her to feel him, to hear what he was saying with no words.

He lowered his body on to her deliberately covering her entirely, like a protective male guarding it's territory so that no other could get close to what was his. Alease couldn't get enough of him. She pulled him down onto her even more, almost begging to be smothered by him. Having him on her was like being cloaked in a protective shield that nothing could get past. Her need for him forced it's way to him through her kisses as she pressed further into him, longing for every part of him to claim her. She felt his arousal and the searing heat coming from between his powerful legs. Her body was not waiting for her instructions, it was pressing against him, pleading for him, she couldn't stop it. Just as she felt herself fighting to regain the control that she knew she was losing, she felt him slow the pace with his body, his kiss and his touch. He deepened the passion by forcing her breath to relent and slow down. With his touch, he was wordlessly insisting that she relax and feel every single thing he was about to do to her. She had no choice, her body was his, and he knew how to control it.

She pulled his face up and took his lips to hers. She kissed him with more need than she had ever felt before. He responded, and then forced her to slow again. He was steadfast in his focus to put her over the edge and she knew it. Her heart was pounding, her body on fire, she hardly knew how to stand it. He slowed her, eased her, relaxed her back down with the power in his kiss and his body. Every time he slowed the pace, she was forced to confront the overbearing emotions she felt for him. The power of her feelings for him were so intense that it frightened her. He must have sensed it, because he moved his lips from hers, up to her ear and he whispered, ever so softly to her, "I've got you." Her entire body shivered at his words and she felt herself fall into him, needing him in ways she had never known. He put his lips back on hers and instructed the pace again. She relented under him and he took control.

His hand ran down her side, in at her waist and out again at her hips. He followed the trace down her leg. She felt the massive size of his hand and shuttered under the power it invoked over her. He stroked her up and down several times, exploring her, reveling in the touch of her skin and sending her into an endless fall of pleasure. Then his hand came up the inside of her leg, her thigh, and her center. He was seducing her with every brush of his fingers. He danced his fingers around the spot that was calling for him, needing him…he toyed with her, tracing his fingers close then pulling them back again. Every time he got close to her clit, her breathing quickened, so he slowed her with his kiss and his hands, forcing her to experience every slight movement of his fingers on her…she was mesmerized by how he could so easily command her body to his whim. It was thrilling to be so vulnerable under him…she found herself daring to follow his lead and let herself go for him. As she relaxed and softened her grip on his back, he moved his fingers again. Closer…closer…slowly…she remained as still as she could…her breath almost non existent…on the edge for him to touch her…and then he did. A sound she had never made before escaped her mouth. His fingers on the button of her womanhood…it shot through her like lightening. Like electricity. The silver pulse of unbelievable pleasure was incredible. She could do nothing to stop it. She could hardly breathe. She could hardly move. He had her, and she let him. He moved his finger in concentric circles on her, each circle bringing more intensity then the last. It was building…she could feel it in every fiber of her being. It was the most extraordinary thing she had ever experienced. He had complete power over her. It kept building…she felt the second nature defenses in her wanting to make her reach for him and stroke him into her…to help settle her instability at the mind boggling burn within her. Her hand started to go for his shaft, and he stopped moving his finger. She gasped at the loss of the pleasure.

His lips found hers, kissed her deeply, then moved to her ear to whisper again, "Let me touch you. Give in to me."

Her entire body melted under his words and she pulled her hand back. His finger moved again, filling her instantly with the building sensations. Her need for him was so great she felt like she would die. She pushed her hips up into him and he slowed his finger again until she relaxed. When she did he continued teasing, rubbing, gliding, and pulling every inch of desire from the depths of her core.

Alease couldn't think straight. She only knew she had to have him. She was desperate for him. She couldn't control anything. "Cal, fuck me, please." She heard the words come out of her mouth as if someone else was saying them.

Cal's voice was smooth, sexy and whisper quiet, "I will. But I want you to come for me first."

She gasped and moaned. He continued to dance his fingertip on her pleasure center. She was so wet, so hot. Never in her life had she felt raging passion like this. The build up was so intense, she had never known it past this point and she felt completely lost under it. It was thrilling, terrifying and completely uncontrollable. She heard herself calling his name, begging for him, yearning for his entrance into her.

With a quick smooth motion, Cal repositioned himself behind her; spooning her with his full arousal at her flood gates, ready to enter. His finger was back on her clit, forcing the build to reach it's breaking point. The silver lightening shooting through her was outrageous and she could hardly stand it. He placed his shaft right at her entrance, like a racehorse ready to be released. She moaned and cried for him. He whispered in her ear as he continued the build. "come for me Alease. Please…come for me."

Then the build hit the point of no return. She could not fight it, she could do nothing but be caught up in the wave of passion that overruled her entire being. Her breathing was fast, just as fast as his breathing in her ear, begging for her to release into him. The break was flooding through her entire world. Then it happened. She came. The explosion came from depths she didn't even know she had. She screamed her release into Cal's mouth as he covered her lips with his. Rapid, uncontrollable pulses raced through her lower body up to her chest. Cal shifted in a flash and was on top of her. He entered her, driving his shaft deep inside her. The feel of his huge cock inside her made the pulsing increase. She screamed in pleasure again, arching her back and clawing her hands into his skin for dear life.

The electric shocks of powerful pulsing and quivering inside her body was all over him. It pulled such pleasure out of him he lost his breath. Her entire body was reacting and erupting in such ecstasy that it forced his cum right out of him faster then he thought possible. The feeling was overwhelming as he shot his load deep inside her, throbbing to the point of explosion. He had to cover his mouth with hers to keep the sound from escaping too loudly. He moaned into her and she did the same. He was still coming. Her body continued radiating with electric pulses that were vibrating all over him. Jesus, he was *still* coming. It was euphoric.

When the very last drop of cum flew out of him and the overbearing pleasure exceeded his strength, he collapsed on top of her, unable to hold himself up any longer. He felt her pull him into her. He rolled slightly to the side to make sure he didn't crush her. She folded right into him, desperately trying to get closer than physically possible. Her entire body was shaking. He pulled her into him, protecting her in his embrace. As she melted into him, he pulled the thick blanket over them, softly breathing in her ear as the firelight reflected around them.

He held her as they both tried to regain control of their breathing. He stroked her hair and calmed her with his touch, gliding his hands softly on her arms as he pulled her into him.

He reveled in the realization that she had given into him. She trusted him. She needed him. There was so much he wanted to say to her, but the feeling of her clinging to him the way she was…he did not want to disturb that for anything. He just wanted her in his arms.

As she drifted to sleep safely in his embrace, his mind went back to the questions surrounding the guy who attacked her. It could only be one of two things; either someone just dropped the ball and the file got dumped because the guy is dead and it was over, or, this was connected to something bigger. If this guy was still out there, he could be a threat to her still. Cal doubted very much that the man's obsession with her would have just faded away. He felt spikes of anger shoot through him at the thought of this man (or anyone) trying to harm her. He pulled her into him even tighter.

His hand softly caressed her silky skin and he kissed her head, careful not to wake her up. Having her in his arms meant everything to him, and the idea that she could be in danger, in any way, infuriated him. Her safety was his top priority. He wondered if there might be a way to bring up the idea of her getting a gun and letting him teach her how to shoot. He didn't think she had any disagreement with guns, but how could he casually suggest it without her wondering why, and he did not want to tell her. The more he thought about it, the more he realized that could set off her defenses and he didn't like the idea of it. Maybe the best additional protection for her, besides him of course, would be for her to get another German Shepherd. Two shepherds around her whenever he wasn't, would be a good thing. Max and another; and he knew just who to contact for that.

He listened to her breathing and knew she was deep asleep. He very gently pulled himself away from her, making sure she was covered with the blanket. She moaned in her sleep and hugged the pillow he left in his place. Standing over the bed looking at her, he was still blown away by how beautiful she was. Her long hair cascading down the sheets and the firelight reflecting off her perfect face. It made him even more determined to set in place every safety measure he could think of for her.

He pulled his cell phone from his jeans that were laying on the floor, and texted his friend James Falker who was in charge of the K9 unit not too far from Joe's house. James is the one who gave him Max. His dogs were brilliant. Most of them ended up serving with police and troops. James always told Cal if he needed anything to call him. So Cal decided he was calling in the favor now. He texted him what he was looking for and hit send.

He didn't expect a reply considering it was 2:00am, but to his surprise, James texted right back.

'No problem. I'm up. Can I call you?'

Cal threw on a pair of sweatpants from his bag, and quietly closed the bedroom door behind him so he would not wake Alease up.

Alease's eyes slowly opened to the sound of rustling across the room. She sat up and saw Cal placing another log on the fire in the fireplace. He was trying to be quiet as he sat back down on the floor in front of the fire, leaning against the small sofa. He looked magnificent in his sweatpants and nothing else. His phone beeped with a message alert and she saw him smile and nod his head as he texted back.

"What time is it?" she asked in a sleepy voice.

Cal looked up and that warm smile of his seemed to touch her from across the room.

"Hey. It's about 3:00am. Did I wake you?"

Alease slid out of bed, pulling the sheet with her, modestly covering herself with it as she crossed over to him. The sheet fell open towards the bottom, like a very high slit on a woman's dress, and her hair fell all around her shoulders. "Who are you texting with at 3:00am?" she asked as he reached for her.

He pulled her down on his lap and she sat facing him with her knees on either side of his strong legs. She felt his heat immediately and could feel his rod react to her as she placed herself on him. He put the phone down to the side and reached up to pull her into him.

"A friend of mine. I had an idea for a gift I want to give you and I texted him because I figured he had what I was looking for." He kissed her and she could feel him relish in the moment.

When he parted his lips, she spoke. "Cal, you don't need to get me any gifts. I'm not like that."

He smiled warmly. "I know, but this is something I really want you to have, and it turns out he has exactly what I wanted for you."

She smirked. "What is it?"

He shook his head. "It's a surprise; but actually, he is only about twenty minutes from here, so there is a good chance he may bring it by later today."

"On Thanksgiving? Wow, he is a good friend."

"Yes he is." Cal's hands were caressing her back as the sheet dropped slightly off her arm, exposing her breast. He took advantage of the slip and lowered his lips onto her, kissing her exposed nipple and pulling her into him even more.

Alease wrapped her arms around him and ran her hands across his back. She could feel the scars as she floated her fingers on his skin and set shivers ablaze on him. He lifted his head to look in her eyes.

"God, you're so beautiful," he said it with such honesty in his tone that she couldn't help but believe he meant it.

A shyness came over her and she broke her gaze from his eyes to look at the scar she was caressing on his shoulder.

"Where did you get this scar?" she asked him as she

continued to glide her fingers to and fro above it.

"Syria," he said simply.

"And the ones on your back?" she asked.

"Afghanistan and Iraq," he paused, then asked the question that had…been on his mind. "Do they bother you?" he asked.

She was surprised at his question, "No, of course not. I mean, I'm bothered that you got hurt, but the marks themselves…no," she smiled. "Cal, you're the sexiest man I have ever seen. Your scars just remind me of how brave you are…which makes me even more attracted to you." There was a look of relief that seemed to wash over him as he pulled her into him and kissed her with forceful passion. He leaned her back, carefully changing their positions so that he was on top of her. She let go of the sheet and it fell open, exposing her complete nakedness underneath him.

He held himself above her as she caressed his face. "Were you worried that your scars would bother me?"

He hesitated with his answer, which was unusual for him. "Yes. A little."

"Why?"

He took a breath. "Some women don't like the physical evidence of…the ugliness that I've been part of."

She knew what he meant and she lifted her lips to kiss away his concern. Her fingers lingered on his cheek after she pulled her lips from his. "I'm in awe of you. The way you have put yourself in harms way for our country…it's remarkable." She could see in his eyes that he was deeply effected by what she said. She meant it. She felt like there were not words big enough to explain her admiration for his service.

His look deepened into her eyes. "I would do that for anything that is important to me…or *anyone* that is important to me." He kissed her again and she felt a wave of multiple emotions rise up in her as he did. She knew he meant *her* when he said that, and that sent a rush of fear and panic through her. It was the same kind of guilt that surrounded her regarding König…but far, far worse. If he got hurt because of her…she couldn't even bear it.

She broke the kiss and looked into his eyes.

"Cal, promise me…promise me you will never put yourself in harms way because of *me*." He looked at her as if she was speaking Chinese, and he didn't answer her. "Cal, promise me that."

He took a long moment. There was a very distinct look in his eyes as if he knew he was about to say something she didn't want to hear.

"Alease, that is the one thing I cannot promise you." Tears formed in her eyes at the thought of it and he stroked her face. "I could never let anyone hurt you."

She moved to sit up and Cal went with it, pulling her up into his lap again, but not letting her distance herself from him. "Cal, you can't…if anything were to happen to you because of me…I couldn't handle it…just the idea of it…" tears fell from her eyes and he held her to him.

"Alease, it's ok." He gave her a moment to catch her breathing. She was trying not to let her mind wander into the dark abyss of her worst fears, but the emotional reaction to the thought of losing him, like she did König, was too much for her and she couldn't stop the tears from flowing. She felt his arms around her and his hands stroking her hair as he whispered in her ear. "Hey…," he pulled her face to his and looked her in the eyes. "Alease, I'm a Navy SEAL. I'm going to be ok. Nothing is going to happen to me, and as long as you are by my side, nothing is going to happen to you either."

She hated that tears were falling from her eyes and she desperately wanted the feeling to go away, so she chose not to speak any more of what she was thinking, but she swore to herself that she would never allow him to get hurt because of her. Never. She would rather die than see the day that would happen.

She kissed him with force, and felt him immediately respond to her. She cleared herself from the bedsheet and her hands found their way inside his sweatpants to the place that would pull his attention from her tears. As soon as she touched him he moaned and was on top of her again. She desperately needed him; every part of him. Her world felt the safest when he was on her, and inside of her. Nothing else in this moment mattered, but that. He answered her need and laid her back down, covering her completely with his body. He entered her and filled her core with himself, driving in and out until he exploded with his white hot liquid, releasing it deep within her. Marking his territory inside her, while sheltering her body from above.

When the pulsing stopped and their breathing slowed, he wrapped her in his arms and lifted her with ease to bring her back to bed. He lowered her onto the silk sheets and enveloped her with his body. She felt the feather blanket come down on her as he made sure she was covered and warm. He kissed her several times and as she drifted off to sleep in his arms, she was sure he whispered something in her ear…but she couldn't quite hear what it was.

Chapter Eight
Thanksgiving

By the time they made it to the kitchen, Dana, Joe and the gang were well into preparations for the big Thanksgiving meal. The inviting smell of the roasting turkey was already filling the house, and the holiday celebration was underway with several mimosa's being passed around.

Joe had the oven door open and was basting the 27lb turkey, while Dana and Elizabeth were filling more glasses with champagne. Dan and Eddie were chatting about football, Tom and Erika were getting breakfast ready for the kids, and Sarah was over by the coffee machine filling cups. Sophie and Jake were at the counter finishing up their cereal and toast.

When Alease and Cal walked in the room, they all cheered.

Dan looked at his watch. "OK, who had 7:30am?"

Sarah spoke up in delight. "I did! Pay up folks."

Everyone reached in their pockets and put a dollar bill in the pile.

Joe closed the oven door and added his dollar. "Damn, I had 10:00am," they all laughed.

"You guys had a bet about when we would get out of bed? Jerks." Cal snickered as he accepted the coffee from

Sarah with a thank you. Alease felt her cheeks flush a little.

"Yes, and I won. Everyone else had you coming in after 9:00am," Sarah said as she proudly took her winnings.

Dana smiled at Alease. "Coffee or Mimosa?"

"I'll start with coffee. Thank you," she answered as Dana handed her a cup. She took a sip, "What can I do to help?" she asked.

"Oh, enjoy your coffee first. Have a seat." Dana pulled out a bar stool at the counter and motioned for her to sit. Cal stood right beside Alease with one hand on her back and the other on his coffee mug.

They chit chatted about various things, sipping their drinks, and slowly continuing the food preparations. The kids bounded in a little while later, full of energy as only kids can wake up with. As Alease and Cal finished their coffees, she saw Cal motion to Joe, and Joe nodded.

Cal put down his empty cup and leaned in to kiss her sweetly. "We will be back in a few minutes." He looked to his team. "Gentlemen?"

Joe pushed away from the counter he was leaning on and kissed Dana. "We will be down in my lower office for a little while." Dana smiled and didn't seem surprised by it. Joe led the way, "Let's go."

Cal gave one last reassuring sweep of his hand on Alease's shoulder, and followed the men out of the room, down the stairs that went into what has been called Joe's lower office…it seemed mysterious to her every time it had been mentioned.

When the men were clear from view, Dana told the kids to go get dressed and get ready to play outside. Sophie told Jake the same thing, and the women found themselves alone together. Dana drastically changed the energy in the room and the rest of the women huddled with her in doing so.

"So, now that the men are out of earshot, tell us how things are going with you and Cal." She sipped her mimosa with an inquisitive smile.

Alease was a little flustered…her mind was still on what the guys were doing. "Uh…fine." She felt her cheeks blushing.

"Oh come on," Elizabeth chimed in. "'Fine' is not going to cut it!"

"Seriously. I have eggs that are frying themselves on the shelf inside my refrigerator right now from the heat between the two of you! Tell us," Dana insisted. They were all suddenly like high school girls wanting to know every detail.

Alease circled back to the overriding thoughts on her mind. "Wait, what is the lower office? What are they doing?" she asked.

Dana brushed it off nonchalantly. "Oh don't worry about that sweetheart. Each of them have a lower office. It's kind of a secure room where they can exchange information that is otherwise…protected."

Sarah clarified it. "Classified. They stay up to date on what's going on and sometimes they need to talk about stuff that we are not cleared to know about. It's ok."

"It's part of being the girlfriend or wife of a SEAL. You'll get used to it." When Elizabeth said that, Alease felt a flash of energy rush through her. She hadn't really thought of herself that way.

Elizabeth looked puzzled. "You seem surprised!" she laughed. "My dear, if you don't know how much Cal loves you, you are blind as a bat!" The women laughed as Alease tried to push down the emotion threatening to rise up through her. All she could do was shake her head in an attempt to dial it down.

Dana put her mimosa glass down with a lite thud. "Alease, come on. You must know he is in love with you." Alease felt at a loss for words. She hadn't really let herself think about that so far. Dana looked to Sophie. "Does she honestly not know this?"

Sophie kind of chuckled. "Alease, I've known my brother longer than anyone here, I can tell you unequivocally that Cal is in love with you."

Dana chimed in. "Completely. I've known him for years, and I have never seen him like this with any woman, including Becca by the way. He is lost in love with you!"

Alease could feel herself getting nervous. "He hasn't said that you guys, so…who knows what he is feeling," she tried hard to downplay it.

They all laughed and spoke simultaneously. "*We* do!"

"Trust us Alease, you have his heart, hook line and sinker," Sarah said as she finished her mimosa. "And it's a good thing. Cal is a fantastic guy and, I think I speak for everyone here when I say, you are perfect for him." She smiled as the others agreed.

"And it seems pretty clear to me that you are just as in love with him as he is with you. Am I right?" Elizabeth asked as the women waited on edge for her answer.

She knew she was, but admitting it out loud was not something she thought she would have to do so soon. She felt even more flustered, but her smile and the flush in her cheeks gave her away.

"I knew it!" Elizabeth cried.

Sophie couldn't help herself. "Have you told him that yet?"

"Heavens no. Sophie…we haven't talked about any of that. He hasn't said anything of the sort."

Sophie brushed that away with her hand. "That's just because he knows you're scared of it. Trust me, he would tell you in an instant if he thought you were ready to hear it."

Alease looked at her curiously. "Has he told you that?"

Sophie paused. "Uhh…I don't want to betray my brother's trust."

"Oh, you mean like you just did?" Sarah laughed.

Dana spoke up again. "Please. There is nothing to betray. It's clear as day to everyone. I knew it the second I saw the two of you together. It's obvious. He would do anything for you. He's certainly already made that clear," she stated with emphasis.

Alease was struck by that last statement. "What do you mean by that?"

Dana looked as if she got caught saying something she shouldn't have, and it seemed to Alease that Sophie stepped in to bail her out.

"Nothing. Just that it's obvious he loves you," Sophie said.

Alease couldn't help but feel like there was something more to that accidental divulgence. Dana seemed to catch the thought process going through Alease's mind and jumped in.

"So, come on…give us the juicy details."

The women all talked over each other in attempts to prod Alease for particulars, which she stayed very vague about. Their conversation continued as they started to put together the dishes for the Thanksgiving meal.

Joe's lower office looked the same to Cal, except for the addition of a new computer and a second phone line. He had several large displays on the wall, each connected to the main computer hub controlling the flow of information to and from this room.

Joe had the phone connection on speaker as they dialed Darrin at the CIA to discuss any additional information he may have found.

After a few rings, Darrin answered. "Joe. Good timing," his voice sounded a little unnerved.

"Darrin, I have the team here with me," Joe said as he looked to Cal to take over the direction.

"Darrin, it's Cal Winters. First of all, thank you for your help," Cal said.

"Anything I can do. I know what you guys have done, so whatever I can do for you, it goes without question." He paused and Cal could sense some trepidation.

"What do you have?" Cal asked.

"More questions than answers, and some heat for looking into this guy, but I did find something you should know about. Joe I'm sending some encrypted files, let me know when you get them."

"Ok, send it." Joe sat down at the computer to download the files and open them. "Got them. Downloading now."

The files were still scrambled, but the download was almost complete. A few seconds later, four images appeared on Joe's big screens. Cal's eyes sharpened and he felt that deep-seeded rage within him boil as he looked at the photos. They were of him and Alease. Recent pictures. There was a close up shot of Cal kissing Alease in his truck. Another of Alease through the window of her kitchen. One of him with his arm around her, and one close up of Cal looking into Alease's eyes, that one had red markings written on it.

Eddie spoke up. "What the Hell are we looking at here?" he asked.

Darrin's voice came from the other end of the line. "These were the only pictures from the drive I was able to access, but I know there are more. There are also several pages in the file that have been blacked out. This thing has been combed through and changed to classified. When I asked about it, I was ordered to discontinued looking into it."

Joe and Cal exchanged glances, and Cal's voice spoke, deeper and more insistant than before.

"Darrin, this makes no sense. Even if this jackass is still alive and targeting me to get to her, why would that be classified?" Cal asked.

Darrin's voice got a little quieter. "Cal, take a closer look at the red markings on that photo. What do you see?"

Cal asked Joe to enlarge that image so they could have a better look at what Darrin was talking about. Joe did so, and almost at once the entire SEAL team took a collective breath. After it sunk in, Joe spoke.

"Fuck me."

Cal looked to his team. "That's Arabic writing."

Darrin interjected again. "Joe, there is a small audio file I sent over to you yesterday - you didn't get that from me, ok? I don't know what it means, but it is part of a larger audio file that has been restricted. This was the only portion of it I was able to open."

Joe found the audio file he was talking about, and clicked it. It was very short, two male voices talking in another language.

"Arabic," Cal said.

Dan shifted and his voice was filled with a dark forewarning.

"That's not just Arabic…that's Levantine."

All the SEALs went quiet. Cal felt a cold shutter run through him as he pieced it together.

"Levantine…the dialect spoken along the Eastern Mediterranean Coast of Syria." He looked to his team to see if they connected the dots.

Joe spoke in complete surprise. "You've got to be kidding. How could this have anything to do with that?"

Cal was confused too, but he learned to read the facts and sort them out later.

"I don't know. But if this is somehow connected with our last mission there…then this is bigger than we thought."

Darrin chimed in again. "Yeah. No shit. My ass is in hot water over here. I have a chew out session coming my way right after this phone call. I don't have the clearance to know anymore details…but you guys do. The only connection I am aware of is that the terrorist group that Abdagan was running was on the Eastern side of Syria, and you were the SEAL team that took out Abdagan. If something is going on that involves that, I suspect you will be getting a call about it soon. Listen, Joe, keep your ports open; if I can get anything more to you I will send it over."

Joe took his eyes off Cal. "Thanks Darrin. Sorry if your Thanksgiving is in hot shit because of us."

Darrin kind of laughed. "Fuck the turkey. I'd do anything I can for you guys. Good luck."

Joe clicked the phone off and leaned back in his chair studying the pictures.

"How does this lead to Mohamad Abdagan?" Dan was just as confused as the rest of them.

Cal looked to Dan. "Can you translate any of it?" he asked.

Dan studied it and then shook his head. "I can only recognize the dialect. Translation was always John's thing. I don't know what it says."

Cal turned his attention from the images on the screen to Joe. "Can you print these out? They don't leave this room, but I need time to memorize them." Joe nodded and hit a few commands on his keyboard. Cal addressed his team. "OK, listen up. It goes without saying, but, this does not leave this room. I don't want anyone upstairs catching wind that something might be going on." They all were in agreement on that.

"What do you want us to do?" Eddie asked Cal.

"For now, we walk out of this room and act as if everything is fine. We have a great Thanksgiving meal together, and later tonight, we meet down here again and we dig into this. We reach out to every connection we have to get to the bottom of it. Copy?"

"Copy."

The Thanksgiving spread at the table was beautiful. Alease was sure it could have been taken right off a magazine cover. Dana was pouring the last of the champagne, and they all raised their glasses. Joe stood up and addressed the group for the Thanksgiving toast.

"My friends, my family, there is nothing I am more thankful for in this world than everyone sitting at this table with me right now. May the blessings of all that is good surround each and every one of you for the rest of your days." They all toasted, taking in his words as they sipped their drinks.

Joe sat down and they began the feast.

Alease had a sense that there was something bubbling under the surface…Cal denied it, but Alease had that feeling creeping under her skin. She caught a few looks between the SEALs and, once again, she had trouble reading them. She couldn't help her curiosity of what transpired in that lower office, but she did her best to put that aside and enjoy the meal.

The turkey was divine. Dana had everything that goes with it; apple chestnut stuffing, port wine gravy, sweet potatoes with perfectly browned marshmallows (thanks to Sarah as she took charge of that dish.) There were mashed potatoes, green bean casserole, fruit salad, homemade rolls… it went on and on. It was the exact kind of Thanksgiving Alease had always pictured, but never quite had. She couldn't help but fall in love with it, and she found her concerns drifting from her mind.

Cal shifted back and forth between having his hand on her thigh and using it to eat the fabulous meal. Every time he put his fork down, he was touching her in some way, and Alease found it very comforting.

The kids were the first to finish their meals and begged to be excused so they could go play. Instead of worrying about cleaning up right away, the adults adjourned to the living room, lounging on the big wrap around sofa in front of the fireplace, enjoying the view of the late afternoon snowfall in the warmth of the house.

Joe had put on some soft Christmas music in the background and the snow was falling behind the sparkling tree in front of the picture window.

Alease was curled up in Cal's arms, as the other women were in the arms of their husbands. With drinks in their hands and full stomachs, they talked and reminisced with each other. Alease felt like she could stay in this moment forever. The peace and love in the room was overflowing and it washed over her like a luxurious hot bath.

As Eddie was recounting a funny story about when Johnathan decided to repaint his bedroom with green Jello, Cal's cell phone rang. He pulled his phone out of his pocket, and the startled look on his face as he saw the caller ID caught everyone's attention.

Joe was the first to ask. "Who is it Cal?"

Cal looked up to Joe and his SEAL team. "It's Kilton."

Everyone in the room seemed to hold their breath, except for Alease. "Who's Kilton?" she asked. As she waited for a response, she was trying to ascertain the look on everyone's face, but she didn't understand it.

Cal pulled Alease in for a kiss, and then stood up. Dana answered her as Cal exited the room to take the call.

"General Kilton…as in Special Operations Joint Task Force."

Alease felt a wave of unease wash through her. She looked to Joe. "Why is he calling Cal?"

Joe had concern in his eyes but he masked it quickly. "Cal is the captain of our team. It's common that Cal would get the call if they needed to reach out for something." He looked to Dana and Alease knew there was a silent communication between them that they understood, but she didn't. The men got up to follow Cal out of the room.

Alease looked to Dana as well. "Is everything ok?"

Dana smiled at her reassuringly. "I'm sure it's fine."

Alease felt her heart rate increase. She knew what Cal had done in the past, but it didn't really occur to her that he could possibly have to do it again. Risk his life again.

"Are they going to get deployed?" Alease asked, unable to hide the fear in her voice.

Dana answered quickly. "That is highly unlikely. They were the top SEAL Team, but they've done their bit for king and country. For all intents and purposes, this team is retired."

"They've earned it after some of the missions they went on," Sarah said.

"Yeah, if something is up, SEAL Team Beta 5 is next on the list, not them," Dana said.

"Then why is Kilton calling them?" Alease was still trying to control her heart rate.

"They might just need some information from them. The boys have seen a lot and they know more than anyone about certain terrorist groups. Could just be probing for info." Dana put on an air of assuredness, but Alease wasn't convinced.

After a good twenty minutes, the men came back in the room. Alease was starting to recognize the forced reassuring looks, and she knew something was up.

Cal walked right in and crossed over to Alease. He reached for her hand.

"Can I talk to you for a minute?"

Alease felt a thud of fear smash through her. "Is

everything ok?"

Cal smiled trying to reassure her. "Yeah. I just need a minute with you." He escorted her into the other room to talk with her in private.

She turned to him as soon as they were alone. "What's wrong Cal?" Her voice was filled with worry that she couldn't hide.

He softly put his hands on her face, and smiled. "Everything is fine. It's just that my team is needed in DC."

"What? Why?" She was battling the fear swelling inside her. She had no idea what any of this meant, this was all very new to her.

"It's not a deployment. Don't panic. It's just a debrief. Just a meeting." He kissed her trying to calm her fears.

"When do you have to go?" she asked.

He took a breath, and she saw in his eyes that he was about to tell her something he didn't want to. "Now. They are sending a car to pick us up."

Her breath dropped from her lungs. "What?" Her eyes filled with tears and she didn't even know why. She just knew there was a growing pit in her stomach that was rapidly blossoming into a tree of panic.

He pulled her into his embrace and tried to reassure her. "It's ok. Everything is fine." He pulled back to look her in the eyes. "It's only for one night. We will come right back tomorrow afternoon." He kissed her again.

Something was biting at her and it didn't feel right. A thousand thoughts seemed to fill her head at once. Her mind began to race; making connections that she didn't understand yet. Something in her stirred uncomfortably and was reaching a boiling point. A deep fear started to break out inside her. She remembered Cal's questions yesterday about her attacker…his preoccupation of wanting to know who he was…and his attempts to drill down about the guys death. Ever since Cal asked her about what the cops were doing when she was taken into the ambulance…she kept picturing it. The cops standing over the body with their guns drawn. Why were their guns out? It kept running through her mind. She didn't think much about it until she had seen the look in Cal's eyes when she said it. Jesus…fear shot through her.

"Cal, this doesn't have anything to do with me, right?" In the silence that filled the air before he answered, she saw it… that look he had last night when she asked him to promise never to put himself in harms way because of her. The look in his eyes now was identical, and she felt herself grow cold.

He paused briefly, then, after a heavily layered breath, he spoke.

"I can't tell you what it's regarding. It's classified." But that look in his eyes was there *again*…she couldn't shake it. She had a feeling in her gut that somehow he was not being completely honest with her.

"Cal…" she was going to push him but he stopped her by

kissing her. Then he pulled away to speak.

"Please don't worry, Alease." He kissed her again. Alease could feel him conveying as much emotion in his kiss as he could, but her fear had kicked up and she was having trouble understanding why she was reacting to the situation with such trepidation. She knew he sensed it and he pulled her into him trying to hug it all away. He released her after a moment and looked at her again. "It's going to be fine. I want you to just stay here with the women while the team and I do this. We will be back before you know it. It's just one night." But even as he said it, she could see an unsettled look in his eyes.

"Jesus Cal, what are you not telling me?" Instead of answering her, he pulled her lips to his and kissed her deeply.

He drew her into him. "Please just trust me. It's going to be ok."

For some reason that made her feel even worse.

Joe quietly walked into the kitchen where they were talking. Cal saw him but did not let go of Alease. Joe gave it a few seconds and then spoke softly.

"Well, the good news is that James is here."

Cal pulled himself back to wipe away Alease's tears, and smiled. "Your present is here. I think you are going to love this."

She tried to smile, but she was so uneasy about everything that it was harder than she thought. "I don't need a present, Cal…"

"Oh, I think you are going to want this one. Come on." He kissed her again, and gazed deeply in her eyes. "I do not want you worrying. Everything is fine." She managed to smile and did her best to put her fears aside for the moment. Maybe she was just overreacting…jumping to the wrong conclusions because that is what scared her the most. That must be it. Logically, how could that phone call have anything to do with her.

"Ok. Sorry. I guess I just panicked." He hugged her, and with a smile, he led her towards the front door. Cal grabbed his coat and put it around her. Sophie and Jake had big grins on their faces; they obviously had been told already what Cal had gotten for her.

"Is it James? Is it here?" Jake was really excited.

"Yep," Cal said as he smiled at Alease and opened the front door.

They stepped out and Alease saw a tall man in a dark winter coat getting out of his truck. He waved to Cal.

"Happy Thanksgiving," he said.

Cal led Alease over to the truck, as the others followed behind all excited to see this gift…she had no idea what this was going to be. Cal reached out his hand to James, "Good to see you James. This is Alease Taynes."

James smiled brightly at her. "It's very nice to meet you Alease. Are you ready for your present?"

"Uh…yeah. What is it?" she asked.

James opened the passenger side door and the most beautiful German Shepherd puppy came bounding out; tail wagging and happy as can be.

"This is Kenya, and she is yours," James said.

It was amazing; it was as if the puppy knew it…with all the people who were standing there, Kenya came right over to Alease. She knelt down and the puppy almost flew into her arms. It was an instant bond that hooked Alease in immediately. "Oh my God!" She exclaimed as Kenya licked her face and let out a few little squeals of excitement.

"Kenya is nine weeks old. She is destined to be huge, so I hope that's ok with you. One of the biggest puppies I've ever whelped," James said. "Cal picked her out especially for you."

She looked up at Cal who was smiling down on her.

"I thought it was time you had another one; and clearly, Kenya loves you, so I think I picked the right one."

Alease stood up and Kenya sat down right by her side looking up at her with that loving puppy grin. Alease was surprised at how great it felt to have a new German Shepherd by her side. Even one that was just a puppy. She had always shied away from the idea of getting another one because of her guilt about what happened to König. But somehow, this little one got right through all of that, and Alease was sold. She was so touched by what Cal had done by getting this for her, that she almost forgot about all the fear that had just been sweeping through her.

"Cal! Thank you so much. Oh my goodness…she is so beautiful."

Cal knew the moment he saw the picture of Kenya last night that she was the right one for Alease. He went back and forth with James on if he should get a fully trained adult shepherd for her, but he was concerned that might be harder for Alease to accept than a puppy. An adult dog might remind her too much of her guilt about König, and also might trigger her concerns about why he thought she needed a trained protection dog again. So he chose to go with a puppy instead. It was clear from the instant bond between Kenya and Alease that he made the right call. Kenya would grow into a large, strong dog, and until then, Max was there. It was the best choice. Besides, the smirk on this little puppy's face…he knew she could not say no to that.

As everyone gathered around Alease to pet Kenya, Cal shook hands with James.

"Thank you again, James. I really appreciate it."

"No problem. I'm glad I could help. Kenya comes from a great line. I doubt you will even need much training with her. Her line has a strong protective instinct almost bred right into them. She's a great dog. Let me know if you need anything else."

With a friendly wave, James got in his truck and turned

down the drive. Cal stood back a bit with Joe, just out of earshot of Alease and the group admiring the playful puppy.

Joe spoke quietly. "How did she take it?"

Cal kept his eyes on Alease as he answered him. "Not great. Its definitely kicked off some...questions in her."

"Do you think she has any idea this involves her?" he asked.

"Jesus, I hope not. I did everything I could to make it seem routine."

"Did it work?" Joe wondered.

Cal wasn't sure. He let out a breath. "It better have. I don't want her to figure that out."

"Did Kilton give you any other clues at how this is connected to her?" Joe asked.

"No, but they are flying us to DC last minute on Thanksgiving…so I'm pretty sure we are about to find out."

As if on cue, a large black SUV turned into view heading up Joe's driveway.

Joe looked to the men. "That's our ride."

Within minutes, the driver had the doors open for them and their escort pushing them to get in so they could go. Cal could see the uncertainty in Alease's eyes, but had no time to do anything about it. He pulled her quietly to the side as the car waited for him.

He placed his hands on her face and held her gaze.

"Wipe away that look of worry. One night. Just stay here,

watch Christmas movies, drink hot toddy's with Max and Kenya at your feet, and before you know it, I will be walking back through the door." He gave her credit for trying to hide her unease behind her beautiful smile, but he knew. He kissed her warmly, and broke the kiss with one last thought in his head. "Alease, don't pull away from me and hide back into yourself. I know you are bothered by…the things I can't tell you right now. But when I can, I will. For now, don't think about it." He kissed her again as the driver honked his horn. Cal could hear Joe chewing him out and telling him to hold his horses.

As he broke the kiss with her and pulled away, he almost said out loud to her what he had whispered last night…when he knew she was drifting to sleep. He wanted so badly to tell her, but doing it now would make his exit even harder on her, and on him. So he said it to her inside his mind with a last look to her before he got into the car.

I love you, Alease.

Alease did everything she could to suppress the river of concern coursing through her after Cal's departure. She didn't want to come across as weak or needy to these women who didn't seem to bat an eye about it. They carried on as if this was normal. It didn't seem to slow down their holiday joy in the least. Maybe that should make her feel better…maybe her concerns were all in her mind.

Stephanie pulled Alease's attention from her internal monologue as she came bounding up to her, "Can I play ball with Kenya?" Her smile was adorable as she gushed over the puppy.

"It's already dark outside…I'm not sure your mom wants you out this late."

"It's an indoor ball. I can play with her over by the Christmas tree. I won't throw it hard." She giggled as Kenya licked at her hands.

"Yeah, of course," Alease smiled, "She likes you!"

Stephanie called Kenya over to the other side of the room and she went happily. The little girl was all smiles, as she played with the puppy, and her laughter helped fill the house that now felt empty at the departure of the men. Alease picked up a few dirty dishes and brought them over to the kitchen where Dana and Sophie were softly talking.

Sophie went quiet when Alease walked in and smiled.

"How are you doing? I know this is probably strange for you, huh?"

"A little," Alease admitted as she set the plates down in the sink.

Dana crossed over to her. "Joe asked me before they left to set your mind at ease."

Alease looked up at her. "Why was Joe worried about me before they left?" Dana got that look on her face…like she, once again, said something she wasn't supposed to. "Dana, do you know something about what's going on?"

There was a distinct pause before she answered. "No, of course not. I'm sure he just knew that this would be offsetting for you, that's all."

Alease saw a tense look on both there faces, and had the un-mistakable sense that they were both hiding something from her.

"OK, I'm calling Deep Dive on both of you," She tossed the dish towel down. "What's going on?"

They looked at each other, unsure what to say.

"How do you know about Deep Dive?" Dana asked.

"Cal. Now spill it. I know you guys know something and are not telling me. What is it?" Alease insisted.

Dana let out a breath as she ran out of ideas on how to deflect the question. "Alease, we don't know anything that's classified. Deep Dive has no power over classified info. The guys would never disclose that, not even to us."

"Fine. Then tell me what is not classified." Alease saw the exchanged look between them and she knew she was onto something. "Guys, listen; no one can fall down a rabbit hole faster than I can. If you don't tell me, I am bound to come to my own conclusions and freak the fuck out, and that will ultimately cause me to pull away from Cal…is that what you want?" Clearly that argument had some pull with them and they shifted uncomfortably. Alease kept going. "I can see it in your eyes that you guys are hiding something from me, and my trust in other people is limited enough as it is. Please…the best thing you can do for me is tell me what you know."

Dana let out a breath and gave in. "I overheard Joe and Cal talking about it on the phone. Joe asked me not to say anything to you because Cal insisted on it. I was only talking to Sophie about it because she already knew and came to me," Dana confessed.

"Please don't make us say anything. Cal will be so mad at us if we do," Sophie begged her.

Alease crossed her arms and stood her ground. "Out with it right now, both of you."

Dana took a breath. "Ok, ok…but you can't let Cal know we told you. He will never forgive us."

"He is so protective of you Alease, he just doesn't want you to worry," Sophie added.

"Worry about what? What is it?" Alease was done beating around the bush on the subject.

Dana spoke up. "Cal has been intent on finding out all he can about the man who attacked you in New York."

Alease felt a flush of dark energy flow through her. She looked at Sophie. "He told you about that?"

Sophie jumped in quickly. "No he did not. *I* asked *him* about it." Alease looked at her questioningly. "After we found out you wrote 'Christmas Mountain' and performed with Kenny Keep, I did some digging around. I was so impressed with your career and what you had done, I wanted to know more. I found a few newspaper articles about what happened and it upset me that you had gone through that, so I asked Cal about it."

Alease took a breath unsure whether she was embarrassed, upset or touched that Sophie cared about her that much.

Sophie continued. "Cal didn't tell me anything you confided in him, other than to tell me he had talked with you about it. He did not betray your trust in him at all, I promise you. But he did tell me he was…looking into it."

Alease tilted her head. "What does that mean?" Sophie looked to Dana.

"Joe has a lot of connections in law enforcement and… other agencies. So Cal asked him for help," Dana said.

"Help with what?" Alease was unclear what she was getting at.

"In finding out who the guy was." Dana saw the shocked look in her eyes. "Alease, he just wants to know as much as he can so he can help you. That's what these guys do for the women they love."

Alease's temper flared a little, more out of discomfort rather than anger. "Help me with what? The guy is dead." A very uncomfortable quiet instantly fell inside the space between the women, and Alease felt as if an ice cold whisper was seeping through her skin. "What?"

After a pause, Dana answered her. "Umm…there might

be a slight question about that…"

Sophie must have seen the rush of fear that eclipsed her face and she spoke up.

"Alease, most likely the guy is dead and there is nothing to worry about. In fact, I'm sure he is."

"Most likely?!" She felt a little dizzy and the women brought over a stool for her to sit on. Dana got her some water and they stood around her doing their best to undo the panic they had just set off in her.

"I'm sure he is dead too. Nothing to worry about," Dana tried to sound reassuring.

Alease had a gazzilion thoughts running through her head; each of them with their own sled of fear attached to it. Then she had a sudden and very loud concern go off in her mind. "Does this have anything to do with them going to DC?"

Dana genuinely seemed to dismis that. "I don't see how it could. The DC trip has to do with something classified. I can't imagine how this could fall into that."

"I'm sure that was just a really bad coincidence," Sophie placed her hand on Alease's.

Alease took several minutes to gather her breathing and adjust to the shocking possibility that had been unveiled. She suddenly felt embarrassed that she was behaving like a frightened school girl.

"I'm sorry guys. I don't mean to be so…weak about this."

The ladies brushed that off. "Nonsense. Are you kidding? I would be freaking out," Dana said.

"Yeah. You are anything but weak. I think you are the strongest woman I know." Sophie had her hand on her still.

Alease looked up to Dana. "Did they find something? Why do they think he could still be out there?" She felt herself shutter as she said the words out loud.

"No, they didn't. I don't think. As of yesterday, my understanding is that they couldn't find the files on it. That's why they were confused. It's probably nothing," Dana assured her.

"That's what got under their skin. SEALs are notorious for needing complete specifics, everything in order and details perfectly lined up. If something is off, even a little, they hyper focus on it. I'm sure it's nothing. Probably just filed in the wrong place or something stupid like that," Sophie's voice seemed confident. She handed her some more water as Dana cut in.

"Please, fuck water! I'm getting us shots." Dana crossed to the bar and brought back a bottle of WoodFord. She poured three shots and they all threw them back. "Better?" Dana asked.

"Yes," Alease lied. She was still very flustered but she didn't want them to know it. "Do Elizabeth, Erika and Sarah know?"

"I don't think so" Dana answered. "Listen, the guys take

trust very seriously, especially with each other. The only reason we knew is because we accidentally found out, and when we confronted them, they didn't lie."

"I haven't heard the women say anything about it, and I'm pretty sure they would have if they had heard something," Sophie said as she poured more shots.

Alease wanted to lighten the mood. "Where are they anyway?" she asked.

"Upstairs I think. Erika and Elizabeth were doing laundry and Sarah was putting Johnathan down for bed," Dana answered as she threw back her second shot.

"OK." She took a breath. "I'm fine you guys, don't worry." She knew she was lying, but pretty sure they didn't know that.

Stephanie wandered in. "I lost the ball. It rolled down the stairs and I'm not allowed to go down there to get it. Kenya went down after it."

Alease stood up. "It's ok. I'll get it."

"Can I get some water for Kenya? I think she is thirsty," Stephanie asked.

"Sure." Dana called her over and helped get a bowl down from the cabinet as Alease walked to the stairs she was playing near.

Alease turned on the light and started down the stairs. It dawned on her as she descended that these were the stairs the guys took to get to Joe's lower office. When she got to the bottom, she saw the door to the right was slightly open, and heard Kenya's squeaky ball from inside the room.

She couldn't help her curiosity. She wasn't sure if this was the lower office or not, but, since the door was open and her dog was in there, she felt justified in going in. Hell, if this had to do with her, she felt justified anyway. She pushed the door open and switched on the light as she stepped in.

First she saw Kenya, wagging her tail with the ball in her mouth, but the smile that should have crossed her face at that sight never materialized.

The screens across on the far wall were lit up, and Alease saw the pictures that were still there. Her brain suddenly felt like it was being filtered through cold, thick molasses. She crossed closer as she tried to understand what she was seeing. Her heart pounded louder with every step. She stopped. As if someone flicked a switch, the molasses feeling was replaced in an instant with a flood that felt like ice cold water was being pushed through her veins. Jesus. She saw the pictures of Cal. Of her. Of them together. One of the close ups of Cal had red markings on it. She didn't know what the scribbles were, but clear as day, she understood the red dot that had been drawn on Cal's forehead. A target mark.

Holy fuck.

She couldn't breathe. She couldn't think. She could hardly feel any part of her body. Then she saw an incoming message flashing on the screen from someone named Darrin.

She moved her hand slowly to the keyboard to open it. She clicked it with a fear she thought couldn't get worse. And then it did. A new picture appeared on the screen and bolts of horror streaked through her. It was him. She felt as if the floor had given way underneath her. He was looking right into the camera; right at her with a bone-chilling look on his face, and in the background, what made the picture all the more horrifying…behind him in the photo she could see Cal's Red Ford pickup truck, the fire pit, and her little white house.

Jesus fuck…he is alive…and he is here…

Chapter Nine
Drastic Measures

Alease stood frozen. Time seemed to stop, as all of her fears overcrowded her thoughts at once. She wasn't sure how long she was locked there, staring into the pictures on the screen; maybe seconds, maybe minutes. Her first thoughts were of the danger Cal is in now because of her. Her heart broke at the realization. She looked again at the photo with the red mark on his forehead. She felt like her world was caving in on itself. How could this be happening? It didn't even have to be formed in her conscious mind; she knew what she had to do. Leave. If this guy was after her again, he would only target Cal to get him out of the way. If she left, he would have no reason to pay any mind to Cal at all. It was the only way he could be safe. She could not allow him to get caught in the crossfire of this man's dangerous obsession with her. It wasn't fair to him, and he didn't deserve to have to deal with any of this.

Tears flooded through her eyes as a wave of nausea filled her gut. Leave…she had to, and it destroyed her very soul to think of it. But the thought of him getting hurt or, God forbid, killed, because of her…the tears gushed out past her eyelids and down her face. She could not permit that to even be a possibility.

Now she understood why Cal had looked at her like that last night when she asked him about not being in harms way because of her. *My God…*

Her world felt like it was imploding. She felt trapped between two horrible choices of complete pain; one where she had to leave him and the other where he could be killed for being with her. There really was no choice then was there? She had to go.

She heard Dana calling for her, so she did her best to wipe away her flood of tears. She picked up Kenya and turned to leave the room. She got up to the top of the stairs and was startled by Jake.

"Hey Alease. Are you ok? You look pale," Jake said.

She felt like she was going to throw up.

"I feel a little sick to my stomach actually. I think I'm going to turn in early," Alease's voice was shaky and she hoped Jake didn't notice it.

"Too much food. Thanksgiving does that to you," Jake said it with a smile, so Alease felt like she had convinced him nothing out of the ordinary was wrong.

Max started to follow Alease to the patio door, and Alease realized she had to make sure Max stayed here. He wasn't hers to take, nor could she stomach seeing anything happen to Max either. For that matter Kenya, but it would look to obvious if she left Kenya in the big house as well. She would figure that one out later.

She turned to Jake. "You want to take Max tonight? It might be better for Kenya to have her first night here with just me. Cool?" she asked.

"Yeah, that's fine. Max loves sleeping at my feet. Come on Max." Max followed Jake into the living room and sat with him as he flipped on the TV.

"Tell Sophie and Dana I went to bed early. The shots did me in. Good night Jake." Alease felt a heavy rush of sadness at thinking that would be her goodbye to the boy. She hated everything about this.

She darted through the cold night air and closed the door of the guest house behind her. She turned on all the lights and looked around to make sure she was alone; which she was. Of course she was…there was no way the guy could know where she is. He may have found the house she was renting but that didn't mean he knew where she was now.

She packed her bag and got her coat. Now the only problem was where to go and how. Shit, her truck was at her house. They had come in Cal's Ford. He left the keys for it on the desk and she lifted them into her hands. She couldn't just take his truck…it was his. She tried to get a working plan to come together in her head and the one that was forming was dangerous, but she didn't think she had a choice. If she could use Cal's truck to drive back to the house and get hers, she could leave his in the driveway with the keys in it. Then she could get in her truck and go. Where? She had no idea, but she would figure that out later. First, she had to get to her truck…but her truck was at her house…he knew where she lived…what if he was there waiting for her? This plan sucked, but it was the only one she had. She would just have to swallow the overwhelming fear it invoked in her and do it anyway.

She sat herself on the sofa and tried to think out her strategy. Her phone rang. She looked at the caller ID, it was Cal. Shit. If she answered he would hear it in her voice. She knew it. She could hide nothing from this man, and if he caught the scent of what she was thinking, she knew he would make a beeline back to try and stop her. Her only choice was to not answer the phone. It hurt so badly to watch the caller ID sit there as the last rings went unanswered. Her phone fell silent.

She had to clear her mind and think out how to do this. She knew the next call he would be making would be to Sophie. Would he send Sophie over to check on her? Maybe. She should wait until she knew the women were asleep just in case. She looked at her watch; if she timed this right, she could leave when everyone here was asleep, and time it so that she would reach her house after the sun came up. Pulling into her driveway in the dark would not be a good idea. If the sun was up, it was less likely this guy would be there to try anything. Her heart skipped several beats as she thought about this. If she could get there, she could grab what she needed from her house, get the keys to her truck and be gone in a flash. She would figure out where she was headed later. The first objective was to get Cal out of the picture so he would be safe.

Cal clicked his phone off. *Damn.* He really wanted to hear her voice before he got on the plane so he would know she was ok. But she didn't answer. He dialed Sophie and a few rings later she picked up.

"Hey Cal," she said

"Sophie. Just calling to check in. Alease didn't answer her phone. Is she there by you?" he asked.

"No. She turned in already. Jake, Dana and I are the only ones still up," Sophie's voice seemed casual.

"Was she doing ok?" Cal was concerned, he couldn't hide it.

"She was…a little rattled about you leaving, but this is new to her. Dana and I gave her some shots and I think that helped." Cal could hear Jake laughing in the background and saying it made her sick. Sophie spoke again, "She is fine Cal. It was only two shots. Don't worry."

Cal couldn't quiet the unease stirring, but he new he had to go. "OK. Please keep an eye on her. I will call in the morning."

"OK. Love you bro," she said.

"You too." He hung up the phone half wondering if he

should turn around and head back to Joe's. Something didn't feel right. He called Alease again. It rang several times and went to voice mail. *Damn*....

It was 1:30am and Alease saw the lights go off in the main house, she knew everyone was turning in. This was her window, if she was going to do this, now was the time. She clicked off the lights so it would look as though she was sleeping. She grabbed her bag and headed to the front door. Kenya was at her feet. Alease stopped and looked down at her, "I can't take you. I don't want you getting hurt." She knew if she left her here that she would be taken care of. She knew when Cal couldn't reach her in the morning that he would send someone over to check on her, and that's when they would realize she was gone. She left a thank you note for Joe and Dana on the table…she didn't want them to worry so she said in the letter that she just needed to go.

She had written one for Cal too…the hardest letter she has ever had to write. She needed him to know how much she loved him and that her leaving was because it was the only way to keep him safe. She left several tear stains on the paper, but she couldn't do anything to stop the tears from falling.

Kenya squealed as Alease closed the door. Then she barked, over and over. Shit, she would wake everyone up. Alease doubled back and opened the door. Little Kenya was grinning, tail wagging and determined to go with her. Fine.

Alease prayed that since Kenya was so little, she wouldn't be a threat to this guy…if he found her during her escape.

Alease opened the door and put Kenya in the passengers side seat. She threw her bag in the back and got in. Her breathing was quick and she was scared to death. The pitch black of night was all around her and she was about to drive out into it by herself…plus one puppy. As the tears fell from her eyes, she turned the keys and started the truck. She drove down the driveway, checking in the rearview mirror that no lights came on in the house. None did. She made her escape without them knowing. As she was leaving she felt her heart break that she might never see them again.

Alease made it to the interstate and headed towards Big Sky. She constantly checked to make sure no one was following her. There was no one. Even on the Interstate, she was the only one on the road at this hour of the night. She did some calculations in her head…she had to make sure she reached her house just after the sun came up. She did not want to be there in the dark. She figured, if by chance he was there, he would be gone by the time daylight came. She hoped anyway.

Two hours into the drive she still didn't know what the next step of her plan was….she couldn't think that far ahead until she switched trucks and was safely away from the house. Then she would figure it out. Cal hadn't called again. He was in the air flying to DC, so she knew she had a few more hours before he landed and his next calls would come in. She heard a few text messages beep on her phone and she was sure they were from him, but she didn't read them or text back. She had to keep reminding herself how much danger she had put him in and that was the only thing that kept her from reaching for the phone to contact him. God, she missed him already. The pain of having to leave him overrode all of her fear.

Kenya was getting a little restless and started to whine, which told Alease she probably needed a bathroom break. She lowered her eyes to the gas gauge, the tank was almost empty. *Damn*. She looked around her…the dead black of night was heavy like a weighted blanket she was trapped under. The darkness was interrupted only by a few lit roadsigns and the headlights of a car far behind her. She didn't want to stop, but she knew she had to fill the tank or be stranded out here. When the next exit came with a gas station, she put her blinker on and turned off the interstate onto the side road. The gas station was just down on the left. No one else was around, but the station was open. She pulled up and fearfully got out to fill the truck. The station attendant was asleep inside the building with the TV reflecting off his face. Kenya jumped out to do her business and came back to Alease's side waiting for her to finish.

Alease looked up and saw a pickup truck coming from the interstate and heading rather quickly towards the gas station. Her heartbeat instinctively increased. She was almost done filling the tank. It took longer than she thought, but finally it clicked. She turned her back to close the gas cap, that's when she heard the truck pull right up behind her with a sharp stop. She didn't even have time to turn around, but she saw the reflection of his face in her window as he grabbed her from behind and pulled her into him. She screamed and he covered her mouth with a soaked cloth. It smelled horrible, and within seconds she could feel her body going limp as she heard that familiar ghostly voice in her ear, "Hello again my dear. You're mine now."

As soon as their plane landed, Cal reached for his phone to see if Alease had called or texted back. She hadn't. It worried him. He looked at his watch; 8:15 am…that meant 6:15am where she was. It was early, but knowing her, she was probably awake. He knew she wouldn't sleep well without him next to her, so he dialed her number. It rang several times and went to voice mail. Shit. He didn't like it.

Joe saw the look in his eyes. "No answer? She is probably asleep. Dana said they did shots last night after we left. I know Dana is not up yet after drinking like that. I'm sure she is ok." He was trying to reassure him, but it wasn't working.

"Yeah," was all he could say. He texted Alease asking her to call him as soon as she was up so he could hear her voice.

Joe lightly slapped him on the back. "Come on. Let's get to the debrief so we can get the fuck out of here."

The SEALs were led to their pick up car and driven to the JFHQ-NCR building for the much needed meeting. Cal wanted his questions answered now.

When they arrived at the Joint Force Headquarters, they were quickly escorted down the long hallways to a secure back room. The bustling offices were crowded with workers all nodding their heads to them as they passed. Their was an unspoken respect for the SEALs, as everyone there knew who they were. Cal didn't care, he wanted Kilton's explanation to what was going on. He wanted his questions answered.

They were taken to a back conference room, much like Joe's lower office. Computers, phone lines, screens and tracking equipment, all there, all secure. Cal did not take a seat. He stood; he waited, his eyes locked on the door.

Within a few minutes several officials entered, including Darrin, followed by SEAL Team Beta 5, and then General Kilton. Kilton was not as tall as the SEALs but he carried the same kind of "don't fuck with me" energy as they did, and he got right to the point.

"SEAL team Alpha 12, this is SEAL Team Beta 5." The introduction was not necessary, each team knew the other. They shook hands with equal admiration for each other. Kilton continued looking at Cal and his team. "You guys have been poking around and now you've woken the bear."

Kilton's voice was deep, brazen and pissed off.

Cal spoke, unafraid, unintimidated in the least. "Sir, all due respect, what's going on here?"

Kilton slammed the files on the table and pointed to Darrin, "You got this guy into deep shit that's one thing."

Joe kept his mouth shut, though it was clear to Cal he wanted to take the hit for that one.

"Darrin only did what we asked him to, but it seems pretty clear to me that we should have been notified about what ever this is." Cal kept his composure though he was getting to the point where his anger was bound to come out.

Kilton looked right at him. "Well, you got your wish now. So here it is." Kilton clicked on the remote he was holding in his hand and some graphics and images appeared on the screens on the far wall. The team looked at the images as Kilton went into the explanation that was long overdue.

"A year ago, your team went to Syria to knock out terrorist leader Mohamad Abdagan. In that mission, as you recall, several of his family members were killed as well; including his two wives, three kids and one of his brothers."

Joe got a little pissy. "Yeah, we were there when the jack-off instructed one of his wives to blow the damn suicide vest. His family died because of him, not us."

Kilton didn't even look to Joe with his response. "Doesn't fucking matter. Abdagan's followers blame you guys for the death of the entire leadership's family."

Cal wanted to move this along. "So what? My bullets killed Abdagan and his number two. As far as we knew the network fell after those two were taken out. Family dead or not, there was no one left to take it over, so why is this even coming up?"

Kilton hit his clicker again; an image of a villainess looking man with a dark beard and dark hair came on the screen. "This is Adil Abd-Allah, the first brother of Abdagan." The man's eyes were a piercing combination of hate and evil.

Dan broke in. "Our intel said Abdagan only had one brother, and we took him out too."

Kilton answered shortly. "Intel was wrong. Abd-Allah is not only his first brother, but his closest, and it also happens that Abd-Allah's first wife was in the compound during the raid, and was killed by the same blast that took out the Abdagan family."

"So what are you saying, that Abd-Allah is out for revenge?" Cal asked Kilton.

Kilton's answer was short and loaded. "Yes." He took a breath and handed out the files he had for each of them. "Abd-Allah not only took over the terrorist ring in Syria after his brother was killed, but he has committed the majority of his resources into payback…" he looked at Cal, "…against you." Cal didn't blink, he didn't waiver, he simply listened. Kilton continued. "Thanks to an informant we had on the inside we learned that Abd-Allah went crazy wanting to know who did this. After torturing everyone he could find, Abd-Allah got your name Cal, your full name, and every piece of info on you he could get." Kilton hit the clicker again and an image popped up on the screen that Cal immediately recognized.

"Fuck," Cal said as he looked at the same face he had seen huddling behind the air-conditioning units back in Big Sky. "I saw him back home. Who is this guy?"

"This is Adam Dunnlen. A loner from New York who was targeted and radicalized a while back. When Abd-Allah took over, he recruited a huge number of his US based radicalized followers to tail you. He switched them often and kept them at a distance so you wouldn't catch on. The latest tail following you was Adam," Kilton answered as some more photos came on the screen of Cal in Big Sky.

Cal looked to Kilton. "I have been tailed by Abd-Allah and you didn't think you should inform me?" Cal was pissed and he could feel Joe trying to pull him back from letting loose on Kilton.

"Why would you keep that from our team?" Joe asked rather harshly.

"We didn't know until recently; when Adam was sent in. Which is how your girlfriend connects to all this," Kilton said back to Cal.

Cal could feel himself tighten all over. His protectiveness

of Alease spiked out hard through his skin at the mention of her in this conversation. "How does she have anything to do with this?"

Kilton clicked his remote again and another image appeared on the screen. The man in this photo looked very similar to Adam Dunnlen, and had a very distinct mark on his neck that Cal recognized right away as the teeth marks from a K9. "This is Jeffery Dunnlen. The man who attacked Alease in New York. Who is also the brother of Adam."

Cal had bolts of anger flying through him at the image of this man's face looking back at him from the screen.

"So this guy is alive."

"Yes. The long and short of it is that Homeland had an eye on Adam for suspicion of his ties to Abd-Allah, but never had the proof they needed. When his brother Jeffery was identified by the arresting cops, Homeland was pinged right away. They guessed he would be in contact with Adam. They were right. So an undercover was put in when Adam came to see Jeffery. Their entire conversation got on the record. That's when we had confirmation of Adam working for Abd-Allah. During their conversation, Adam convinced Jeffrey to join him in working for Abd-Allah, if he managed to get off for the crime he committed. We saw an opportunity there, and we took it." Kilton was looking at Cal in full anticipation of the anger that was about to be evident.

Cal put it together quickly, and his body flushed with red

hot rage. "You let Jeffry go."

"Yes," Kilton answered coldly.

Cal could feel his fist clinching and he knew Joe saw it. Joe spoke up, taking the focus and trying to deflect the tension that was flaring up.

"You let him go?" Joe's question was layered with unmistakable disapproval.

"We placed bugs in his cell phone and had traces on all his devices. It was a perfect opportunity to put an unknowing informant on the inside of Abd-Allah's US recruits; and it worked" Kilton said as he clicked again and up popped several more images of the extremist recruits, several audio/video files of the terrorist network and many more pictures of Cal and Alease.

"The wealth of information we gathered revealed many things, one of which was that Abd-Allah had you tracked down the day he found out who you were. Then he had you tailed…for a long time…we weren't sure why he didn't strike when he found you. We didn't understand what he was waiting for, but when Alease entered the picture two things became clear; Abd-Allah found what he wanted, *and* he finally had two recruits dumb enough to help him put his plan into action. One in particular, whose obsession with her overruled any fear of danger in going up against you and your SEAL team."

"What plan?" Joe asked.

Kilton clicked on one of the audio files and it played softly. They could hear the Arabic language in the background as Kilton spoke over it.

"Abd-Allah was looking for Cal's weakness. Just killing him wasn't enough. He wants Cal to suffer. So he waited… looking for someone who Cal cared about so he could use her to hurt him. He found that when he saw the photos of you and Alease. He knew she meant something to you and he knew that she was the key to his revenge."

Cal felt bolts of hatred and anger filling his body.

"How exactly do the Dunnlen dicks fit into this?"

"Abd-Allah couldn't find any recruits dumb enough to face you and your team" Kilton said to Cal. "You guys created quite a reputation over there and no one had the balls to go up against you guys. But when Jeffery saw the pictures Adam had gotten of you and Alease…there was his opportunity. Jeffery's fixation with her sucked him right in. Apparently the deal was struck, as long as Jeffery was allowed to…have his way with her first, then the brothers would get her and bring her to a rendezvous point where Abd-Allah's men would take her and bring her to him."

Cal's anger flew out. "No fucking way they get anywhere near her. Where are these two now?"

Kilton let out a breath. "We don't know. They dumped all their devices two days ago and we lost them."

Cal's anger escaped him and he exploded, "God Damn it

Kilton!" His fist hit the table with such force that even Kilton was startled. "This is bullshit that you let this get so far without telling me!"

One of the commanders stood blocking Cal from Kilton. "I wouldn't raise your voice like that to the General, sir."

"Fuck you!" he yelled in the commander's face.

Joe wanted to calm the flare up, but ended up not quite doing so. "Cal is right, General, this is bullshit."

Kilton placed a hand on the commander telling him to sit. "That is why I have had SEAL Team Beta 5 on this since we found out. Their Captain, Aaron Daniels, said the same thing. I disagreed, seeing as how you are too close to this Cal, but then you guys started sticking your nose into it and I knew it was a matter of hours before you put the damn thing together, so I called you in."

Aaron, the Beta 5 SEAL team captain, stood up. "The last audio file we received has got my nerves up. I think you need to play it for Cal and his team."

Kilton nodded and clicked it. "Tell him" he ordered.

Aaron spoke over the recording to Cal. "Abd-Allah's need for vengeance against you has gone mental…there's no easy way to say this…"

Cal cut right in with a bitter tone. "Just say it."

Aaron detached himself as much as he could from the words about to fall from his mouth.

"His plan is to have these brothers bring her to an

exchange point where his men will bring her to him for repeated videos of his…abuse of her, sexual and otherwise, for you to see. He is planning on a long, drawn out revenge using her to destroy you from the inside out." Aaron paused and Cal saw a signal in his eye that there was more.

"And…?" Cal's tone was obviously furious.

"The last recording…he was filled with an urgent and twisted idea to get her pregnant himself, and flaunt it before your eyes in released videos…and then, after the birth of the child that would enrage you, he would kill her." All the SEALs in the room had the same bolts of heavy anger in their eyes, but none matched the fury in Cal's.

"I want a team at Joe's right fucking now! No one gets anywhere near her," Cal ordered.

Kilton raised his hand. "I already sent them this morning. They should be there by now."

"Give me the damn phone." Kilton handed Cal a phone that would work in this secure room and he dialed Alease. It rang and went to voice mail. "Fuck." He hung up and called Sophie, after two rings she answered. Cal didn't waste anytime with pleasantries. "Sophie, where is Alease?" he asked abruptly.

"Good morning to you too. She is still sleeping Cal," Sophie said as she yawned.

"When did you see her last?" Cal knew his voice was harsh, but he didn't care.

"Cal, relax. I'm sure she is fine. I saw her turn her lights off last night around 1:30 am. She has been sleeping since then."

Cal grew cold. "She turned her lights off last night? Fuck. Sophie get over there right now!" Cal barked at her.

Joe crossed closer. Cal looked at him and spoke with concern all over his voice. "She would never turn the lights off, Joe. Not without me there."

"Put it on speaker Cal," Joe said.

After some rustling on the other end of the phone, they heard the sound of a door opening and Sophie calling Alease's name with no answer. Then Sophie got quiet.

"Sophie? What is it?" Cal asked sharply.

"Shit. Cal, she isn't here." She paused, "Fuck. Your truck is gone." Sophie's voice was suddenly weak and frightened.

"God Damn it!" Cal slammed his hands so hard on the table that everything on it flew in the air and several glasses broke as they shattered back down. He knew he had to get his emotions under control. He was filled with such anger, and fear for her. He had to get his head on straight so he could figure this out. Was she taken, or did she leave voluntarily; and if so, why? He took a breath. "Sophie, who was the last person to see her? Think," he asked.

"I think it was Jake," she said.

"Go get him. I need to speak to him right now." Cal's temper was flaring. His face was red with tension and his fists locked ready to punch something, anything. When Jake got on the phone, Cal spoke as calmly as he could. "Jake, I need to know everything about your last conversation with Alease. Tell me what you remember."

"I don't know. She was coming up the stairs and she looked really pale. She said she didn't feel well and was going to bed," Jake said.

Cal paused… "*Up* the stairs? What stairs? Where were you?" Cal asked.

"The stairs by the Christmas tree. Then she asked me to take Max," Jake answered.

She was coming up from Joe's lower office…Fuck. Cal looked to Joe, "Did you lock your office door when we left?" he asked him.

"No. I was in such a rush, I asked Dana to lock it for me." Joe was visibly pissed at himself for the lapse.

Sophie got back on the phone. "What is it Cal? What's going on?"

"Sophie, I need you to go down the stairs and tell me if Joe's office door is open," Cal said.

After several footsteps, Sophie spoke, "It's open, Cal." There was a pause, "Oh my God, what is this?" Sophie asked.

Cal and Joe exchanged glances. "What do you see Sophie?" Cal asked with trepidation in his voice.

"A bunch of pictures on the screen of you and Alease… and a really scary looking guy with scars on his neck…in front of your house." Sophie sounded really unnerved by the images.

Now it was clear. Alease knew. Shit. She had seen the pictures and she knew. His anger exploded as did his fear for her. His rage caused him to throw a coffee cup across the room, smashing it on the far wall. "Damn it!"

They could hear Dana's voice calling Sophie in the background, then Sophie's voice brought them back to the phone. "Cal, there are men in uniform coming to the front door. What's going on?"

Cal used all his skills to calm his voice and bring himself back under control. "They are there just as a precaution. It's ok. Let them in and we will be in touch as soon as we can." Cal was trying to speak and think at the same time. When Sophie started to push for more info, Cal cut her off. "Sophie, I do not have time right now. Please trust me. Let them in and just wait, and if you hear from Alease you call me right away."

He hung up the phone and there was thick, dead silence in the room as Cal got his breathing under control.

Joe spoke. "What is she trying to do by leaving?" he asked.

Cal's voice cracked with emotion. "She is…trying to protect me." He was so upset he could hardly hold it in.

Dan, Eddie and Tom, all on their feet now looked at each other.

"There is no reason to believe they have her," Dan said.

"Yes. Just because they know where your house is Cal, doesn't mean they know where Joe's is," Eddie added.

"You certainly were not followed when you drove up. You would have noticed that." Tom was right, Cal had to agree that was true. He always looked to make sure he was not being tailed, and there were so few cars on the road at that time. He would have noticed.

Cal took a deeper breath and ran his hands through his hair to try and get his rational mind in gear and put the emotions to the side. Her life was in serious danger and he had to get her back. "OK. Top priority; we have to find her and we have to find her right now," he said.

"She is driving your truck. Let's track it." Joe turned to Tom, "Get on that now." Tom took control of one of the computers and started work on it with the license plate and vin info from Cal. Joe looked to Cal, "I have an idea."

"What?" Cal asked.

"Let's get Dan to call his buddies at the police, and have her arrested," Joe said. When Cal looked at him with concern, he continued, "Cal, the safest place for her, until we can get back there, is a jail cell surrounded by cops."

Cal had to concede, he made a good point. "OK. Arrested for what?"

"Well…she stole your car didn't she?" Joe decided. Cal nodded and Dan got on the phone. Cal hated the idea of it, but getting her off the street and out of the potential hands of the Dunnlen brothers was the first priority, and Joe's plan was a good one.

Cal paced the floor impatiently as the time ticked by waiting for the police to get to his truck, which they were able to track. The GPS locator was showing the car not moving and Cal was trying to rationalize the stillness with something logical and safe, like filling the car with gas. It was pinged off the interstate, so that made sense. The police were given the number to one of the phones in the secure room, with instructions to call by video when they got there so the images could be directly linked to the screens for the SEALs to see. The phone rang, it was them.

They answered as the images of the cops by Cal's truck came on the screen. "Do you have her?" Cal asked before they could even speak.

"Negative. There is no one here. The keys are on the ground and the car door is open. Attendant says he woke up to the sound of a pickup truck pulling away at rapid fire speed. He didn't get the make or model," the cops voice was thick and low.

Cal lost his breath and pushed against the table in frustration.

"Are there security camera's there? We need access now if there are," Joe insisted.

After the muffled conversation between the cops and the

attendant, the cop answered.

"Yes. He is pulling it up now."

While they waited for the security footage Cal thought out loud, "How the Hell did they know where she was? How did they find her?" He paused, then continued. He spoke to the cops on the line, "I need you guys to look under the car… is there any kind of tracking device on it?"

The cops acknowledged and began inspecting it. One of the cops towards the rear pulled something out from under the back of the truck. "Found something. I've never seen anything like this before."

"Place it in view of the camera," Cal said.

Both SEAL teams had the same realization. "Tracking device," Cal said.

"Syrian. Look at the markings on the side," Dan added.

Eddie spoke with clarity. "They are definitely working for Abd-Allah, and it looks like he spared no expense to get his plan into action. Those are not cheap."

Cal's worry was filling him fast. "Can we track her cell phone?"

One of the cops spoke up, "I think this is her cell phone right here." He held it up to the camera, and Cal recognized it right away.

"Fuck!" Cal was losing his ability to control his anger, and his concern for Alease was growing exponentially. "How long ago did this happen?" He asked the question while trying to get his mind to be logical again.

"Attendant said around 4:00am," the cop answered.

Cal looked at his watch and felt desperation seep all throughout him. "Jesus. They could be anywhere now."

The security footage was pulled up and they watched it. Cal experienced an overbearing pain surge through his heart when he saw Alease get drugged and thrown into the back of the black pickup truck. It felt like the worst moment of his life; and he had been through Hell before like very few men on this planet. But this…this was worse than anything. He could take any kind of torture on himself, but Alease…dear God he couldn't handle that.

Joe spoke up to the cops, "Put out a BOLO on that black truck." They had the license plates from the video footage, but Joe and Cal both knew they would be chasing their tails always one step behind them without another way to track them. They had several hours head start on them. Tracking the truck was all they had.

As they waited for any reports on the black truck, Joe was doing his best to help Cal stay focused and calm.

"Give us the footage again at the gas station," Joe ordered. "I want to see the entire thing."

Cal watched with the rest of them. He filled with dread again at seeing Alease get out of the truck to fill the tank, unaware of what was about to happen. He saw Kenya jump down, go off and then come back. He saw the truck and the two brothers get out. His fists clenched in anger when he watched the drugged cloth being put over her mouth and her body go limp. Joe was about to suggest that Cal stop watching it, when something caught his attention.

"Wait. Go back a little and play that again."

They watched as Adam pulled Kenya up by the neck and reached for his gun, laughing. Jeffery came back to him after throwing Alease roughly in the back seat.

"Look at this," Joe said.

They watched as there was a small struggle between the two regarding the puppy and then Jeffery grabbed the dog and threw it in the truck.

Joe looked up to Cal, "Why would he take the dog?"

Cal had a sick feeling in his stomach, knowing the answer and how it would affect Alease.

"Payback probably. Her last dog left a nasty mark on his neck, not to mention he almost killed him. He probably wants to kill the puppy in front of Alease as some kind of revenge." Cal was getting nauseous thinking about how traumatic that would be for her…which is exactly what this asshole wants.

What felt like hours later, they got the call. The truck had been found by a private airfield. No one was in it or anywhere around. There was an empty airplane hanger with nothing there. They were gone.

Cal was livid. "They took a fucking plane? They could be anywhere. How the Hell are we going to track them?!" He felt helpless; the worst feeling for a Navy SEAL. He refused to accept this. He desperately tried to focus and push his emotions down.

Dan spoke first after the pause. "They must still be in US airspace."

Eddie had his hands running through his hair in frustration, "Lot good that does us with no way to track them. They could literally be anywhere in the entire country right now."

Tom added, "As John used to say, it's like trying to find a needle in Africa."

Africa. Cal froze. He took a breath and looked to Joe. "*Kenya.*"

Joe didn't get it at first. "What?"

Cal spoke again to the cops at the hanger. "Is the puppy there? Dead or alive?" He waited for their response.

"No. No sign of any dog. No blood either," one of the cops answered.

A daring grin started to creep on Cal's face. "No way…" his mind was clicking a hundred miles an hour and he looked to Joe again, who now got it.

"Do you think?" Joe asked him.

"God, I hope so. Get James on the phone now," Cal ordered.

Joe dialed and handed the phone to Cal. When James answered Cal spoke right away. "James, it's Cal. Please tell me you still tag all of your dogs with the military grade GPS tracking chips."

James almost laughed. "Of course I do. Every one of them at 8 weeks. Why?"

"Kenya got one too?" he asked it as if his entire world relied on the answer, which it did.

"Yes sir. Kenya too," James affirmed.

Cal felt like he had been holding his breath for hours and it finally got released. There was a brief collective relief from both SEAL teams, then Cal continued.

"James, I need all the info on her chip and I need you to send it immediately over to JFHQ-NCR," Cal instructed.

"Joint Task Force HQ? Shit. You got it. Sending now," James said.

As the room picked up into action to get the info and follow the lead, Cal turned to Kilton. "My team goes and takes lead on this."

Kilton stood to object. "Cal, you are way too close to this. Beta 5 should go."

Cal got right in his face. General or not, Cal was not backing down. "My team is taking this." He was not asking and he would not take no for an answer.

Aaron moved in, as did Joe.

"Both teams should go," Aaron said. Kilton was going to argue but Aaron continued. "General Kilton, there are two missions here. One is to rescue Alease Taynes, but the other…

we may have a chance here to find out where the rendezvous point is and use it to track down and knock out Abd-Allah. Two teams might be a really good idea here."

He got Kilton with that. Cal jumped on it. "Aaron is right. We take this opportunity to get right to the bees' nest. We knock him out and his commanders under him, this thing is over for good."

A voice from behind the computer broke the argument. "We have them!"

Cal almost jumped over the table to see the screen. He saw the longitude and latitude of the tracker as the dot moved across the screen.

"Judging by the speed and altitude, I would say they are coming in for a landing," Joe said.

Aaron spoke next. "Near the Everglades in Florida. My guess is they are headed to the port. Easiest way out of the country with a drugged up hostage is not through the airports, it's by water. Lots of smuggling happens with private yachts leaving from Port Everglades and handing cargo off in international waters. I bet you anything that's their scheme."

Kilton cast his order. "Beta 5 you're lead. Alpha 12 you're second. I will get your equipment ready, you guys make up your plan."

When Kilton left the room, Aaron looked to Cal. "Fuck Kilton. You're lead. We all know what you guys have done, and if this was *my* woman, I would want the same. Tell us what the plan is, Captain."

The plan was already forming in Cal's mind. They had to move fast and it had to start now.

Chapter Ten
The Rescue

Alease had never felt so weak and groggy. She had an immense amount of trouble opening her eyes, they felt as if they were taped shut. When she lifted her head it felt ridiculously heavy, like a sack of cement. She tried pulling her hand to her temple but she couldn't move it. Finally, she got her eyes to open and pain filled her even more as the light in the room pierced through her brain like a knife. She couldn't focus her eyes at first, but then she was able to handle the agony of the light and keep her eyes open.

In a sudden wave of terror she remembered the gas station…the reflection in the window and his cold hands on her. She couldn't remember what had happened after that. How long had she been out? She had no idea. She didn't know where she was or how she got here. Her head was killing her. She tried to move her arms again and that's when she looked above her head and saw that her hands were bound to a metal pipe above her. Her feet were bound together as well. She was trapped. She struggled and pulled but she was not able to get her arms free. Looking around, she saw she was in a small room. Some kind of small boiler room. She felt rocking back and forth. *My God, am I on a ship?* That's what it felt like. She was filled with dread and fear. She heard a squeal and looked to her side. Kenya was tied up next to her. Her mouth had been bound and the rope around her pulled tight. Alease went to speak to her but realized she couldn't. Her mouth was bound with something as well. It felt like duct tape. She listened and could faintly hear the muffled conversations of men coming from above her. She couldn't quite make out what they were saying, but she knew one of the voices. It was him.

He had gotten her. Fear iced through her at the thoughts of what was about to happen to her. She tried to calm her breathing and her fears…the only comfort she had was that they had found her without having to kill Cal. He was safe. She had a small sense of relief for that. Leaving had hurt like Hell, but she knew now she had done the right thing. Cal was not a target anymore. She concentrated on that instead of her own fate. Her heart broke at the realization she would never see him again. God, she could hardly bear the thought…it filled her with pain worse than anything this man could do to her. She prayed, but she knew, she was not getting out of this one. Her eyes closed as the tears fell, flooding her face.

The door flew open and a man she had never seen before was standing in front of her with an nefarious grin. He was eyeing her up and down, licking his lips intrusively like a rabid dog. She felt sick.

"Hey sweetheart. My brother would like to see you now that you are awake," he crouched down and got right in her face, "and then, when he is done, I'd like to see you too." His breath smelled like cigarettes and old beef.

He took a knife out of his pocket and taunted her by dragging it on her face. Another man standing behind him with a thick accent and a big gun spoke up sharply with and unmistakable air of authority, "Hey! No marks on the face. Abd-Allah's orders. He needs her recognizable."

"Pity," the man with the knife said. Then, with one strike, he cut her restraints from the pipe and pulled her forcefully to her feet. Her hands were still bound together at her wrists and her arms seared with pain from being over her head for what could have been hours for all she knew. He grabbed the rope attached to Kenya and yanked her behind him as he pulled Alease to her feet and forced her to move. Her feet had just enough room to move in a small shuffle, but that was it.

The man half dragged her from the room through the narrow hallway. The rocking back and forth was more prevalent now, and as she passed a small window, she confirmed she was indeed on a ship. The moon was bright above the water, but the cold blackness of night covered everything else. There was nothing but ocean as far as she could see.

As she was being dragged through the ship, she saw a few more men with guns patrolling the perimeters.

The man pushed her, forcing her to climb the stairs to the higher levels. As she ascended higher, she realized this ship she was on looked more like a large private yacht.

She was led towards the back of the yacht and down the hall where they came to a closed door. The man knocked once and opened it, pushing her inside…and there he was. The man she thought was dead was standing right in front of her with a ravenous look on his iniquitous face. There were two more men in the room, both with guns.

He half snarled and half laughed, "I've been waiting for this for a long time." His gaze screeched through her. He spoke to the men in the room, but he didn't take his eyes off of her as he did so, "You all can go."

The man who forced her up here spoke as he dropped the lead on Kenya, "Don't forget, I get a turn too when you're done," he snickered, then all three of the men left the room closing the door behind them.

Alone with the man she convinced herself was dead, she was terrified. He moved in close to her, a breath away, and made a grotesque moaning sound. She closed her eyes and looked away. His ice cold fingers reached out to touch her and she instinctively whacked him with her bound hands. His face got beet red and his temper flared in an instant. He grabbed her face hard with his agitated fingers and pushed his lips a whisper away from hers.

"You are lucky we have orders not to mark your face up, or I would have split your rosy cheeks wide open just now." He smiled, aroused at the fear he instilled in her. He ripped the duct tape off her mouth and then he pushed his lips down on hers so hard she screamed under the pressure of him. She tried to push away from him but he overpowered her and she couldn't move. "We're gonna have some fun now." He grabbed her breasts and squeezed so hard that she cried out in pain. Lifting her bound hands she whacked him again across the face in a defensive blow. He boiled with anger and knocked her off her feet sending her crashing to the ground. He let out a burst of frustration and then yanked her up to her feet, dragging her to the balcony in the back of the ship.

The night air was cold and she screamed again as he threw her against the wall at the corner of the balcony. He lifted her hands and pulled out another restraint tie, attaching her arms to a solid ring in the wall above her head. He backed away while she struggled, and laughed at her as she realized she was trapped, once again.

"Now, first things first…" he spit to the side and then looked over at the bound puppy. Alease had a wave of fear rush through her.

"Leave her alone. She is just a puppy," her voice was panicked, and that seemed to entice him even more.

His crooked smile flashed across his wretched face and he crossed the room to the dog. He lifted her harshly by the scruff of her neck and dangled her as he walked back out onto the balcony.

"I could shoot it, but that would be too fast." He dangled

her over the side of the boat as Alease's tears seared her cheeks. "I think it might be more fun to just drop the little thing into the ocean, with it's feet bound," he laughed. "Can't swim with no feet. Drowning is such a painful way to go, don't you think?" He held the puppy over the edge, tyrannizing her, relishing in the power he felt at the fear he was igniting in her…and then, he opened his hands and Kenya dropped like a rock into the water. Alease screamed as she watched her fall over the balcony, her heart seething in guilt and pain.

He laughed and delighted in his enjoyment of seeing her devastation. His smile faded and his voice turned harsh.

"Payback for your last dog that left these marks on my neck." He turned his body to face her completely. His hands reached for his belt and he slowly started to undo it. He opened his jeans and then, with the sinister look in his lustful eyes, he started towards her. She closed her eyes trying to gather whatever strength she had left. She had it in her for one more blow, but she knew, after that, her strength would be gone. God help her…

The Sikorsky UH-60 Black Hawk was in position, holding it's moving hover above the cruising yacht. The UH-60 was so silent it couldn't be heard below, and the stealth design made it near impossible for them to be picked up on radar. They were as close to invisible as they could get.

Cal was in position on board along with Dan and Eddie from his team, and Aaron, Mac, Rick and Pike from SEAL Team Beta 5. They were all set, ready to drop on the order. Cal had his Recce Rifle ready, looking through the outfitted Vortex optic. He had a clear view of the back balcony of the yacht, and a clear view of the first target he was here to kill; Jeffry Dunnlen. The two other guards arguing with him would fall too, but Cal's focus was Jeffry. His rage boiled as he looked at the man through his optic. He controlled it masterfully, but that was in large part because his team was here and he had complete confidence they knew exactly what to do when he gave the order.

Cal examined the weapons of the two guards. The Rifles the SEALs had were far superior to the guns the guards were holding. Cal wouldn't have cared either way; he was dropping down and taking them out no matter what. Hell, he'd be happy to drop the Recce and use his damn hands to rip their throats out. His anger was like a massively destructive volcano ready to blow, but he had extraordinary control over it at the moment.

He spoke to the other SEALs through the NSW Invisio M4s they all had for communication. "I've got Jeffry and two guards in the back room near the rear balcony. Two Basic assault rifles, one pistol."

"I'm in position off the front right. I've got 3 guards patrolling the outer deck. Three basic assault rifles, and one pistol," Rick, from Beta 5 said.

"In position front left," Pike from Beta 5 said.

"In position off back balcony right. Say the word," Joe confirmed.

"In Position off back balcony left. Ready," Tom said.

Dan and Eddie confirmed jump ready from the black hawk for any position needing back up.

Cal spoke again, "Tagger? All good?"

"Yes. Holding the CCA in locked position just south of the yacht," Tagger replied from the stealth boat they had in the water.

"Anyone have Alease?" Cal asked it in a very steady voice.

Tagger spoke up. "I have the tracker up. Looks like it's moving towards the back balcony. Don't know if that means her too, but it's coming your way, Cal."

Aaron was also looking through his viewer towards the front of the yacht. "Hold up…Jesus, I think I see Abd-Allah's number Two. Front right. Rick, you got a closer look?" Aaron wanted confirmation of the sighting.

Rick's voice broke in a few seconds later. "Yeah. That's Dizhvar alright. Blue sweatshirt, jeans ripped on left side. Damn…he is here? You know what that means? This Douchebag is never far from Abd-Allah."

Aaron quickly answered. "Heads up. Keep Dizhvar alive if possible. We need to squeeze him for Abd-Allah's location."

"Does anyone have Alease?!" Cal's voice got tense. He didn't mean for it, but he needed eyes on her.

"Tracker five seconds out, Cal," Tagger said.

Cal waited tensely. They all fell quiet…waiting… listening for Cal's go.

The door opened and Cal forced himself to stay cool. He saw Adam throw Alease into the room. Damn, she was bound at the hands and feet. *Oh, the ways he was going to kill this bastard.*

"Got her. Back room. Adam has her, one basic assault, one extra large jagged edge knife on Adam. Everyone hold. She's too close. Bound at hands and feet Joe," Cal said.

"Copy," Joe replied.

"Rick, report?" Cal asked.

"Easy pickings. Dumbasses are sitting down smoking cigarettes. Say the word, and they're gone. Don't see Dizhvar anymore though. He went in on his cell phone."

Aaron spoke. "Damn…we need someone on him. Cal, let me go down and eyeball him. Left side, midsection. No-one there right now."

Cal didn't like it, but he knew Aaron was right. Capturing Dizhvar was the key to getting to Abd-Allah, and if he was close, they had to take this opportunity now.

"Aaron, go. Everyone else hold."

As quiet as a mouse, Aaron jumped. He slid down the

long rope from the Black Hawk down to the side of the boat, landing perfectly over the left side by the mid section. He grabbed onto the boat and cut the line loose.

"In Position," he reported back.

Cal's attention was back on Alease. He saw Jeffery grab her face and rip the duct tape off her lips, then force his mouth on hers. "God damn it, this bastard is dead," he couldn't hold back the words.

"Easy Cal. Remember the plan. We got this. Keep your cool. Tell me when," Joe spoke in a firm, but calm voice.

"Copy," Cal answered, swallowing his anger…for the moment. "Jeffery has her alone now."

Cal's attention was pulled one floor up from where Alease was. "Aaron, affirmative on Dizhvar. Second level, mid. Climb straight up that wall and you have access through an open window right above your position."

"Copy," Aaron answered. Cal saw Aaron begin the climb up the outside of the yacht.

He moved his viewer back to where Alease was. Jeffery had moved her and was heading out to the balcony.

"Joe, he has her, and heading right for your corner," Cal informed him.

"Copy. I hear them," Joe answered.

Cal watched Jeffry tie her hands to the metal ring above where she was standing. He cursed to himself again, itching to put a bullet in this guys head. "Aaron. You in position?"

"Not yet. Almost," Aaron responded.

Cal moved his viewer to spot check Aaron. Damn, almost, but not there yet. He had to hold the order.

Cal went back to Alease's location and saw Jeffry walking towards the balcony dangling Kenya. He had a good idea what was coming. "Tagger, you seeing this?"

"Yeah. I see it." Tagger had an optic just like the rest of the team and was keeping an eye from his location.

"I need you to be ready, you got me?" Cal asked.

"Yes sir. On it," Tagger answered.

Cal saw Kenya drop to the water and heard Alease scream. His blood felt red hot. "Tagger go. Everyone else hold."

"Copy," Tagger answered.

Cal watched as Jeffery undid his jeans and walked towards Alease. Damn, he would shoot the bastard right now but Alease was in the direct line of fire. He couldn't risk her, and he couldn't give the order until Aaron was in position. "Damn it Aaron, are you there yet?"

"Ten seconds," Aaron answered.

"Everybody ready…we are going in five seconds," Cal barked. As the countdown began in his head he saw Jeffery get right up to Alease, he almost called the go order early but then he saw her lift herself with her bound hands and smash her bound feet right into Jeffrey's groin. "That's my girl," he said.

"I heard that. Sounded like a good hit. He screamed like a child," Joe said.

"In position," Aaron said.

Cal didn't wait, "GO, GO, GO!" he ordered.

Suddenly, the SEALs were in action. Cal descended from above and hit the deck in less than three seconds. Tom was up on the left side of the balcony and Joe jumped up directly in front of Alease, standing between her and Jeffery. Cal was on his feet striding towards Jeffery with his rifle ready. Jeffrey was on his feet, he backed up as his mind grasped what was happening. Then his eyes locked on Cal and he became completely terrified; absolutely motionless. Little prick was so scared he didn't even scream.

Cal had his rifle aimed at his head…then he moved it lower to his chest…then lower to his belly…and then even lower… *That's it, target acquired*…he pulled his trigger. Jeffrey screamed in searing agony, and went down as Cal descended on him. Jeffery's face was overcome with horror when Cal reached him, and had him in the grip of his powerful, and exceedingly livid hands. In one quick movement, he threw Jeffrey's pistol overboard and punched him so hard he knocked out a few of his teeth. He did not stop his actions as he spoke, "Joe, you got her?"

"Yes. Cal, I've got her," Joe said.

It had taken everything she had to lift herself and kick the bastard. If she weren't tied up, she would have collapsed on the floor right after she did it. She had been about to resign herself to the punishment he would hand her, when the sudden commotion all around her shocked energy back into her. She looked up and saw the sudden appearance of several men in black and then Joe was suddenly right in front of her. It was them. The SEAL team. Joe raised a huge knife and cut her free from the metal ring, as he told Cal he had her. When he cut her loose, he grabbed her to keep her from falling.

"Cal?! Where is he Joe?" She desperately tried to break free from Joe to see if Cal was really there. Of course she couldn't, even if she was at full strength, she could never overpower one of these SEALs. "Joe please, where is Cal?"

Joe tried to stop her from moving. "Alease, he is fine, but I have to get you out of here now. Please stop and come with me."

She struggled but knew she was losing. She heard Cal's voice.

"Tom, hold him." Seconds later Cal appeared in front of her as Joe stepped aside to let her see him. He grabbed her and kissed her with a quick and urgent force. She felt like she must have died and fallen into a fantasy world. He pulled away much faster than she wanted him to.

"Cal!" Tears fell down her cheeks. "I'm so sorry. This is all my fault!"

"No, it isn't. I need you to go with Joe. Now." He was

short and intense. He pushed her back into Joe's grip before she could argue.

"What? Why? What about you?" Her questions were not being entertained. Cal turned to Joe and ordered him to take her and go. As Joe and Tom were pulling her over the side of the yacht, she saw Cal advance towards Jeffrey with an air of rage that looked like Hell itself.

She felt herself falling, her stomach in knots as the never-ending plummet took over all her senses. Then she felt the ice cold water smack her skin and she went under. Joe never let go of her the whole way down and he pulled her head above the surface within seconds. He had her on his stomach as he swam them backwards, away from the moving yacht that now seemed so far away she couldn't believe it.

"Cal!" she screamed his name. "Joe, you can't leave him there! What are you doing?!" She was so upset she could hardly breathe.

Joe kept swimming, holding onto her tightly as he did so.

"Alease, you need all your energy to breathe. Stop talking and relax. Let me take you in. Just breathe."

She heard Tom talking to someone named Tagger, but just as quickly as the fall had woken her from her exhausted state, it took her over again and she felt herself losing all her energy.

She could hear Joe speaking to someone. "All good. We have her. She is fine. Tagger is here. She is safe. Now focus on your end." There was a pause, then he continued, "you have my word my friend. Switching M4's off. Kick their asses boys. Out."

Suddenly she felt Joe lifting her up and someone grabbing her from above and pulling her on a boat. She fell to the floor trying to catch her breath. With a thump Joe and Tom were on both sides of her helping her up to a sitting position, as a stranger was wrapping a blanket around her.

Joe smiled at her. "Alease, Tagger. Tagger, Alease." He made the introduction as casually as if they were at a cocktail party in line waiting for drinks.

"Nice to meet you Alease. Hell of a jump." He smiled at her and then went back to the helm of the boat.

Alease scoured at Joe. "How could you leave him there Joe! We have to go help him." She tried to stand but Joe easily pulled her back down with one hand.

"What are you going to do Alease? Swim over to a speeding yacht you couldn't catch even if you had a motor attached to you, to do what? Save a Navy SEAL? Sit down and try to calm yourself. Cal is fine."

She was so weak she fell back to sitting. "Joe you left him alone?!"

Joe shook his head. "I did no such thing. He is on that boat with six other Navy SEALs. Tom and I are following orders."

"Whose orders?!" she snapped at him.

"Cal's. Now sit and catch your breath," Joe said as the boat sped up and turned in a direction opposite of the yacht that Cal was still on.

Alease's tears flew down her cheeks as the helplessness of her position hit her. She could do nothing to help him and he had done exactly what she told him not to do. He was on a boat with killers now because of her.

Joe seemed to be reading her thoughts. "Alease, there is more going on here than you realize. This is not your fault."

She started to hyperventilate and tried to stand up again. "Joe, we can't leave him there. You have to take me back. He can't get hurt because of me!" Her shivering overcame her and she became even more weak than she had before.

"Joe, I think she is going hypothermic," Tom said.

Alease wanted to protest but she was overcome. She felt herself start to fall over as Joe caught her, and then everything went black.

"Cal, you copy?" Aaron's voice was asking again on the M4's. Cal did not answer. "Dan, Eddie, what's Cal's situation?"

Dan came on the M4's, "He is…uh…finishing up."

"Is he ok?" Aaron asked.

Cal opened the door from the balcony room to see Aaron standing there. "I'm fine. Did you get Dizhvar?" His voice was steady and calm. He saw the shocked look in Aaron's eyes as he took note of the massive amount of blood covering Cal's clothing.

"Jesus! Are you hurt?" Aaron asked him.

"No. It's not my blood," he said matter-of-factly as he kept walking.

Aaron looked in the room and saw an unrecognizable body on the floor. He knew it was Jeffrey, but just barely. "Jeffrey?" he asked.

Cal very simply answered, "He's Dead."

Aaron laughed. "Yeah, I see that. Made sure of it, did you?" he asked sarcastically.

Cal looked at him with his own twinge of sarcasm. "What? He resisted arrest." Cal focused back on the M4's. "Joe, status?"

"All good. We have her. She is fine. Tagger is here. She is safe. Now focus on your end," Joe affirmed in a very confident voice.

"You have my entire world right there, Joe. Promise me you will keep her safe."

"You have my word my friend. Switching M4's off. Kick their asses boys. Out." Joe and Tom clicked off, as per the plan. There could be no distractions for the team now. Cal knew the only way he could focus is to be assured one hundred percent that Alease was safe, and the only one he trusted for that was Joe. Sending Tom as his back up was just an extra layer of protection Cal needed so his mind could be on the mission knowing she was safe.

He turned back to Aaron. "Status?"

Aaron smiled a cocky smile. "Adam is dead. All terrorists dead, except for Dizhvar. He is badly hurt, but alive. Pike and Rick have him at the Helm."

"Let's go," Cal ordered. "Everyone at the Helm now."

When they got to the Helm, all the SEALs were there and Dizhvar was on his knees, arms and legs bound, clearly he had not been cooperative and had suffered badly in the brawl with the SEALs. His eyes were open, and Cal recognized right away that the evil in Dizhvar's eyes were now matched with an even mix of fear. Good. He would use that; and enjoy doing so. Cal would just assume put a bullet in his head, but Aaron had a point about his usefulness. After all, Jeffrey was just *one* of the two targets Cal wanted taken out. The mastermind behind the danger Alease fell into was because of Abd-Allah, and Cal needed him dead to know Alease would be safe, and this man was the only one who could tell them where Abd-Allah was.

"He is not talking," Pike said.

"He will," Cal said in a very dark, but calm voice. Cal crouched down and got right in his face, with an ice cold stare and a jet-black tone that could strike fear into the Devil himself. "I'm Cal Winters." He saw the terror shoot across Dizhvar's face, which told Cal this would be easier than he thought. Kilton was right, they had created a helluva reputation. At times like this, that was a very powerful weapon and Cal intended to use it. "Let me make this clear. I'm angry." He put down his rifle. "My woman was put in grave danger today because of your boss, and you helped him." He put down his huge jagged edge knife. "That means I don't like you." He rolled up his sleeves and cracked the knuckles on his hands, making sure Dizhvar saw that his hands were big enough to rip his head right from his shoulders. Cal saw in his eyes that his tactics were working. From what Cal knew of him, Dizhvar was actually a very privileged, sheltered man. He never really had to face any of the dangers he was facing now. This made his fear fresh and extremely useful to Cal. He got closer to him. "That also means there are five other deadly SEALs in this room who don't like you either." Dizhvar's horrified eyes scanned each of the SEALs, seeming to register how much bigger than him they all were. "You have one chance, and one chance only, to answer my questions without pissing us off…and when this team gets angry…I promise you…you will regret it." Cal saw him break. Dizhvar could no longer stand the terror overtaking him.

"Ok," he said in a very shaky voice.

"Where is Abd-Allah?" Cal asked.

"He is on the cargo ship; already at the rendezvous point. We are meeting him there in twenty minutes to make the switch and move to a new location," Dizhvar answered.

Cal looked for all the signs of deceit and did not see any. He looked at Aaron. "He is telling the truth."

Aaron laughed. "Yeah. He is scared to death. He just pissed his pants too."

"Where is the rendezvous Point?" Cal demanded.

"It's already set in the ships navigation. You killed our captain before he could change it."

Cal looked to Rick. Rick nodded and went to the controls.

"Affirmative. ETA, 19 minutes," Rick said. "I can pilot this thing easy."

Cal sent his attention back to Dizhvar and saw his eyes glossing over and his balance falter. "He is bleeding out," Cal said. His injuries during the struggle were taking their toll and he didn't have much time left. Good, one less terrorist to worry about. Then Dizhvar's eyes closed and Cal let him fall. He checked his heart rate…there was none anymore. "Dizhvar is dead." He stood and moved on, addressing his team. "Change of plans. We are not leaving quite yet. Mac? You copy?" He knew Mac was still on the M4's, listening as he held the Black Hawk in it's position above.

"Yes sir," Mac replied.

"Rick, is sending the navigation information up to you. Be close and swing in there when we call. Copy?" Cal instructed as he stood to face his team.

"Copy. See you guys there. Good luck," Mac answered, and then he disengaged, pulling the chopper away to remain out of eyesight until needed.

Cal was desperate to get back to Alease. To see with his own eyes that she was safe and have her in his arms. He knew he was the only one who could ease the fear out of her from what she went through. He knew she needed him. He also knew she would never be completely safe until Abd-Allah was taken out, and they had just been given the most important unexpected gift; the exact location of the fanatic himself. Cal had to lead his men right into the fire to end him and his terrorist ring once and for all.

Chapter Eleven
The Resolution

The yacht was coming up on the location of the cargo ship. They could see it in the distance. Cal had a matter of minutes to come up with the plan for this, and he prayed one last time that it would work. It would spread the SEALs apart, which he didn't like, but, if his calculations were correct, it just might work. Or, they might all be walking right into the end of their time on this earth. A risk they all knew they had to take.

The priority was to eyeball Abd-Allah. He had to be killed face to face for complete verification of his death. Not to mention, proof of his death would be needed at Headquarters. Just blowing up the cargo ship wouldn't cut it, and Cal could think of only one way to ensure a face to face with Abd-Allah; him.

Cal stayed dressed in his SEAL fatigues, but ordered the rest to change into the clothes of the killed recruits. With Dan & Aaron dressed as recruits, it would look like Cal had been taken prisoner. None of the men working for Abd-Allah would know what these recruits looked like. The only ones who would know that would be Abd-Allah himself and Dizhvar. Cal only needed a few seconds to get close enough to Abd-Allah to confirm the target and then kill him. He was banking on Abd-Allah's arrogance and elation at Cal's capture. That could distract Abd-Allah just long enough from registering that the guards bringing his prize were not his hired recruits. It was risky as Hell, but vengeance has a way of becoming ones own worst enemy and creating that margin of blindness that can destroy the owner of it's grip; something he was well aware he needed to be careful of himself.

Rick, Eddie and Pike were set to implement the second part of the plan; using the yacht as a weapon against the cargo ship. It was full of stolen weapons and explosives. With the explosives set in just the right places on the yacht, and the added touch of Pike attaching explosives on the lower side off the cargo ship, a collision between the two boats would knock the entire cargo ship out. Sending everything and everyone on both ships up in flames. It spread the team out thin…but it was the only way.

All the bodies of the killed recruits were put in the boiler room below. The door was locked. Dan, Eddie and Pike took their positions throughout the yacht, their weapons in hand.

They were only minutes away from reaching the small cargo ship. Cal stood on deck with Aaron and Dan at either side of him.

"You guys ready?" Cal asked.

"Ready," they both answered.

Aaron put the rigged pair of restraints over Cal's hands. "These should pop off and reverse with minimum effort."

Aaron and Dan had their guns drawn and their hands on Cal as if controlling him.

"Everyone, we are go," Cal said. They all clicked the timers on their watches, and Pike quietly slipped into the water; heading for the under side of the cargo ship to plant the extra explosives.

Now or never, Cal thought.

A lower access door on the cargo ship opened, and a few armed guards were standing their waiting for them. Aaron spoke as soon as they were within earshot of the other vessel.

"We got Cal Winters. Dizhvar said to take him to Abd-Allah right away." The guards seemed stunned to see Cal in restraints. When it sunk in, they cheered. "Enough! Celebrate later. Abd-Allah should be the first to lay eyes on this sight. Let's go!"

It seemed to be working. The guards took them on board and three of them led the way down the hall. As they boarded they heard Rick calling from the helm, "Come on, we need to go back a ways. Cal threw the girl overboard with a life vest. I have her location. If we hurry we can go get her and bring her to Abd-Allah."

Cal heard several of the men jump on the yacht and the engines turn in reverse. The access door closed and he knew their plan was under way. Now if they could execute it without getting killed, it would be a very good day.

One of the guards turned to eyeball them as they walked.

"Where is Dizhvar?" he asked in a heavy accent.

"Went back to get the girl. Can't blame him for not wanting to fail at the job Abd-Allah gave him," Aaron said.

"You the US recruits?" the guard asked. "You seem… big."

"That's what Abd-Allah wanted. How else we gonna stand a chance against someone like the infamous Cal Winters? Or do you question Abd-Allah's intelligence for choosing us?" Aaron asked angrily.

That shut the guard up and he stayed quiet. They knew they would have only a matter of seconds once in the room with Abd-Allah before things would go south very quickly. Cal glanced at the timer…seven minutes and counting.

They were led up to the cargo deck and towards the back, to a silver metal container. The guard knocked and the door opened to reveal a rather nice living space inside, complete with lights, a sofa, and carpeting. In the center of the room stood the man himself. Abd-Allah was cold looking, unkept and skinny. Cal could break him in half easily, except for the three guards around him with guns. The split second calculation of who takes out which guards was easy, so long as Beta 5 was trained the same way his team was. Too late to ask now. Abd-Allah's eyes glowed as he was told who was being brought in the room. He was instantly giddy; which made Cal's position all the better. Cal's calculation had been right. Abd-Allah was focused on him and payed no mind to

Dan and Aaron. Men who get cocky tend to let their guards down. *Should be at four minutes now and counting...*

"Cal Winters?!" Abd-Allah looked him over and laughed with glee. "Ahh yes! Cal Winters...I recognize you from all the photos I have of you on my wall. You look different with your head still attached to your body!" He laughed again. Cal was still and quiet, as Abd-Allah started to move closer to him. *Good...keep coming...*

"You are my white rhino," Abd-Allah said with an air of infatuation. He was sure of himself...*good, another weakness.* Cal stood still waiting for him to get close enough. "I hear the yacht is on it's way back right now with your girlfriend. Ahh, tried to save her did you? Well, now you can see the live shows instead of the videos." He continued to move closer to Cal...to taunt him. *Three minutes and counting...*

"You made a serious mistake Abd-Allah," Cal said.

Abd-Allah laughed out loud. "Tell me how I have done so? You are in restraints. Being held by my men with guns all around you. I have your beautiful girlfriend on her way to me for my personal enjoyment...ahh...over and over I shall enjoy her, right in front of you." He was almost close enough. *Two minutes...shit they had to move...*

"Yeah? Come here and say that...right to my face. Unless you are scared to get that close," Cal toyed with him. It worked. He moved in. That was all he needed. Game over. In one swift movement, Cal had the restraints over his wrists and onto Abd-Allahs. He pulled tight and his hands were bound. He turned him around to use him as a shield, while at the same time pulling his hidden Recce from under his shirt. Simultaneously, Dan pivoted and shot the guards behind them while Aaron took out the guard to the side. Then they both swung back around, but Cal had already shot the guards in front. All five guards in the room were dead within seconds.

Cal picked Abd-Allah up over his head and slammed him with fierce, punishing force to the ground. One swift move and Cal was standing over Abd-Allah with his gun in his face. "Time?" Cal asked it not taking his eyes off Abd-Allah for a second.

Aaron checked his watch, "60 seconds."

"Go!" Cal ordered Dan and Aaron.

"Cal -" Aaron tried to argue but Cal cut him off harshly.

"Now! That's an order!" he yelled, still not taking his eyes off of Abd-Allah.

Aaron and Dan followed his instructions and darted out of the container, heading toward the side of the ship.

Cal switched off his M4. "I wish I had more time to end you right." He jammed his foot into Abd-Allah's groin so hard the fanatic screamed in searing pain. Then he jammed the end of his weapon right into his head. "But your death, anyway it comes, is good enough for me." Cal's ice cold stare didn't flinch as he pulled the trigger, and ended the bastards reign of terror. He took a quick DNA scan and photo for the proof of death…there was nothing left of his face for ID, but he took the picture anyway.

Must be twenty seconds left…

Cal ran out of the container and headed for the side of the ship. He heard the explosions and even felt the heat as he lifted into the air to jump overboard.

The sound of a door closing pulled her from her sleep. Alease slowly opened her eyes and found herself in what looked like a very large hotel suite. Her head was killing her, and her vision took a moment to adjust. When it did, she saw Tom and Joe talking with someone in uniform across the room in the kitchen area. She stayed very still to try and make out what they were saying.

"Yes, Commander Kimmey, we can confirm the explosion; both the yacht and the cargo ship late last night, but there is still no update on your men nor confirmation of enemy deaths." The words came from the young man in uniform that Alease did not recognize. "I'm sorry I don't have better news." The young man's face looked very concerned.

"What's the latest on Mac and the Black Hawk?" Joe asked.

"Doing another sweep of the area now, sir."

"Cal should have reported in by now…" Tom was going to continue but he saw Alease sit up and stopped short. He put on that forced reassuring smile that Alease could now see through. "Hey, look who's up."

Joe excused the young man in uniform and he and Tom walked over to the end of her bed.

"How do you feel?" Joe's tone was very soothing and calm, but it did not quiet the nerves shooting through her at what she heard.

"What's going on? Did you say Cal hasn't reported in? What does that mean?" She couldn't hide the panic in her voice, but she didn't much care.

Joe sat down on the far end of the bed. "It doesn't mean anything. Very typical. I'm sure he and the rest of the guys are fine."

"What do you mean you're sure? Why don't you know?" She tried to get up but Tom crossed over to block her from doing so.

"Alease, you are really weak, don't try and get up yet." Tom was putting on the same facade of confidence that Joe was.

Another bolt of pain shot through her head and she winced. Joe saw it, of course.

"Are you ok?" He asked as he crossed over to feel her forehead. "Fever still," he said. Joe picked up the phone and Alease heard him ask for the doctor to be sent up.

"Am I in a hospital?" she asked as she laid back down on the pillow.

"Private suite, private doctors. Nice huh?" Tom was trying to relax her, she knew, but her mind was all over the place trying to sort out everything she went through.

"God…what happened?" Alease was having a hard time keeping all the images from crashing into each other and creating havoc in her mind.

Joe crossed over to join them at the side of her bed. "Well, I tell you, you took that jump off the yacht better than most rookies." Alease suddenly remembered the drop. "But you were in a weakened state, and not dressed for the cold water. It took a little longer to get to the rescue boat than we had originally planned. You went hypothermic on us."

"How long have we been here?" Alease asked.

"Just under 24 hours," Joe replied calmly.

Alease tried to sit up again. "Cal's been missing for 24 hours?" She wanted to stand up, get out of the bed and go find him, but she couldn't fight the pain in her head enough to even sit up all the way. She heard Joe chuckle.

Joe looked at Tom. "Cal warned me she was stubborn. This one keeps thinking she can run out there and save the best SEAL the Navy has ever seen." Tom chuckled too. Joe looked back at her and tried to reassure her, "Alease, Cal knows what he is doing. He just needs time. Believe me, I know beyond a shadow of a doubt, he is trying to get back to you as soon as he possibly can."

There was a knock on the door and the doctor came in the

room. Alease had a foggy memory of him.

"Good evening. Alease, how are you feeling?" the doctor asked. As he approached the bed, Tom and Joe moved out of the way and crossed back to the kitchen to give them some privacy.

After an examination, the doctor gave her some medication for the fever and something he said was for the pain. She heard Joe asking the doctor for an update on her condition and the doctor reported that she was fine except for a slight fever and exhaustion. He was concerned that she hadn't eaten, and made clear they needed to get some food in her. Tom was on it and picked up the phone to order something up to the room. Alease had no desire to eat. All she wanted was Cal; to know he was ok. To feel him holding her. She needed him and she felt broken without him there.

She laid her head back down on the pillow and the images of the nightmare of what happened streaked through her mind. The gas station, the yacht, seeing her attacker alive and right in front of her, Kenya…her eyes filled with tears remembering what happened to Kenya. Her heart raced and broke with pain at the same time. She sat up trying to rid her mind of the image. Joe saw her and crossed over.

"You OK Alease?" His voice was very kind and concerned.

She shook her head. "I'm just remembering things… Kenya was…" her voice cracked and she stopped.

To her confusion, she saw Joe smile.

"Kenya was the hero of the entire mission." Joe turned to Tom and nodded his head. As Tom dialed on his cell phone, Joe turned back to her and continued. "If it wasn't for Kenya, we never would have found you. She saved your life…and depending on the outcome of Cal's mission…Kenya might have saved thousands of lives."

Alease didn't understand most of what Joe was saying, "I don't think I follow."

"Kenya had a military grade tracking chip. It was only because she was with you that we could track you and figured out where you were." Joe paused and looked at her in a slightly stern, almost fatherly way. "I do hope you never run off like that again. Cal would have died if we had lost you."

Her eyes filled with tears. "That's exactly what I was trying to prevent." Her tears fell down her cheeks in droves. "Jesus, this was all my fault." She covered her face with her hands as the uncontrollable sobs flushed out of her.

"No, Alease, it's not. There is a lot more here that you are unaware of."

She spoke with a cracking voice through her tears. "Like what?"

Joe took a breath. "I'm going to let Cal explain it all to you when he gets back. He will make it back, Alease. I know it. I know him. Cal doesn't lose."

Alease could feel her body weaken again. Her eyes were

wanting to close and she had a sinking suspicion the doctor had given her something to make her sleep.

She heard another knock on the door and she recognized the man they called Tagger. He entered with a big smile.

"Hey Alease, I've got a surprise for you." At that, the door opened wider and in bounded Kenya. Happy as ever, tail wagging, and that fabulous puppy grin that Alease never thought she would see again.

"Kenya!" Her excitement caused her to bolt up to sitting despite the searing pain it shot through her head. More tears escaped her eyes in the joy at seeing her alive and well. She hadn't died! She hadn't suffered! "Oh my God! Kenya!" When Kenya heard Alease's voice, she squealed and ran top speed over to the bed. Joe picked her up and placed her on the bed with Alease.

She was so overcome with emotion she couldn't even speak. As she hugged the puppy, she looked at Joe, and he answered the question she didn't have the voice to ask out loud.

"We were right there, Alease. Cal was right above you, I was right below you, and Tagger was out in the boat. As soon as Cal saw that jackass walking to the balcony with Kenya, he knew what he was going to do. So he ordered Tagger to adjust our plan and go get her." Joe was warmly smiling as he recalled it. "That dog led him right to you. No way was he going to let her die."

Tagger crossed over. "And I got to her in plenty of time. Even had a vet check her out today. She is perfect. Not a scratch on her and no worse for the ware. She is a really strong dog." He patted Kenya on the head sweetly.

"Thank you so much, Tagger." Her feelings were so raw and overtaxed that she couldn't get anymore sound out than that.

As the waves of emotion settled, the pain in her head pounded and she lowered herself back on the pillow. Kenya curled up right next to her and she felt her eyes closing again.

"Joe?" Joe came closer to the bed side so she wouldn't have to speak too loudly and drain more of her energy. "Please promise me you will wake me if you hear anything. Anything, ok?"

Joe nodded. "OK. I will constantly be here in the room with you. Tom and Tagger are here too. So if you need anything, just speak up."

"Am I still in danger?" Alease asked as her eyes started to close.

Joe spoke softly but confidently. "I highly doubt that. I am just following the orders I was given. Until Cal comes walking through that door, I am not letting you out of my sight. Tom and Tagger are following his orders too. Just sleep, you need the rest."

She felt her strength vanish and her eyes close before she could say anything else.

* * *

The sounds of voices woke her. The pain was gone and her vision cleared. She saw that young man in uniform again; the one passing information to Joe and Tom. She didn't wait to eavesdrop, "What is it Joe?" she asked.

Joe turned to her and a big smile crossed his face, "He's fine, Alease. They got them."

Alease bolted out of bed. Joe and Tom rushed across the room towards her as she fought to gain her balance and steady herself. "Where is he?"

Joe reached her side first and grabbed her so she wouldn't fall. "Good lord, Alease. If you fall over and break something Cal will have my hide! Are you trying to get me in trouble?"

Tom laughed and chimed in, "You and Cal are definitely meant for each other. Both impatient and stubborn as Hell."

"Where is he you guys?" Alease insisted.

"He is supposed to be in a debrief downstairs, but apparently, he is so focused on getting up here to see you that he told Kilton to fuck off. For the moment anyway. He is on his way up," Joe said as he let go of her when she found her footing.

And just like that, the door opened and Cal dashed into the room. His eyes found hers immediately and Alease lost her breath. Tears flew from her eyes and if he hadn't bolted across the room to pull her into his arms as quickly as he did, she would have fallen to the floor from the weakness that swept through her at seeing him.

Joe, Tom and everyone else in the room faded out of her mind as she felt Cal's strong arms around her, pulling her so tightly into him that there wasn't even air between them. He held her as she cried in his arms. She tried to speak, but no voice could break past the thick wave of feelings crashing through her. She buried her body into him and lost herself in his embrace.

He couldn't let go. He had her safely back in his arms and he just couldn't let go. He heard the door close and knew Joe and the rest had all left the room to give them privacy. He held her for an eternity and then finally had the strength to pull back just enough so he could kiss her. And he did. His mouth planted on hers and he took her into his very soul through his lips. His hands on both sides of her face, touching her; making sure she was really there. The feel of her was a Heaven he was unwilling to ever live without.

He found the strength to release her, just enough to look her in the eyes.

"Don't you ever run from me like that again. Please." His emotions got the better of him and he found himself unable to do anything but pull her back into him again, and hold her.

"I'm so sorry Cal. I had no idea he was alive. I didn't know he would -" She wanted to continue but he cut her off, and pulled back to look at her again. His hands on both sides of her beautiful face, holding her with all the love he could offer.

"No, Alease. This was an evil from my past that caused this. Not yours. This was not your fault," he tried to keep his voice as soothing as possible.

"Cal, his obsession with me almost cost you your life!" She was full of self blame and tearing herself up with it, he knew.

"No. Listen to me. He would not have come after you again had it not been for someone wanting revenge on me. This was not your fault. It was mine." He held her close knowing this was not the time or place to try and fill her in on what really happened. "I will explain it later, but for now I need you to hear me. This was not your fault. It came from a situation you had nothing to do with. But it's over now. It's done. Everything is fine now. I promise." He kissed her again clutching her to him with everything he had. He tried to ignore the harsh knock on the door.

"Cal, Kilton says now," the voice from the other side of the door yelled.

Alease pulled from his embrace. "What does Kilton want?"

Cal swept his fingers across her cheeks to wipe away the tears that were still falling down her beautiful face. "I have to debrief about what happened. It's protocol. I will be right downstairs and as soon as it's done, I'm making a beeline right back here to you, OK?"

"I just got you back…" Her tears fell again and he kissed them away.

"You have me for the rest of your life, I hope you know that." His smile seemed to go from his lips to hers and she smiled back.

"I better. Cause I can't let go of you." His heart filled with joy at the words that fell from her mouth.

"Good. Don't. Don't ever let go. Please." He kissed her again as the next pound on the door came bashing through the room. "I'm coming." He looked back to Alease. "Please, just get in bed, relax and wait for me. As soon as I'm done, I am getting in that bed with you."

He lifted her in his arms and placed her back down softly in the bed. Leaning over her, his lips fell on hers one last time before he found the strength to pull himself away and head towards the door. As he left, Joe stepped back in the room, still following Cal's orders to keep his eyes on Alease until he returned.

Leaving her to do the fucking debrief pissed him off. He hated it. He needed her, he needed to feel her under him, and to be inside of her. As if to make sure the entire world knew that she was his and no one else's. He knew the debrief was vital and Kilton would have it one way or another, which meant if he didn't go down, Kilton would storm into the room and have it right in front of Alease. He didn't want that. He still wanted her shielded from as many of the details as he could. There were particulars she would never need to know about.

Cal entered the debrief room and a very pissed off Kilton was there with the rest of the SEAL Teams.

"About fucking time Winters," Kilton said as Cal walked in and took his seat. "Where is Joe?" Kilton asked.

"Watching over Alease until I get back there," Cal answered without hesitation.

Kilton looked at him strangely. "Team should be here for debrief."

Cal shook his head. "I'm not leaving her alone after what she's been through. You can have me or Joe. Not both."

Kilton was pissy, but considering the outcome, it seemed to Cal he would not push it, and he was right.

Kilton went on without Joe. "We have all the DNA you collected and the photos. Abd-Allah, and Dizhvar are both confirmed dead." Kilton looked to Cal, "Abd-Allah looks really, really dead, judging from the photos."

Cal just shrugged his shoulders refusing any comments on the massive destruction to the guys face. "Dead is dead."

"I agree. Clever use of their stolen military weapons. Bringing the yacht around again with explosives in it… attaching explosives on the side of the cargo so they would both go up in flames. Risky plan, but well executed."

Kilton continued. "…and the Dunnlen brothers? Do you

have confirmation of their deaths?"

"Yes. They are dead, sir. Both of them," Cal answered simply.

"Any photos of them for confirmation?" Kilton asked.

Cal just shook his head. "No sir."

Kilton tilted his head curiously. "Anything you want to tell me about how they died?" Kilton asked.

Cal had no intention of explaining it, nor did he feel he needed to. "No sir. Just…dead. Jeffery by my hand, Adam by Aaron's." Aaron nodded offering no further details either.

Cal thought he saw Kilton smile ever so slightly. Kilton was not stupid. He knew some level of personal vengeance had taken place but, considering the evil nature of these two men, he didn't think Kilton would care. Cal was right, dead is dead.

"Well, some very bad people were wiped off the face of the Earth. I'd say that's a very good days work." He looked to Cal. "Get out of here. Go up and be with your woman. You have earned it. I'll debrief with the rest of the team from here." Cal rose and Kilton saluted him. "Well done Captain. Very well done."

When he got back to her room he opened the door softly. Joe was sitting at the counter in the small kitchen drinking a coffee. He looked up and smiled at his friend.

"Hey Cal. She is sleeping. Fell asleep about thirty

minutes ago," he spoke quietly so as not to wake her up.

Cal closed the door and crossed over to Joe.

"Joe…thank you."

Joe stood up and hugged him. "Cal, you are my best friend; my brother. I would do anything for you." He smiled at him, "But leaving you guys on that boat was the hardest thing I've ever had to do, I'll admit it."

"I needed you to. My head would not have been focused if anyone else had her. It had to be you." Cal knew Joe understood, but he said it again anyway.

"I know that. She did great. Damn if she didn't try several times to swim back to the fucking yacht in an attempt to save you though."

Cal laughed. "What? Really? She is stubborn that one."

"That she is. Perfect for you," Joe paused, "So, when are you going to marry her?"

Cal grinned. "Joe, that woman has been my wife since the moment I saw her."

"I know that," Joe smirked.

"But officially, I am marrying her as soon as I can."

Joe slapped him on the shoulder. "Your best man is ready and waiting." Joe picked up his coffee and headed towards the door. "Permission to get the Hell out of here so you can have some quality alone time with your wife?"

Cal laughed. "Permission granted. Thanks Joe."

"Always." With that, Joe went through the door and

closed it. Cal locked it and headed over to where Alease lay sleeping.

Cal softly picked Kenya up and placed her on the sofa. He took his clothes off and got under the blankets, pulling her body into his. As soon as she felt his touch she woke and turned into him.

"Cal" she said in a soft, sexy voice. She moaned into his kiss and the flare of passion that always sparked between them lit the room. He rolled on top of her, hovering above her, sheltering her with his body a breath away. She pulled him down onto her and pushed her hips up to meet him. He needed her with such urgency he could hardly stand it. He needed to feel every part of her. To reclaim her as his and push away any trace of anyone else who had their hands on her. He felt her curl in under him, seeking his protection and his comfort, which he gave a thousand fold. She was his, and the world would know it; now and forever. He clasped her hand in his, and kissed her deeply, and passionately. He used his powerful body as an endless source of protection of her, and he entered her. He kissed her as he pressed into her and she sighed yearning for more of him. Her body pulled him in with such need he could do nothing but give her everything he had. As he moved in and out of her he relished in the feel of her. He savored the feel of her. He immersed himself in feeling her needing him.

He touched her as he drove into her and made her come

as his own build inside of her intensified to the point of euphoria. He lost track of time, he lost track of everything but making love to her. When he came, it was deep, it was powerful and it shot through him like a never ending fire storm. The tremors of their climax lasted forever before they started to calm back down. He kissed her again, over and over. She gave him every part of herself and he felt her lose herself in him. He pulled back and looked into her eyes, his hand still wrapped around hers.

"I love you, Alease," He said in his deep, masculine voice. "I am so in love with you."

She breathed in his words and looked him in the eyes, "I love you too, Cal."

His lips met hers again in a kiss that seemed to sear their very souls together forever. When he broke the kiss, he rolled to one side and scooped her into his embrace, holding her with everything he had in him. He lifted the covers over them both and pulled her as close to him as he could get her. He whispered his love for her again in her ear and felt her melt back into him with the words coming back to him from her lips.

He drifted to sleep knowing what his future would hold. He would build that new beautiful deluxe log cabin style home on his property, where he would live with this beautiful woman in his arms. The evils from both their pasts had collided and been knocked out forever. He had won. In every way, he had won. He had the woman of his dreams safely in his arms. She was his, and he was never letting go. He sent his gratitude up to whatever God had sent her in his direction.

Thank you for sending her to me...thank you for sending her to Winter Mountain...

***

Alease could feel her heart pounding. She gripped her weapon in her hand and lay as flush against the snow bank as she could. She tried to quiet her breathing and listen. Cal had taught her how to shoot, how to attack, and when need be, how to hide. She heard footsteps not far…her heart skipped. She only had one shot left. The footsteps ran off in the other direction. She felt a moment of relief. She was just about to gauge her next move when she heard a sound that sent a chill through her; she heard Cal call out. *No…was he hit?* She always knew it could happen one day, but she never thought it would happen this soon. She flipped over trying to decide if she could sit up and look down the hill to where his last location was. She carefully looked and then she saw it. She could hardly breathe. She was filled with denial….*it couldn't be…oh my God…*

"Cal!" It came out of her mouth, she couldn't hold it back. She didn't even care if she got hit. She got up and half ran half slid down the snow covered hill over to where he lay on the ground motionless. She stood over him looking at the red stain above his heart and the splash of red scattered on the snow bank behind him.

"Cal!" she cried. Part of her still couldn't believe it.

His body lay still as his eyes slowly opened and he looked at her. Alease was shocked at the sight.

Then she tilted her head, and threw her hand on her hip.

"Do you mean to tell me our twelve year old daughter got you? And right in the heart?" She lowered her paint ball gun and shook her head in astonished bewilderment.

Cal's smile shot across his face and he bolted upright, his face beaming with pride.

"Oh my God, Alease! You should have seen them!"

"Them?" Alease asked.

"Yep!" their twins yelled with elation. Joanna and Christina jumped up to standing; Christina from behind the big snow bank, and Joanna from behind the half open barn door. They were laughing and running towards each other with high fives and hugs.

"I can't believe it. How did you two do it?" Alease asked.

"Dad fell for a girl trick!" Christina teased. "It was Joanna's plan," she said looking proudly at her sister.

"Yeah. Christina is a better performer and I'm a better shooter, so we worked together to bring dad down!" Joanna cried in triumph.

"I pretended to fall down the snow bank and hurt myself. I cried and everything! Dad bought it hook, line and sinker! He lowered his weapon just like Joanna said he would," Christina added with glee.

"Yep. I knew he would fall for it. Then I popped up and took the shot. Bam! I hit the target dead on! Ha! I got the Navy SEAL! I finally won the Annual Winter Mountain SEAL Challenge!" Joanna was beaming with pride.

Cal was laughing with delight and joy at his daughters. He got up to hug them both.

"I have never been more proud of being so stupid! That was amazing. You both did exactly what I taught you to. Use the gifts you have. You guys worked together and took me out!"

"Hey, I helped!" Kevin popped up from behind the snowbank.

"That's right. Kevin helped. He was my cover in case I missed, then he was going to shoot you dad," Joanna said with a smile.

"I was protecting Christina. Just in case Joanna missed," Kevin said.

Cal smiled over at Kevin. "You were protecting my daughter? At your own risk?"

"Of course. Always, Mr. Winters," Kevin said proudly.

"Kevin Keep, you are a good young man," Cal hugged him too.

"Where are the rest?" Alease asked.

"All dead," Joanna said it nonchalantly with a shrug of her shoulders. "I got Kathy and Jenny. Dad got Stephanie, Jake and Johnathan,"

Sure enough, Alease saw them all waiting on the front porch with big paint ball splotches all over them, laughing and celebrating Joanna's win.

A black Escalade turned up the driveway. "Hey my dad

finally got here!" Kevin said.

Alease turned to see. Yes, it was Kenny's car. She turned back to the group. "OK, Everyone is here. Time to go in and celebrate Christmas!"

All the kids ran over to greet Kenny as Cal wrapped Alease in his embrace. He kissed her and still could not stop the smile on his face.

"Did you really fall for their trick?" she asked.

"I really, truly did. Joanna won fair and square. I'm so proud of them." Cal kissed her again, before they walked over to the group in the driveway.

Kenny had a huge red bag filled with Christmas gifts for everyone and was walking towards them as they met in front of the house.

Cal hugged him. "Hey Kenny. How was the concert?"

Kenny smiled brightly. "Great." He looked to Alease and hugged her as well. "They loved your new song, Alease. Gonna be another overnight sensation, I'm sure of it."

"Wonderful, I can't wait to watch it tonight when it airs on TV," Alease said with a smile as she hugged Kenny's wife Charlotte.

"How are you feeling, Alease? Morning sickness?" Charlotte asked her.

Alease rubbed her slightly swollen belly. "Yes, I have to say. I don't know if it's because its the second set of twins, or because one of them is a boy, but it's a little more uncomfortable then the girls were. How about you?"

"Not too bad. Funny that we are looking at the same birthdate for these new additions." Charlotte said. "We decided to find out today…it's a girl."

Alease hugged her. "That's fabulous news."

When they walked through the front door, the crowd was already bustling about Joanna's win. Everyone was cheering her and greeting Kenny and his wife at the same time.

"I can't believe it. She really got you, Cal?" Joe was laughing. "I always knew she would, just didn't think it would happen so soon." He leaned down to Joanna very seriously. "You know what that means don't you?" he asked her with a grave for-warning.

"Yes, uncle Joe, I do. That means next year I have to go up against two SEALs. You and dad."

"That's right; and we learn, so your trick isn't going to work again. You will have to come up with another strategy," Joe advised as he patted her proudly on the head.

"I will. I've got a year to think one up," Joanna said, as she took her boots off and crossed into the living room.

Cal turned to Kenny. "And your son…I've got to tell you, I like that kid. You know, he risked his life twice during the game today to save Christina?"

Kenny laughed. "Well, I raised him to be a gentleman… and also to have a healthy fear of disappointing you." Cal laughed as he handed him a glass of hot spiced wine. Kenny cheered him with his glass. "It also doesn't hurt that he is sweet on Christina. I think she won him over with that voice of hers."

Cal smiled proudly. "She can sing. She gets it from her mother." He kissed Alease on the cheek and pulled her into him.

"Kenny have you heard the song those two wrote?" Alease asked.

"Not yet, but I hear they are going to perform it for us tonight. I can't wait to hear this. They may just be the next big thing. Put me right out of business," Kenny laughed.

"I'm starving. Can we eat now?" Sophie asked.

"Of course," Alease said with a smile as she handed her and Aaron fresh glasses of wine. Aaron kissed Sophie sweetly and Alease felt a surge of happiness flow through her at the love they found in each other. "Come on everyone, let's celebrate Christmas!" Alease said.

Their home on Winter Mountain was even more beautiful than she had imagined. They had knocked down the two houses and built a gorgeous, luxurious mountain home in it's place. Four floors, huge fire places and wide open rooms where all their friends and family came to celebrate the holidays together. Both SEAL teams and their families, Kenny Keep and his family; everyone who meant everything to them, all here in their home. They sat down at the extra large Christmas tables, rejoicing in the company of each other. Alease looked at all the faces of her friends, her family…her home was filled with the people she loved more than anything, and filled with the magic of everything she had always wanted in her life. Her incredible husband Cal, this amazing man who saved her life in more ways than one, stood to give the Christmas toast. "My friends, my family… on behalf of my beautiful wife and our girls (and soon to be boy,) I want to wish you all a very Merry Christmas. The love we all share with each other is the greatest gift human kind could have. Every one of you reminds me of the unbelievable good in this world, and I am thankful to my core for all of you. May we be in each others lives forever, blessed in the love we have found in this great big family of ours." He raised his glass and everyone else did the same.

As they all toasted each other with smiles and happiness, they began the festivities of the Christmas celebration.

Alease couldn't help but think back to the very first day she arrived here. Little did she know that she would find such love, such warmth and such family. Cal was right, her life had started over that day, and bloomed into more than she could have dreamed, and it all happened right here.

She thanked what ever force of fate or God it was that whispered to her all those years ago…that magically illuminated the path that guided her right here…to Winter Mountain.

The End

L.A. Liechty

Lyn Liechty

Lyn Liechty has recorded and performed the hit duet **"Here In My Heart"** with the world renowned Scorpions off the platinum selling album **"Moment Of Glory."** She has also created a big name for herself performing leading roles in world premiere blockbuster shows such as **"Jekyll & Hyde,"** **"Dance Of The Vampires," "Miss Saigon,"** and **"Dracula."** She has worked closely with Lionel Richie, Roman Polanski, Jim Steinman, Frank Wildhorn and Leslie Bricusse to name a few. Lyn's first single **"CaveMan!"** off her album "At Last", has gotten over 1.6 million views on YouTube, and charted at #11 on the Billboard hot Singles Charts. Lyn is the author of several books including **Hollywood Fire**, **A Wynken, Blynken & Nod Adventure** (Children's book,) **The Magic Of Poems, The Magic Of Night** (Children's poems,) and two cookbooks; **Recipes Of Home** (The Main Collection and Sweets Treats and Desserts.) For more info, please go to:

www.LynLiechtyMusic.com

9 780578 718453